JENNI DAICHES was born in Chicago, ~~~~~~ England, and has lived in or near Edi~~~~~~ ~~~ars of part-time teaching and freelance writing, including three years in Kenya, she worked at the National Museums of Scotland from 1978 to 2001, successively as education officer, Head of Publications, script editor for the Museum of Scotland, and latterly as Head of Museum of Scotland International. In the latter capacity her main interest was in emigration and the Scottish diaspora. She has written and lectured widely on Scottish, English and American literary and historical subjects (as Jenni Calder), and writes fiction and poetry. She has two daughters, a son and a dog.

Daiches manages her double narrative with dexterity... this is an accomplished book. ALLAN MASSIE, SCOTLAND ON SUNDAY

This is a novel that the discriminating reader will value. It is strong, it is searchingly honest, it is passionately realised, and it is utterly free of ideology or polemic. NORTHWORDS NOW

Daiches' debut novel has considerable virtues. Her evocation of travelling around China is sharp and effective... The prose is efficient... The final pages are the best, and are very well done. SCOTTISH REVIEW OF BOOKS

By the same author:

Chronicles of Conscience: A Study of Arthur Koestler and George Orwell,
  Secker and Warburg, 1968
Scott (with Angus Calder), Evans, 1969
There Must be a Lone Ranger: The Myth and Reality of the American West,
  Hamish Hamilton, 1974
Women and Marriage in Victorian Fiction, Thames and Hudson, 1976
Brave New World and Nineteen Eighty-Four, Edward Arnold, 1976
Heroes, from Byron to Guevara, Hamish Hamilton, 1977
The Victorian Home, Batsford, 1977
The Victorian and Edwardian Home in Old Photographs, Batsford, 1979
RLS: A Life Study, Hamish Hamilton, 1980
The Enterprising Scot (ed, with contributions), National Museums of
  Scotland, 1986
Animal Farm and Nineteen Eighty Four, Open University Press, 1987
The Wealth of a Nation (ed, with contributions), NMS Publishing, 1989
Scotland in Trust, Richard Drew, 1990
St Ives by RL Stevenson (new ending), Richard Drew, 1990
No Ordinary Journey: John Rae, Arctic Explorer (with Ian Bunyan, Dale
  Idiens and Bryce Wilson), NMS Publishing, 1993
Mediterranean (poems, as Jenni Daiches), Scottish Cultural Press, 1995
The Nine Lives of Naomi Mitchison, Virago, 1997
Museum of Scotland (guidebook), NMS Publishing, 1998
Present Poets 1 (ed, poetry anthology), NMS Publishing, 1998
Translated Kingdoms (ed, poetry anthology), NMS Publishing, 1999
Robert Louis Stevenson, (poetry, ed), Everyman, 1999
Present Poets 2 (ed, poetry anthology), NMS Publishing, 2000
Scots in Canada, Luath Press, 2003
Not Nebuchadnezzar: In Search of Identities, Luath Press, 2005
Smoke (poems, as Jenni Daiches) Kettillonia, 2005
Scots in the USA, Luath Press, 2006

Letters from the Great Wall

JENNI DAICHES

Luath Press Limited

EDINBURGH

www.luath.co.uk

First published 2006
Reprinted 2008

ISBN (10): 1-905222-51-3
ISBN (13): 978-1-905222-51-3

The author's right to be identified as author of this book
under the Copyright, Designs and Patents Act 1988 has been asserted.

The paper used in this book is recyclable.
It is made from low chlorine pulps produced in a low energy,
low emission manner from renewable forests.

The publisher acknowledges subsidy from

 Scottish
Arts Council

towards the publication of this volume.

Printed and bound by Bell & Bain Ltd., Glasgow
Typeset in 10.5 point Sabon

For Diana, without whom it would not have happened

I

I PROMISED AN explanation. But how can I explain? Not here, sitting on this warm stone, my back against the parapet wall, late afternoon, the sun hanging just above the mountains, still hot to my sun-starved skin. Fewer people now. Most of the buses have gone. A little while ago it was like a fairground, looking down on it all from this distance. So many people, so many colours, shapes forming and splitting, buses reversing and honking, dust burling, incongruous camels in bright leather trappings, stalls selling T-shirts and soapstone and cans of coke.

The fact is I no longer want to explain. Nor do I want to apologise. I realise apology might be considered appropriate but it doesn't seem to belong now. I no longer feel I ought to.

It's as if they chose the steepest, highest pinnacles to build on, that's what I don't understand. They did not build a wall to keep out barbarians – I see them assailing the barrier with daggers between their teeth. Typical occidental's stereotype. We impose our own pictures – we can't help it. They built a wall to demonstrate the building of a wall. There is no compromise with the landscape here, no acknowledgement of the contours of hills. No one sought – or did they, and lost their heads? – an easier way. The wall actually seems to loop and twist so as to follow the most spectacular, the most difficult, the most astonishing route. It seems organic to the mountains. At the same time it proclaims itself man-manufactured, woman too, perhaps. I don't know, though I've seen women carrying stone and mortar, a weight at each end of a carrying pole. Whoever they were, thousands of them died in the building of it. Humankind's mark upon the earth, and in it.

A wall for the sake of a wall. I can't tell you, though I owe that to you, I know. Owe, ought. These words are cousins, but second cousins I think. My 'owe' should suggest not obligation but a wish to give. I can't tell you why I left, why I came, what I am discovering here. No, that's not true. (Why do I want to tell the truth? Does anyone else? I doggedly tussle with language and truth. I don't care for lies but I tell them, of course I do.) I had good reasons to leave. But I should go back to the beginning again. What I should say is that I don't want to. Like a truculent child I want to toss my head and say, why should I? Why can't I do as I like? I hear you drawing breath to give me some answers, sensible answers. Of course, I know the answers. There was always room in my head for sensible answers, in the days of those private, precious conversations, but I don't think I'm interested in them any more. Have I cast off the yoke of obligation and guilt? That's too much to hope for. If there have been miracles I've been blind to them. You need sharp eyes for miracles.

A lot of questions. My flesh drinks in this eastern sun. The warmth of the stone, hard on the bum, is wonderful too, the very hardness making me feel as if the heat is reaching my bones. (Bones are everywhere. So much flesh and blood above the earth, so many tombs and trenches of bones beneath.) Suppose there were a cancer, I suddenly find myself thinking. Would this warmth penetrate the maverick growths in my body? It seems so much kinder and more healing than the savage things they do to attack the wildly splitting cells. There are times, though, when we need some savagery. I hate to say that – you know I have always believed in being kind. It's not done me much good, or I've not been much good at it. The sun is dropping, way beyond the wall and the cone-shaped hills. The sky to the north and west is a murky yellow, freighted with desert dust. That's where the threat comes from.

I remember deciding. I'll tell you about that, it might help.

It was a cold March afternoon, over a year ago. Thousands of miles ago. I was writing an article I'd put off all term and there were books I needed. It now seems remote and ridiculous. At the time it was important, a deadline to meet. I drove to George Square and parked the car nose to pavement. There were clumps of snowdrops in the grass, and crocuses. I could see the little dots and dashes of gold and purple through the railings. There's nothing like spring in the dark, northern countries of the world. The trees were bare and black against a pale orange sky. It was late afternoon, as it is now.

I sat in the car for a bit, looking at those fragile scraps of colour, my hands and feet getting cold, and for the first time, suddenly and clearly, my head articulated my unhappiness. Until then I'd just felt a mush of dissatisfaction, worry, maybe fear, sometimes waking in the night with a stab of panic. But now something spoke. You are unhappy, it said. Your past, your present, your parents, with being here and doing this, with driving to the university to consult books, with writing an article that will say nothing of any real significance, or even make-believe significance. You are unhappy with what awaits you when you return home. What are you going to do about it?

I got out of the car, shut the door, locked it, walked. You know what it's like when you suddenly see yourself performing actions you've performed a million times before. When you suddenly become a stranger to yourself. I watched myself get the books, return to the car, key, ignition, seat belt, reverse gear, radio on (Radio Three – CPE Bach with that almost tinny woodwind which I love). Traffic lights, left turns, right turns, cyclist snaking in front of me, elderly man jaywalking ten yards from a zebra crossing (I thought of my father, of course). Parking, only three doors down from the desirable urban residence I share with the man I now know I can't marry. In through the street door and up the stairs. Front door key.

How easy. My mind made up. I can't marry Roy. I can't go on living in my fine and comfortable home. I can't forgive my mother. I never loved my father. I can no longer tolerate my snarling colleagues. I can't forgive myself. I have to go away. I stood, only seconds probably, looking at the white painted door of the flat, and I couldn't believe how clear everything had become. All my life I'd been making things unnecessarily complicated, agonising over decisions, should I apply for that job, make love to that man, fail that student, confront parents, boss. Should I speak or stay silent? Should I flee or attack?

I didn't tell Roy at once. But the perspective changed, and when perspectives change the people in them take on a different shape. The scenery, the quality of the air, the temperature, changed too. When he came in, later, he seemed diminished. He had no idea that I had a huge, expanding secret. I had just been sitting. I had taken off my jacket and was holding it against myself. The books were on the floor beside me. He hardly looked at me, saw nothing strange, smiled as he always did. Without that smile I'd never have been there. He won me with that smile.

As he went into his room – he had his room, I had a corner of what my mother called the lounge – he threw back a question. What are we having for dinner? Shall I open a bottle of wine? It was Friday. We always had a bottle of wine on Friday.

I didn't feel sorry for him at all. I sat. A while later he emerged. Are you alright? His expression benign and preoccupied. Just tired, I said. Roy never complained. He took me as he found me. No reproof, that wasn't his style. I'll make omelettes, I said. I didn't care, then or now, if I hurt him. Or his pride. He's a nice guy really, I thought, clutching my jacket. Want a drink? Roy asked. I nodded. A pity, I remember thinking. I'll have to move. I can't go on sitting like this. I'll give the game away.

Well, I moved. I left my jacket and my books on the floor and sat at the little writing desk under the window, the desk I found in that junk shop in St Stephen's Street. Roy handed me a glass, turned on the television, and sat down on the sofa on the other side of our large, high-ceilinged living room. Or lounge. I'll go out for a pizza if you like. The offer was rhetorical. It was Roy being considerate, though we both knew that I would demur, so I did. Not that I mind omelettes, he said at the same time as I said, it will only take minutes. And there's some nice rye bread, and I'll make a salad.

For the first time I began to understand the attractions of space travel. For being here is as I imagine the experience of another planet. If I were to describe the landscape, the curious conical hills, the dark scrubby trees, the dry crusted earth. Or the city, the stark new buildings, the forests of cranes, the canopy of dust, the startling fragments of another time. A green and yellow gateway, curling roof tiles, faded courtyards. It would at once be familiar as a known world, a different idiom maybe, but the same planet. If I were to describe the people, their movements, their expressions, their bundles of belongings, the clothes they wear, the smells, it would be recognised as a humanity we're all acquainted with, if only through words and images. But it is also entirely different, different from anything I've ever encountered, frighteningly different. This is humanity on a scale beyond imagination, life concertina-ed, layered, fused, fractured. Like all the multiple activity that batters the earth below and above its surface.

I will go on writing to you and hope that I can clarify this in my own mind. It is important to me – the experience itself is not enough. But I don't think it is something I can purposefully describe. I hope you will understand that discovering this is the most important thing that has happened to me. The writing about it is part of the importance. There's never been anything to write about until now, except other peoples' words.

A child has stopped to stare. I am getting used to this now. Never have I attracted so much attention! Imagine the fascination that lies in my thick, rather coarse light hair in a land where hair is smooth and dark. My blue eyes are dazzling. Fingers reach out to touch my freckled skin. At home I am of medium height and slenderish build. Here I am big and bulky, with rough pale limbs, patchily tanned, in a land where young flesh is smooth and lustrous.

The child still stares, beautiful, unsmiling. Yellow shorts and a white T-shirt, round face fringed with cropped black hair, skin subtle as silk, tilted eyes. I smile. She takes a step back and looks round quickly to check if her parents are still within reach. But her eyes swerve back to the foreign devil. Her parents are walking slowly away from her, the man, early thirties I'd say, about my age, the woman in a rather short white skirt, the edge of a nylon petticoat just visible as she walks, a yellow nylon blouse. The sleeves of the man's shirt are rolled above his thin elbows. I recognise the ubiquitous thin cotton of his navy trousers. They walk side by side and begin the steep climb up one of the wall's great arcs. After a few steps they pause, turn, and call the child. She hesitates, takes a last look at me, and trots after them in her little canvas shoes.

There is such joy in observing.

A child. That would be an easy explanation of it all, prefabricated, there to pick up and present. Everyone would nod, murmur to each other, ah yes, of course, poor Eleanor, a child, of course. I suppose it was Roy, they'd say, so ambitious, wouldn't want his life cluttered up with a child. And on the other side the troops would also mass. Eleanor, what a pity, no space in her life for a baby, she'll regret it later. You should have your children young. She'd be happier if she settled down. Children being necessary to settlement, as if without them there is nothing to hold you steady. If you wait too long, it may be too late.

That's what hurt my mother, or at least I guessed it did, though she hardly seemed to notice when I told her that Roy and I had finally decided to marry. By that time I think she'd got used to it, our cohabitation, though a child without marriage would have been beyond her, and I was sure she'd immediately calculate on a grandchild when I told her yes, at last, we'd even set a date. Roy wanted a child. One of his arguments was that it was cruel to deny my mother a grandchild, though her son had already given her two.

No, it wasn't Roy who opted out of children. He comes from a big family himself, has several sisters and nephews and nieces I've never met. When he raised the subject of marriage and children he always took me unawares, for he never chose

6

those intimate moments which, to me, suggest possibilities of close communication, but would, perhaps, come into the kitchen straight from the computer and without noting my activity, chopping onions or my hands in rubber gloves, would say, Eleanor, we should think seriously about marriage, you know. I don't want you to wait too long before you have a child. Marriage was on his agenda, the decision deferred rather than dropped, which meant that I could dodge the issue without ever having to say no.

Something changed after my father died. I used to see, or imagine, reproof in my mother's eyes. After my father died that vanished.

Roy required a child, two probably, just as he required a woman, not to depend on, not to share with, not for sex or housekeeping or hot dinners, but to complete his image of himself. That's my ungenerous view. It was to do with status, with masculinity. The expectations of others. I glimpsed deep-rooted feelings about a son and heir, inheritance, carrying on the line, maintaining the name. He is the only son, perhaps that has something to do with it. I don't think he's ever taken his sisters seriously, although he clearly likes them. Sometimes I teased him. I'll have a daughter, I said, who will bear my name. He smiled his wide, good-humoured smile. He didn't take that seriously either; he knew I didn't mean it.

The little family is returning now. I've done my climb, calf-aching, to the crown of the first arc to the east. From there you can see the wall dip and curve over the green and brown landscape. I wish I could convey the nuances of colour here to fix them in my mind. Green and brown are in no way adequate. It's a particular density of green, a quality of brown, something of red in it, something of yellow, and it's a tenacious green, a green against the odds. And all these colours seem influenced by the colours you find on T'ang tomb figures, horses, camels, lovely beasts built for burial. The eye is so imposed on by these colours, human creation, that the landscape too looks as if splashed by rich glazes. There's nothing untouched by humanity. Not only is the landscape disturbed, we cannot avoid interpreting it as if art came first.

The wall is crumbled beyond this stretch of reconstruction, but its progress is distinct as far as the eye can see, and indeed further, for you know, not because of what words tell you but because of its conviction as a wall, that it goes on and on. Just as you feel that China itself cannot have an end. In some parts the wall has almost disappeared; much of it was never more than mud. This does not matter. In other parts just the watch towers survive, turrets like teeth on top of the highest peaks. And it didn't keep them out, the barbarians. Whether it was treachery, or skill, or sheer weight of numbers, they crashed through from time to time and streamed east and south. Now the barbarian hordes drop through the air. But there is still the need to define territory. China does end. Other countries begin.

They are quite right to regard me with suspicion, the little family, all three of them staring as they pass. A northern barbarian from a rugged, limited land, gnawed by sea, walled and corridored by mountains. Child of hard-hewn, limited parents. Growing up in a small town with sandstone relics, a roofless grey palace, hollow reminder of hollow ceremonial. A defunct marketplace and dead distillery. Taught to expect too much and too little. Taught to respect money and morals, to respect respectability. Taught to be clean and orderly. But I mustn't blame my parents, indeed I have no wish to, and what use is blame? Children blame parents out of convenience, not out of need. There is usually nothing else to blame.

It was hard for them to explain their daughter. Achieving yet feckless. It wasn't the need to understand that bothered them, but the need to explain, to put into acceptable language that fitted the requirements of their small world. Other peoples' daughters sang in the church choir. They needed more help than I did. Though God knows there were times when I've wanted to weep for lack of it. When I did weep. And my mother now? Perhaps I shouldn't worry. She was always able to rationalise – me too, of course. Perhaps I learned it from her, though I tried so hard to absorb as little as possible. Sometimes my mother seems as resilient as a child. She still surprises me. My father was always more brittle, in spite of his granite exterior. I am quite sure my mother is not saying, Eleanor's done a bunk. No. Eleanor will be taking advantage of a wonderful opportunity. And so she is. It is probably not often she tells the truth about her children. It is wonderful. But all the same, I know I've done a bunk, a wonderful bunk, a bunk I'd never have thought possible.

But I really don't want to think about my mother, because I know it's no longer possible to see her in quite the same way as before, and I haven't yet figured out how the picture has changed.

I stopped there, stiff with sitting and writing for so long with my pad on my knee. Though I stayed a little longer, leaning my head against the pale stone, catching the last of the sun before it dipped behind the dark hills. Then I had to gather myself together, shoulder my capacious bag – notebook, pens, money, traveller's cheques, passport, sunglasses, aspirin, sun cream, paperback (*The Butterfly* by Wang Meng) and my precious camera, and make my way down to a bus that rattled me back to the Beijing Hotel, a magnificent assemblage of Edwardian and Stalinist architecture, my baseline for Beijing.

I went into its dark, vaulted lobby. I'm not staying in the Beijing Hotel, but I soon discovered that I could get cold beer there, brewed and canned in Shanghai, the legacy of German brewers who came to China in the nineteenth century. The corridors are lofty and cluttered. Everywhere there are 'Europeans', by which I mean mainly Americans and Australians, who wander aimlessly, it seems, among the little boutiques where you can buy silk and curios at inflated prices.

The cool, dim lounge where I sip my beer is not yet full of pre-prandial drinkers but in the corner there's a noisy group of tanned Australians in shorts and polo shirts sitting round a table stacked with cans. I take out my notebook again, and acknowledge the ambivalent need to talk. Yesterday there was a couple from an

English university, Reading I think. He a geneticist on a lecture tour, she a faithful companion who at home works for the local Citizen's Advice Bureau. They were sipping gin and tonic in a rather conspiratorial fashion, talking in low voices, unlike the other occupants of the lounge. They turned out to be waiting to be picked up and rushed to another tourist site, or lecture hall, or banquet – whatever was next on the packed agenda. They thought it was all wonderful, but seemed confused.

I identified well-placed hearts and an engaging enthusiasm, like children, though almost old enough to be my parents. They had kindly turned to talk to me when they saw I was alone. They were anxious about what to take back for their teenage children. And anxious that I should miss nothing they had seen. Had I been to the Ming tombs, the Tibetan temple? How long had I spent in the Forbidden City? Had I walked in Beihai Park, and where was I going next? I explained that I had commitments in Beijing, that I, too, was giving lectures. But that I hoped to get around a bit later. On your own? they enquired. That's very brave.

They were nice people, very nice people. I almost hoped to see them there again. They wore quiet clothes and were full of wonder, as much at the way every moment of their time was organised, as at China itself. Tomorrow, they told me, it was the Summer Palace, the day after, a flight to Cheng Du. A brisk lady in a grey suit and spectacles, a professor at Beijing University, arrived and whisked them away. They had not finished their drinks, but made no protest. I left soon after, and caught an overflowing bus to the Friendship Hotel, the place where 'foreign experts' stay.

I have hardly started. There is some shape to the story, I think, though there can be no end of course. If only one could write on one's deathbed, issue a statement as it were, write the last words of one's own story. This was what it was all about, this is what I meant to say. But it will be someone else who has the final say, and how can someone else possibly get it right?

2

WE EAT IN AN echoing dining room, distinctly institutional yet with vestiges of grandeur, as if chandeliers were suspended above us. But there are no chandeliers, and the high ceiling has a dark and dusty look. The noise is clamorous. Conversation bounces around the room like the sound of breakers in a sea cave. There are students, researchers, visiting academics, advisors. French, German, American. I am disinclined to talk.

Last night I found myself with a group of students, mainly French. The talk was of democracy. They say that Chinese students are not quite open in their disaffection, in their eagerness to be involved. Those I have met have been politely insistent in their questions about 'England'. I have not yet tried to explain 'Scotland'. They ask about politics, education, and how to get books and how to improve their English. They want to go to England. Or better, America.

Tonight I am sitting next to a bearded Canadian. He is tall and bulky, with brown curly hair and square hands. I quite like this place. Most people complain. I have a dingy little room with heavy dark furniture and a small window. The food is quite good. It's also very cheap and there's plenty of it. Steve has an attractive, warm voice. He is an ethno-musicologist.

I am giving two sets of lectures. Last week it was the nineteenth-century novel. The hall was packed. Students sat on window sills and stood at the back. Tomorrow I move on to Dickens. At the same time as listening to Steve my mind is fishing for similarities between Beijing and the London of Dickens. They are both foreign territories.

I am eating noodles and spicy vegetables. Steve is wearing a checked shirt with the sleeves rolled to the elbows, and I notice his beard is greying. He comes from Vancouver. He says, waving his chopsticks for emphasis, that Chinese music is more richly and complexly tuneful that anything written by Mozart or Beethoven, and if I'd care to listen to his tapes he would demonstrate. Western music, he says, depends on harmony. Without harmony most of the melodies would be banal.

I am interested, and Dickens slides out of my mind. I like his brown eyes, which are slightly prominent, but warm, like his voice. Back in Vancouver he has a collection of oriental instruments. He lives near the university. He is drinking beer, and when he gets up to buy more, from a little booth, he asks if I'd like one. I say yes, and an hour later we are the sole occupants of the dining room. Then we go to his room to listen to his tapes, Steve carrying a couple of beer bottles by the neck in each hand.

I like the music. Once you get past the barrier of strangeness that these curiously congested sounds throw up, once you learn to listen to the currents of the pentatonic, it becomes amazingly open and flexible. Its sinuosity winds itself around and through you. When Steve discovers I come from Scotland he points out, almost with a degree of triumph, the kinship between Scottish and oriental music. He hums sonorously to demonstrate. One thick-wristed hand is raised above his head, and slowly, gracefully, descends.

In the night I had to get up to pee. It meant a long walk down the corridor, lit only by a single hanging lightbulb, which seemed fierce, though the light it cast was so weak. The silence is also fierce, and I am relieved to get back to my room and into my narrow bed.

I've walked for hours in the Forbidden City, crisscrossing the vast courtyards. Grass and weeds grow through the cracked marble. Neglected artefacts rest among the dust. The surging crowds of visitors overlie the desolate passivity of the place, but when another tour group has passed, emptiness reasserts itself. It could never have been like this.

The great bronze cauldrons and tortoises, dragons and lions, glint under the heavy sun with a vibrant but alien insistence. The scale of the expanse of white stone, of the sweeping steps laced with marble dragons, of the winged buildings, seems to diminish rather than enhance the human. I am not happy with such grandeur, yet I cannot stay away.

I shoulder my camera and make another traverse in the sun. The lone traveller is a rarity here. The space is not adequate for a human being alone. And although there are so many people, they tend to remain in clumps. It is easy to step round a corner into an architectural backwater and to reflect on my small presence. My camera gives me a purpose, for just to look doesn't seem enough. Through a lens I can almost take it in better, as if I am cutting it down to size. I feel more comfortable with my camera in my hand, less alone.

In April last year I was with Roy at a conference in Bologna. It rained. I don't think I saw the sun at all, so I think of Bologna as a dark city. I accompanied him because I thought of an Italian spring, a Florentine spring. I thought I would go to Florence. At first I walked round and round Bologna's arcaded square, out of the rain, pausing to examine stalls piled with cheap sweaters and shirts, until I began to know them by heart. Finally I bought two sweaters. Roy was mildly scornful. We quarrelled in the hotel room. We didn't often quarrel, not seriously, well, not really at all. I don't think it was because of the sweaters, but perhaps it was the rain, or my difficulties in being a conference-goer's partner. What were they supposed to do? Why didn't I join the other wives on tomorrow's trip to Ravenna? At dinner, Roy was in animated conversation with his colleagues, and I was silent.

The next day I got on the train to Florence. In the Uffizi I imagined the roar of tramping feet to be tanks in the narrow streets outside. Botticelli was pierced by an American voice explaining, explaining. I didn't want anything explained. Dutiful students moved, tramp, tramp, from one picture to the next. They massed in front of oval faces and festoons of waving hair, extraordinary, compelling fabrications. On the Ponte Vecchio I was wedged in a sea of tourists, and struggled off the bridge to look down at the khaki-coloured Arno moving lethargically at my feet.

But the sun was shining in Florence. Back in Bologna I crossed and recrossed the dark square in the rain, to the university where I listened to a paper delivered in a ponderous monotone, then back to the hotel where I stood at the window and watched the ebb and flow of people in the street, or lay on the bed with a book. I sat silent at dinner while Roy and colleagues bandied anthropology. From time to time he glanced at me, and I read discomfort in his look. A wonderful city, one of his colleagues said, smiling with perfect teeth, when he gathered I'd spent the day before in Florence. No other city glows like Florence.

Beijing in June doesn't glow. Sitting at the little desk in my gloomy room with the window open, I'm acutely conscious of the dry darkness beyond. I am here because I choose to be, which is why I find myself thinking of Bologna. Here of my own free will, as they say. Choice is exhilarating, even when it isn't real. Frightening too, of course. I know people who disintegrate in the face of choice, others who retreat from it. And there are those who make choices but deny they are doing it, deny the responsibility, the effect on others. The ultimate justification, and perhaps the only explanation I feel the need to offer, is that I decided to come here. The decision came out of my own head and heart. Exactly how a decision on an arrival became also a departure I am not quite sure. It remains to be examined, if not to be explained.

I do think of Roy sometimes. I think of my mother. I think of my dead father, though without thinking of him as dead. I think of my brother George, and Sally his wife, and Fiona and James, their children. I think of their house in Newington where Roy and I went often for Sunday lunch. I resented this example of normal, familial life foisted on me so regularly. Roy, on the other hand, seemed to enjoy it. George and Sally felt, or so I thought, imagined, that I needed this not so subtle reminder that I too could share in the delights of marriage and children. Nothing was ever said.

I'm fond of Sally, although I don't like to be alone in the same room as her. There is something that makes me uncomfortable – even her voice seems to have a glossy skin to it. George often told me, in the months before they married, how sensitive she was, but I can see only the poise. She is convinced I will grow out of my wrong-headedness. George tells me that too. Sally says nothing directly, but has a way of smiling on her children and turning to catch my eye. I am George's little sister. She never openly reproves her children, only suggests that they should behave differently. George doesn't beat about the bush. Like his father he is abrupt, not raising his voice, but adopting exactly the same unbending tone with just a hint of sarcasm. Fiona and James are no worse than other children, it seems to me, but being George's children they are required to be better. George and I were also required to be better than other children.

Memory tells me that I always did as I was told. I don't think that can be true, because I feared that iron voice – my grandfather worked in an iron foundry, perhaps that's where it came from – and my mother was always there with the terrible blackmail of disappointment. Oh Eleanor, how could you. Oh Eleanor, I asked you. Oh Eleanor, you haven't. I can't remember these things I did or didn't do. I would rather have been shouted at, and watching George and his children I wonder if that's what they would prefer. Anger is easier to understand than the taste of metal.

But I often say to myself, Eleanor how can you? How can you live with Roy? How can you do this to your mother? There's nothing wrong with Roy. A promising young academic with a doctorate that impressed my parents greatly. They could hardly have wished for anything better, except, of course, that I should marry him. When my mother came to visit she laid her good tweed coat and silk scarf (a Christmas present from her daughter) on the bed that Roy and I shared. What was she thinking? I wondered. Roy escorted her to an armchair and poured her a glass of sherry. She had come without my father, the family harbinger. She admired the flat, the spacious rooms, the olive-green curtains (left by the previous owner), the trendy pine panelling in the kitchen (also the choice of the previous owner).

My mother did not usually drink sherry, or anything else, at lunchtime. She sipped it with a certain gravity. I had spent hours tidying, dusting, pushing the vacuum cleaner nozzle into unfamiliar corners. I had never met Roy's parents, or visited the large untidy house in the south of England where he had grown up. The house of my childhood, where my parents still lived, was a 1930s bungalow into which my father never quite seemed to fit. He seemed to have to fold his height when he came in through the front door. Perhaps it affected his temper.

Mother must have reported back favourably, for after a while father came too. Roy behaved impeccably. He was very polite to me as well as to my parents. Not that he wasn't normally polite, but his behaviour on that occasion must have suggested that we were bound by an almost formal courtesy rather than anything remotely like passion. I had agonised for a week over the menu. My father didn't like fancy food. Avocados? I found myself wondering, in the middle of a class on the Brontës. No, perhaps not. Then, yes, why not? Avocados, definitely, but then reduced myself almost to tears when I failed to find ripe ones on the day they were coming.

We didn't exactly pretend, but we colluded in presenting an image of an upwardly mobile young married couple, for that was what my parents wanted us to be. Roy talked cheerfully. Mother responded, almost smiled. Father gradually unbent. I had arranged the table carefully. Everything on it could have been a wedding present. Here we are, mother, I was trying to say, here we are, happy, respectable, doing well. Look at all our nice things, our nice lives. Roy poured wine as if my parents drank wine with their dinner every day. My guts were knotted in my anxiety that nothing should be allowed to distort their appreciation of the scene. What worries me now is that I don't understand why I tried so hard to fool myself as well as them. Neither am I quite sure any more why I didn't want marriage while I accepted, at least for a while though always with shrewish doubts, so much of what marriage is. Was there a thrill, perhaps, in not being married, an added lustre? There was nothing very lustrous about life with Roy. Perhaps I was trying to manufacture it. But there was an air of promise, and that was what appealed to my parents. They looked around them, Roy smiled and filled their glasses, and they responded to that inimitable suggestion of potential.

Roy made love in a way that was considerate but somehow non-committal. As if his body quite liked what it was doing but his mind was somewhere else. Perhaps that's one of the things I've run away from. I did want to engage Roy's mind as well as his body, and I didn't succeed. I didn't know him. I liked him. But I watched him taking off his clothes at night, removing socks from his white feet, and had no idea what was in his head. I think about this quite a lot and ask myself if I was expecting too much. After all, you never can intrude into the mind (the heart is easier to get at) and the body is awfully good at performing illusions. I'm sure Roy was troubled by none of this. If I had tried to tell him about my difficulty he would have been puzzled, so I never tried. I would only have felt inadequate, and he would have fallen back on his kind smile.

The way I was brought up suggested that there was no place for passion in ordinary life. No tidal waves of lust that overwhelm you before you reach the bed, no sex on Sunday mornings, no longings that draw you from the food on the table to richer tastes. No making love on the hearth or in the bath. But also no hugs or impulsive embraces. No thank you kisses or farewell tears. Tears won't make it better, my mother used to say. I discovered that wasn't true. And I discovered other things, but not from Roy. Roy saw, and it seemed loved, the reserved and careful, even sometimes fearful, child of Robert and Margery Dickinson. He did not see the Eleanor Dickinson who learned to give absolutely everything she had, and didn't know she had. I can't blame him.

It's not passion I'm looking for now. I'm satisfied that I discovered it, but if I wanted it now I'd be disappointed. I detect no currents of passion here, and although I look at Steve with interest and see tenderness in his large hands and a kind of fatherliness in his manner (not, of course, the fatherliness of my own father), passion with another foreign devil, seeking some non-oriental oblivion, seems unlikely. Passion seems now an irrelevance. Perhaps it is the privilege of the indulged third of the world. Here it is work, persistence, dedication, survival, that take hold. I see earnestness in the talk of participation, democracy. Conviction, huge seriousness – we're talking life and death here – but not passion. But it may be that I am failing to recognise it, as others failed to detect it in me.

There were beggars at the railway station the other day, when I went to buy my ticket for Xian. Two brothers, I guessed. One was blind, led by the other, who yanked him by the hand and pointed silently at him in the hope the spectacle would bring forth money. They were appallingly dirty, their skin mottled with grey patches of grime. Their clothes were shreds of dirt-caked cotton. They seemed about fourteen. The seeing boy looked cunning. The blind boy's teeth were bared. They went from group to group of those who camp in front of the station, waiting perhaps a day or two for a train, but as I watched no one gave them money. The little knots of people, squatting on the ground with their bundles and cats and chickens in bamboo cages barely glanced at them. They carried on throwing dice or eating noodles from small enamel bowls, or simply did not open their eyes but continued in apparent slumber. Some of the bundles were people, wrapped in blankets, in spite of the heat.

3

STEVE HAS A bicycle, and today he borrowed one for me. It's
Sunday, and I had no lectures. We set off along one of Beijing's
ring roads that are wide as car parks. Imagine a city with acres
of new but dust-covered buildings, half-built multi-storeyed
structures topped by cranes; then suddenly you turn a corner
and you're in a narrow lane, flanked with crumbling, patchy
walls with flaking gateways and doors. If you look carefully you
can find traces of faded paint.

Thousands of men and women on bikes, children behind
or before their parents. Every time you hesitate at a crossroads
they come towards you like a cavalry charge, obeying rules and
impulses that I don't understand. The intersections are vast and
you have to pedal across an endless arena of space, a kind of
no man's land without definable frontiers. I clung to Steve, or
tried to. I was on the edge of panic, and if his bike pulled too
far ahead the thought that I would lose him brought tears to my
eyes, already stung by the dust. He says the trick is never to look
behind or to the side. Fix your gaze steadily in front of you and
whatever happens don't stop. But several times I wobbled to a
standstill and was engulfed, sure I would never get started again.
I was ignored, or the target for hostile stares, in my helpless
hesitation, while Steve's broad shoulders and greying, curly hair
vanished into an ocean of people.

I forced myself to launch across a vast space in a stampede
of bikes intermingled with ramshackle buses and trucks. And

there was Steve, grinning, his red-checked shirt dark with sweat. Then suddenly we were out of this great surging torrent and in a narrow lane, a little tributary stream which seemed centuries away. We were in amongst the hutongs. We got off our bikes and pushed them over the cracks and gaps in the road surface. Here most people were on foot, although a few Chinese on bikes bumped and wove in and out of the pedestrians. There was a smell of garlic everywhere, garlic threading through the dust. On windowsills there were pots of garlic growing. And flowers. People with almost nothing, or so it seemed, had their garlic and their flowers.

It was hot. My feet, bare in my sandals, were gritty with dust and dirt. We peered through gateways into courtyards. A single standpipe for perhaps six families. More flowers, red, pink, in battered enamel containers and plastic tubs. Bedding hung out to air. Washing hung out to dry. The dust-laden breeze catches the sleeves of a white shirt, a pair of faded cotton trousers. A man stripped to the waist washes his hair in a basin of water set on a leaning wooden table. Children. Three men squatting on their haunches, playing cards. An old woman filling a bucket. A young woman wheeling a bike in front of us with spring onions and cabbage tied to the back in a green bouquet. A small boy with his hand in that of an old, white wispy-bearded man, perhaps his grandfather, two pairs of eyes, young and old, at different levels, watching us.

My mother's mother was a teacher. We visited her sometimes, in the cottage at Dechmont which she shared with her sister, also a teacher. Grandfather had been killed in the war when his ship was torpedoed. My mother a teenager. Sometimes I tried to imagine what it was like. Growing up in a West Lothian village. The news of the ship going down. I could connect none of this with my mother, who shrank from anything out of the ordinary. She too was to have been a teacher, but marriage put an end to that.

Each gap in the decaying walls offered a window into a totally private world. Strange, remote, impenetrable. Who was I to wheel a borrowed bike down a lane in Beijing and gawp at other people's lives and point my camera at their little intimacies? I photographed the old woman's bent back. I photographed the bright squares of washing on the line. I photographed the flower pots clustered at an open door. Would I have opened the door of my smart city flat, with an invitation – watch, watch my dissatisfaction grow, neither useful nor beautiful? Examine my bright kitchen, festooned with gleaming pans and whisks and shelves of food, my bathroom hung with thick Marks and Spencer towels in stylish muted colours. Photographs of my muted life, neither beautiful nor useful, decaying out of self-neglect.

Perhaps it was self-pity that spurred me. Poor Eleanor, wasting her time with students who have no wish to learn, who flash accusatory glances if they're criticised. Circumscribed by colleagues, mostly men, clinging to the conventions that shape and dictate the criteria of success. And a few women striving to prove their worth in a world they could not bring themselves to challenge.

The professor invites us to dinner cooked by his wife and we all make a point of praising the skilfully fashioned food. The chicken breasts are cooked in an almond and cream sauce. The wine, Californian, is poured by the professor with a self-deprecatory smile. It is a subtle reminder of his triumphant year at UCLA. He describes his visit to the vineyards of the Napa Valley. The sunshine. The tastings.

We turn a corner and there is a market, with a woman buying a small slab of bean curd which she carries away gently in the palm of her hand. There is no need for Steve to say anything, and he remains pleasantly silent. We wheel our bikes. From time to time I stop and with the bike propped against my hip focus the camera. The action of taking a photograph satisfies me, although each clicking of the shutter is an intrusion. I am conscious of it, but nevertheless relish the pleasure.

I have turned a corner, but I'm not at all sure where I find myself. There have been stages on the route that are worth mentioning, if only as a kind of checklist. Or perhaps this urge to write about them is because I am so very far away and am experiencing a sensation of absence that distances me even further. It is a year ago, almost exactly. A chilly evening in early June. It has been raining all afternoon, a Saturday. I have been marking exam papers, forcing myself to concentrate, allowing no space for the thought that fairness is impossible, that the whole process is absurd. Roy is not at home. But now I am surfeited. The tortuous handwriting, the inadequate spelling. I can take no more. I can't settle at my desk with its little elegant drawers not big enough for A4 paper, nor on the sofa where I can spread papers round me on the floor. I had agreed as, glowing with possession, we wandered through the empty rooms of our newly purchased flat, you must have a study. And so the second bedroom, with its window onto the quiet back green, became Roy's study and was in due course fitted out with a handsome desk and ample bookshelves. I had a drawer in his filing cabinet.

I get up and go into the kitchen, where I read half a page of the *Scotsman* which is lying on the table. I go back into the living room and stand by the window. The evening sunlight is filtering through the breaking cloud. I've been in all day. One sheaf of exam answers after another. There wasn't even a need to go shopping to break the flow. But now I want to get out, propelled by a feeling that I might be able to catch something, absorb something, from that pale lemon light. So I pull myself from the window and snatch up a jacket, put on an old pair of trainers and, as if afraid that I might change my mind, run down the stairs from the third floor with the car keys in my hand. I'm not aware of making a decision, of thinking shall I go out? Should I stay in? Where can I go? What about the work on my desk? What will be the consequences for tomorrow if I don't do it today? But I am on my way and I know where I'm going, and for some reason there is a feeling of urgency.

By the time I get to Swanston village, tucked under the steep slopes of Caerketton and Allermuir, it is nearly nine o'clock. There was a little rain on the way, but the gleams of sunlight which drew me out are still there. I leave the car and strike up through the almost too pretty hamlet of smart whitewashed cottages and through a cluster of trees. Once on the hillside I follow the burn. I've forgotten what a steep climb it is. How long is it since I was last here? It must have been when I was a student. I remember coming with my friend Jan, after our finals. We hardly noticed the climb because we were talking, talking in the heart of a great wind which swept the slope, about men and sex and marriage.

There are a couple of golfers on the course that flanks the village. They are like automata. Golf has always seemed a strange activity. There is no one else about. A few sheep, a few fat lambs. Birds scattering like dead leaves in the wind. Mud and bog water seep into my trainers. Sharp stones reach my feet.

But I climb fast, getting out of breath, pausing, turning to see how the city and the firth broaden out below me with each few extra yards upward. I see the little coloured cars silent on the city bypass, the fingers of new building creeping into the green of unripe wheat and barley. The higher I climb the more insignificant seem the small humps of Blackford Hill and the Braids. Arthur's Seat loses its familiar shape and looks both older, more primitive, and undeveloped, unformed, as if it has not yet grown to maturity. The grassy path gives way to scree. My feet skid. I have to slow down. The air around me is thin and grey, but to the west it is bright and as I near the summit the sky fills with a smouldering pink.

I reach the ridge and pause to get my breath. I remember sitting here with Jan, it must have been the same time of year, but in the afternoon and the wind stinging our faces. We sat perched high above Edinburgh under a blue sky shredded with cloud. We only had jerseys on, and pushed our hands inside our sleeves to warm them. I don't like Edinburgh much, Jan said. I know it sounds silly, not what you're meant to feel when you finish uni, but I want to go home. Everybody talking about their plans, going abroad, getting a job, and I want to go home. She did go home, to Elgin, and married a man in the Forestry Commission. The last I heard she was working in a travel agent's, and pregnant. I think she had a boy, but we haven't kept in touch.

I have to move carefully now for on my left is an almost perpendicular rocky bastion that goes a long way down. And then suddenly the view to the south, a dense gathering of dark hills rolling beyond me, deeply shadowed, gloomy, sinister, with tassels of mist drifting in the black hollows. That on one side, and on the other a sky so radiant with gold, so extraordinarily iridescent, I can almost see gods and fiery chariots taking shape in that cauldron of colour, stabbed with fingers of cloud. For it seems alive, seething. I understand, which I have never done before with all my love of literature, how it is that humankind can have visions. It is a moment almost of ecstasy, I can think of no other word, and for the true visionary perhaps there would be no doubt about it. That sensation of being taken out of the body, of being drawn by some power beyond oneself. I cannot imagine ever experiencing it again, and I am desperate never to forget it.

I stood on that ridge, still breathless from the climb, triumphant, knowing that the presence of another would have drastically dissipated the moment. It's only a small hill, yet I felt an immense sense of achievement, intensified, perhaps even engendered, by that blazing sky. I felt that it was all mine, that I had in some way created it. No one had helped, no one had done it for me. There was no one to share it, to take any of it from me, to intrude comment or interpretation, to demand explanation or reaction, to say look at that. How marvellous. How beautiful. Offer banal words. There it was, all for me, without the aid of drugs or alcohol or poetry. I looked south again and the black hills loomed with threat. I remembered battles had been fought there. These hills that are part of my everyday landscape, even when I was growing up there were places where I could see them in the distance, green, rounded, friendly.

The mist suddenly thickened and crept round me with a cold touch. The intensity turned, for an instant, to fear, and though I looked back to the west for reassurance from the richness of the sinking sun I knew I had to get off the summit before the mist and the darkness blinded me. I started to descend, too hasty, for

I put my foot on a loose stone and fell and slid for several yards, bruising my thigh and hip. I was half lying on the slope, with a grim presentiment of being trapped on the hillside, on a night near to midsummer when frost was still possible.

Cautiously I felt my leg and ankle and then got to my feet, shaken. When I put my weight on my right foot there was a stab of pain. What a fool, Eleanor, what a bloody fool, to come up here alone. The mist had followed me down the hillside. I began to edge my way slowly on, making my left leg work harder than my right. After fifteen minutes I was aching, another ten and my muscles turned to water.

Each tiny shift of scree brought me to a halt. I could now see only a few steps ahead of me, and was shivering. Then the mist lifted as suddenly as it had descended. I reached the grassy slope and limped the rest of the way down, with a steady view of suburbia flattening before me, and came out of the territory of silence where only the curlew punctuated the current of my own thoughts, and was only a woman walking late on a June evening as the dusk was falling. The golfers had gone home, or to the nineteenth hole. It began to rain again. The car sturdily awaited me. I drove home slowly, my right foot gentle on the accelerator. When Roy returned, my muddy trainers stood in the hall, their laces trailing. He never asked where I had been. He never noticed my limp or my bruises or my swollen ankle.

Let me leave you there. In fact, maybe that was what I did, for you were not with me on the ridge between Allermuir and Caerketton. In bed that night I turned away from Roy, wincing when he unconsciously knocked my bruises. I have felt the intensity of that hilltop vision all over again, here in my shabby little room where through the open window comes the sound of bicycle bells and buses. I am tired. I'll go down the hall in a moment and shower the Beijing dust from me. I have a lecture to give tomorrow, and another meeting with Steve. I now know that he is married and has three children. It's dark outside and the lightbulb hanging crookedly from the ceiling gives only a feeble light. My eyes are aching. I have been writing for too long.

4

EVEN HERE A kind of routine takes shape. There is safety in routine, though I am troubled by it, thinking of those blind, tyrannical days, when I rose and dressed according to my occupation and walked to work. A ritual which was both refuge and prison. The walk up the hill to Princes Street, the route unvaried, across at the lights, along the side of the National Gallery, up the Playfair Steps, Roy and I together, going to work, and passing other couples coming down, going to work. Professional couples side by side. We got to know them, almost.

And the day of classes and lectures and tutorials and tedious admin and queries and letters to be written. Desperately, but hardly consciously, hoping for something that would make things different. A new student, a new face, an unexpected voice, a fresh idea, something out of the blue. Anything to stir me, to take me by surprise. The institution has ruled me for fifteen years, since I first arrived as a student. I remember the day. I remember the threadbare carpet on the floor of the room I rented. I remember the huge emptiness when the door closed and how nervously I ventured out. I had never gone away. And unlike Jan I had not even a place to go back to, at least nowhere significantly distant, for home was less than twenty miles away.

Well, I've gone away now. The vision stayed with me, that hilltop vision, and also the fear, the threat. I was, I know, silent. On most days Roy and I walked to work together, separating in George Square, he to his department, I to mine. But we usually returned separately. His days, it seemed, were longer and more complex than mine, though I was never sure why, and almost always I was home before him (felt that I should be home before him). Walking down the hill in the winter dark, or on summer evenings when I would see the blue of the firth, impossibly near and vivid, in front of me.

What would we have for dinner? Sometimes I shopped on my way home, a pound of onions from the greengrocer, something from the fishmonger who stayed open till six. Putting water on to boil before I took my coat off. My mother used to do that. Straight into the kitchen, a meal under way before she'd taken a breath. Because it wouldn't do to be late. Father would be wanting his tea.

Roy put a friendly arm around me, poured his whisky, pulled papers out of his briefcase. We ate in the kitchen. Often there was a concertina of word-processed script at his elbow. I had my sleeves pushed up, an apron on. I asked how was his day, what did he say to the difficult research student, how did the meeting, the lecture go. And he'd tell me and I'd half listen and try to remember, who was Tim or Jim or Nicky, and was Nicky male or female? What about you, love? Had a good day? He'd ask, and smile, almost indulgently. He found my devotion to the written word idiosyncratic. What could people do with a degree in literature but teach it to others who then could only teach it?

My Chinese students tell me that by reading Dickens they can understand capitalism. Most evenings Roy and I talked in the kitchen over our evening meal. Occasionally our words met and mingled, but after a while I began to feel that he saw what I did as a pastime, like patchwork or crochet. A girl thing. In spite of the fact that most of my colleagues were men. He never read novels. He could not understand why people should want to read made-up stories. When I pointed out that the societies he studied were full of stories he replied, patiently, that they were different, they were the way pre-industrial peoples explained the world. I made no comment.

If Roy took off his jacket I knew he was going to wash the

dishes. But often he picked up his briefcase and papers when he'd finished eating and went straight to his desk. I was fond of him. There was something reassuring about him, comfortable. But after that June night I felt myself becoming quieter and quieter. And not just a verbal quietness. It was as if my body, too, had withdrawn from conversation. As if there were an internal silence, as if something was growing there. But it wasn't a child.

There was a night he came home late after entertaining a visiting examiner. He had been drinking, and was amiably tipsy. Unlike some of his colleagues he didn't get loud or pugnacious when he'd had a few drinks, or revert to schoolboy attention-seeking. I was in bed, reading. He came into the bedroom, his eyes bright, sat on the bed and kissed me, pulling the book out of my hand. I couldn't respond. I felt remote, physically and emotionally at a great distance from this perfectly nice man who was climbing into my bed, a perfectly nice man whom I'd known for years. I did try. But I don't think he noticed my distance from his embraces. It didn't seem to matter.

Who was this woman? I asked myself that, although he did not. How had she been spending her time? What filled her head? Had she been out? Talked to anyone? Felt anything? Did she have views on the issues of the day? Had she washed her hair or changed her clothes? Telephoned her mother?

I could have slipped away and left someone else in my place, in my skin. As long as the woman lying in bed with her knees drawn up, a book propped on them, had seemed vaguely familiar, as long as the customary objects were around him, the alarm clock and the glass of water, the colour of the sheets and the wallpaper recognisable, there was nothing to disturb, nothing even to attract his attention. A different surface, a change in the shape of the breast under his hand or the texture of the skin – these might have been noticed. But beneath the surface? A difference in the rhythm of the heart, the configuration of the mind? One expects too much. I know that, but it's important. Without expectation, would life be worth living?

It became part of the fear. Living with someone who not only did not know me, but showed no sign of wanting to know me. The amiable Roy, who had been so nice to me in those early weeks and months when we went to concerts and ate curries in the Royal Bengal. He rarely lost his temper. He could be scathing about his colleagues but always retained a kind of geniality. And they seemed to like his company, and respect him. He was rarely critical of me. I began to wish he would be. It would have been a way of registering that things were not quite right, of making me feel relevant. As it was, I was little more than part of the base from which he pursued his career. Built success upon carefully planned success. Published another paper, gave a keynote address at another conference, was commissioned to write a major book, took part on a programme on Radio Three. These spelled progress and fuelled further aspiration. The really important milestones were marked with a bottle of champagne. I represented comfort, I think, comfort and security. In other words, what I had thought I needed, and got, from him.

The fact that we were not married did not seem to interfere with this. He was confident in the foundations of his life, for a home, jointly purchased, appropriately furnished, holding within its walls a woman who cared for him, were ample evidence of security. And besides, he always believed that marriage was just a matter of time.

Let me digress and talk about marriage for a moment. And perhaps it's not a digression, for although what I lived within was so like marriage, in many ways the reasons for my resistance to marriage remained unweakened. I guess most women accept that when they marry they are taking on not just a personality but a job, an occupation, a profession: an existence, an ethos, a way of life which in effect excludes them. For generations, centuries, women have lived with this, and it has not often been the other way round. Man's independence is tied up with man's work, and that doesn't need to mean paid employment though for most men it does. Especially now when the ability to earn, or make money somehow, is an essential feature of male identity.

In agreeing to set up house with him, I took on Roy Dunlop the anthropologist (his name Scottish, though his family had been in England for generations). And he? What was he taking on? He saw himself, I have no doubt, sharing his life with Eleanor Dickinson, not with Eleanor who had lived and breathed the written word from the age of five, who had discovered books as a way of shutting out the everyday disturbances of her growing up. Eleanor the dreamer. Eleanor the idealist. Eleanor's literature and Eleanor's idealism were frills, productive frills perhaps, attractive frills, but something to be indulged rather than taken seriously. The real Eleanor Dickinson, Roy's reality. Medium height, light brown hair, occasionally bleached nearly blonde by the sun, greyish blue eyes, a tendency to freckles, a size twelve figure, a pleasant, lively sort of girl, intelligent, alert, amenable. A companion on the journey of the high flyer, a passenger, not a co-pilot.

But Eleanor wants, wanted then, to pilot her own modest lift-off from the ground. One day she was in a pub at lunchtime, eating a toasted sandwich with a fellow graduate student, who was working on a subject eighteenth-century and esoteric. As Eleanor picked at fragments of escaping lettuce he talked at length about romanticism and landscaped gardens. Eleanor's subject was safer and simpler (and reinforced her passenger status) for she was writing about children in Victorian fiction. It was neither threatening nor of any particular interest to any of the men she knew.

I was content to listen to Bernard. His glasses made his eyes look small and round. For months I had been reading worthy fiction, much of it mediocre. I felt I was plodding, though I enjoyed it. Bernard wasn't a plodder. Nor was Roy. As I was listening to Bernard that day two young men came in and sat at the same table. One of them she knew slightly. The other was Roy. He had just come back from fieldwork in East Africa. He was very tanned. His teeth shone white and regular when he smiled, and he had a smile that spread slowly, almost uncertainly, until it lit his entire face, while at the same time his eyes widened with an apparently innocent pleasure. It was an otherwise ordinary though quite pleasing face. It was only the smile that was exceptional.

And she, Eleanor, I remember, in black jeans and a cream sweater with shapeless cuffs, her mass of unruly hair, longer then, tied round with a head band, and gold hooped earrings, which suggested a slightly gipsy air, in spite of her fair colouring, and made her look perhaps a little older and less fragile than her twenty-two years. The three men talked. Eleanor watched Roy. She liked what she saw, and from time to time his eyes included her in the conversation.

I wonder what people think they're doing when they decide to share their lives, what they think it means. Do they consider its possibility? I didn't. It's easier to share bodies than thoughts, and perhaps that's what is so misleading. (Though even sharing bodies defeats me sometimes.) I mean sharing rather than simply giving. Giving isn't so difficult. I know what Roy likes to eat, his favourite TV programmes (he is less discriminating than you might think), the whisky he likes, and that he is also partial to vodka and ginger ale. I'm familiar with the shape of his upper arms and the muscles on his back, the feel of his hip bone jutting against mine. His habits are second nature to me now: the way he comes in through the door and drops his coat on the chair in the hall. The way he gathers up his mail and takes it into his study before he does anything else, even – especially – if he's been away. The way I'm rewarded with his exceptional smile. The way he'll perform certain routine tasks, stacking dishes after a meal while he's talking so there's a curious disjuncture between words and actions. A thousand little details rooted in familiarity. This is security. This is what most people crave. And I suppose this is what gives people the illusion that their lives are shared.

I am writing in the present as if we are still together. But we are not together, and won't be ever again. I am sure of that. The habits of 'we' and the present tense are hard to unlearn. These, too, foster the illusion. To be able to say 'we'. The 'we' that so many people cling on to, that little fragment of a word, forced to carry so huge a burden, and never so bold, so distinct, so unequivocal as 'I'. And it's not 'we the people', it's not a great, expansive, all-embracing, collective 'we'. It is inward and exclusive. 'We', not 'you'.

And what about Steve? The thought inevitably intrudes at this point, though what indeed has Steve to do with any of this? With Steve I have been riding the broad city highways, swept along by streams of bicycles more alarming than the buses and the trucks, or the many fewer cars, all of which ignore red lights and regard road junctions as sectors of combat. There are collisions sometimes, but only minor ones. Or so I am told.

Steve is my guide. He has taken me under his wing. He loudly insults the mothers of those drivers who will not give way to his bulkily-pedalled made-in-China bike, or at least that's what he says his Chinese means, but no one pays much attention. We wheel down streets I have already walked, today past the long red wall of the Forbidden City, tree-lined, speckled with sun and leaf shadow. Past the bicycle park where hundreds of bikes are banked and numbered, their chrome catching the broken sunlight, tended by a woman in a white cap who looks oddly clinical, like a nurse.

I walked up this street just two days ago, making my way back from Beihai Park where I spent an afternoon. Walking circumspectly through the three youths kicking a football down the street as they ran, skipping on and off the kerb, backtracking, gracefully arcing round me, grinning, one pausing to eye me. Sweeping a hand through a swathe of black hair. Past the walls that look and feel like ancient baked clay, now crumbling and pitted, and the doors of faded carved wood set into them. They were once the homes, facing the Forbidden City, of influential men, merchants and statesmen. They were once furnished with slender, delicate chairs and couches and tables and draped with silk. They were once cool with blue-veined porcelain and fragmented light. Now they are occupied by several families, sharing the standpipe and the privy in the yard, hanging their cotton and nylon garments on a length of plastic line.

At Beihai we leave our bikes and join the crowd pouring across the bridge into the gardens. The lake is pale, hazy, with figures in boats shimmering indistinctly under the dust-laden sunshine, like an Impressionist painting seen through clouded glass. When we reach the top of the hill, an artificial hill built by an emperor, the water and the tiny figures seem miles away. The lake too, gently curved, was created at an emperor's command. Beyond it the tall misplaced, misjudged buildings of modern Beijing, criss-crossed by the long arms of cranes.

You can think of this as a vast job creation scheme, Steve says. Power depends on keeping the population occupied or suppressed. Occupied is more productive.

It's a people's park now. They move slowly. Steve adjusts his large body to a small-scale pace. I feel purposeless. I have intentions and some of them I fulfil. But I am not used to living from day to day like this, without deadlines, without responsibility, except to give a few lectures. Yes, I think, my thoughts could easily turn to revolution. Instead, they seem to have turned to writing, yet though that seems a necessary task it is too private to define my function.

We are at the top of the temple on the hill. We look out across the Forbidden City, laid out below like a vast parterre. Except that even at this distance it is dead and sterile. Waves of curled-roofed buildings, huge courtyards, gleaming marble. Steve puts a heavy arm around me. My dad was a truck driver, he is saying. Logs mainly. Steve grew up in Nova Scotia. His dad wasn't around much. Steve's arm is warm and damp on my shoulders as I look out over the red and green and marble of the emperor's palaces and think about his father driving a truck from Sydney to Halifax, places that mean nothing to me.

I was eighteen before I got to Halifax, Steve says.

I am quiescent, as if there is nothing I can do to suggest that maybe Steve should remove his arm. As if it means nothing.

But I know that's not true. Steve's wife is in Vancouver, and his children. But that is a long way from our hot dusty rides round Beijing and seems to have nothing to do with me. As Steve talks, pictures take shape. A truck roaring through dense Nova Scotian forest. A family gathered on the porch of a wooden house, like an old black and white photograph. We had a dog called Buster, Steve is saying. Another family in a neat North American garden, occupying my head as I look out on the playgrounds and palaces of emperors. Alice. Danny, Rick and Kate. The sort of names I would have expected, clean, clear North American names. Another picture, in colour this time, a painted clapboard house with mountains and cedar forests behind and the blue Pacific in front. Now we have a dog called Sandy, a golden lab. There is warmth, pleasure, in Steve's voice. Alice and Danny and Rick and Kate and Sandy. And Steve. They seem so right and comfortable. I can see Alice, slim and tanned, wearing shorts, long legs. She looks much younger than Steve. And Danny, the elder of the two boys, on the beach, throwing sticks for the dog who plunges barking into the surf. And Rick, in blue jeans and baseball cap, picking up shells and driftwood. And Kate, the youngest, not yet at school, curling her toes at the water's edge. The picture is vivid, precise, but not intrusive, a snapshot I can look at and admire and put away and forget.

Vivid but marginal. Fixed but expendable. Perhaps it doesn't matter. Perhaps being friendly means going to bed, and perhaps it doesn't. That doesn't seem to matter either. Perhaps that snapshot is entirely spurious, and Alice is dumpy, nagging, unfaithful and the boys spotty and uncouth and Kate a bundle of tantrums. But the labrador barks and wags his tail. Steve talks cheerfully, lets his arm drop. I was hoping to bring Alice this time, he is saying, but she couldn't manage it. She's doing a summer school course. Couldn't get away. The blue Pacific stretches westward and the sun is just above its rim.

Look, Steve says, his fingers touching my bare arm, its freckles deepened by the sun. A little troop of schoolchildren is filing up towards us, like miniature soldiers. They are wearing white shirts and red scarves. They give us shy looks as they pass, but don't break ranks. They can't be more than six or seven years old.

Discipline, Steve says. And they're so cute.

I'm smiling. Yes, they are. I don't want Steve. Not particularly. Yet I don't not want him. I follow him down the hill. His thick hair curls at the back of his neck. His broad shoulders are balanced by stocky hips. He looks, I reflect as I walk behind him, more than twice the weight of most Chinese, solid, steady. I like that solidity. I like his enthusiasm and the assumption that others share it. There is something safe about Steve.

5

ROY WAS SAFE too. He took note of me in the pub. We met again, and again. And so it went on. But Eleanor wasn't going to marry, not our Eleanor. She doggedly, irrationally, you might say, chose this one issue to take a stand on. Was she jealous of her own identity, or not sure enough of it? She did not pause long enough to enquire of herself what it was she was trying to protect. It was instinct. Instinct warned her to hold back from marrying the man she unquestioningly, or almost, agreed to live with nearly a year after meeting him.

So I am back with my digression, and wonder if I am stating the obvious. Lots of people have been where I was, I have no doubt. Should I have tried harder? Was there a way I could have insisted that Roy accepted what I did? Not just accepted, but genuinely acknowledged its importance to me? What kind of woman would I need to be to achieve that? The business of earning a living in the way that I had chosen – I was lucky – occupied most of the hours of my waking life, the most important hours. Roy should be able to understand that. The fact is, I never tried to make him understand. The test was that he should understand without me trying. He failed the test.

What is he thinking now? Would he like to speak to me? Would he like to write me a letter? He's never written me a letter. When he's away, on fieldwork or at conferences, he sends postcards. Would he like to send some words to the Friendship Hotel in Beijing? A message to be found by me as I pass the desk on my way to breakfast, or out to whatever the day has to offer, to be read on the steps, perhaps, as I hesitate between bicycle and bus, to be stuffed into my pocket when Steve appears. For, although Steve has wife and children, it doesn't seem quite right for me to have Roy. Or to preserve a link which I have tried to sever.

But there isn't a problem. There is no message from Roy. There is no Dearest Eleanor, come back, I need you, my heart is breaking. I'll be whatever you want me to be, do whatever you want me to do. I promise I'll take you and your work seriously. I promise I will no longer smile affectionately when you talk about your work, as if you were a child home from school.

Bullshit. Never in a million years. And I don't want transformations, I would have to say to him. If he can't be what I want (whatever that is) there's nothing to be gained from masquerade.

Steve is working today, a few loose ends to sort out. In a few days he will be leaving. I promised to see two students this morning, both girls. They want to discuss their dissertations. I talk with them for nearly two hours, in a dirty-windowed classroom. They are heartbreakingly eager, but desperate for books. I lend my copy of *Our Mutual Friend* with my notes pencilled in the margins. They promise to return it in two days. Two days? How can they each read it in that time? We got onto the subject of women's suffrage. I'd been trying to explain why Dickens wrote about women as he did. There's no need for feminism in China, one said. And the other, gathering her notebooks into her shoulderbag, bit her lip, looked at me, looked away. Democracy is the important thing, she said, the words slipping into the dusty corners of the room as if they had never been spoken.

They are late for their next class. Thank you, thank you they say, smiling, waving as they hurry away. I take the bus to the Beijing Hotel and pass again into its dim imperialist depths. After a coffee I walk up Wangfujing and go into the big department store to escape the hot, grainy air. It is gloomy inside, dingy. But it is packed with people shuffling over the uncovered floor. When

I first came I thought they were buying everything from plastic washing-up bowls to stereo radios. I watched for a while, and realised that most people were not buying at all. It was the same today. People move slowly and lingeringly from one section of the store to another. The assistants stand with their hands folded in front of them. Very little money changes hands.

I want a pair of sandals and go upstairs to where there are imported clothes. But I see nothing I like. I might be better off with Chinese plastic, or with cheap canvas slip-ons. In the dull light everything looks drab and colourless, and the dust seems to have filtered in from the street. I, too, have to move slowly with the crowds, and I feel I have become part of what I am looking at, listless and opaque. And I am aware that I am being observed.

Abruptly, I need to get out, but it cannot be done quickly. I have to hold myself to the slow movement of the press of people filling the spaces, clogged at the doors, breathing all the oxygen. As soon as I am out on the street I take a gulp of abrasive air. I spend maybe a quarter of what many people earn in a week on an ice cream. It is thin, watery, not very sweet, but I enjoy its coldness. As I am eating it, standing on the pavement, an old woman in black cotton trousers and jacket minces towards me with tiny strides, reminding me of a bird with clipped wings. Her stunted feet are in little canvas slippers. But I am the oddity, huge and light-skinned, licking an ice cream, watching an old woman with mutilated feet in Wangfujing.

Tomorrow, Steve says, he will take me to meet some friends in Jianguomenwai, where the foreign diplomats live. We'll go to the Friendship Store first, then drink duty-free gin with his friends. But today I am alone. Steve has written down for me, in English and Chinese, the names of places I might visit. If I walk back to the Beijing Hotel I can get a taxi. I can't face the bus in this heat, or negotiating for information as to which bus I should get on. I reinforce my uncertain pronunciation by pointing to the words on Steve's paper when I attempt to communicate with the taxi driver. He screws up his eyes and sucks the end of the thin moustache that outlines his upper lip. Finally he nods. As the taxi moves away from the kerbside he switches on the radio. We make our journey across town to the accompaniment of UB40 and 'Red, Red Wine'.

Music and smell are the most suggestive triggers to memory. Sitting in the back of a Chinese taxi and not entirely sure I am being taken to where I want to go, I am suddenly whisked back two years, three years, when that song floated through pubs and public places and an intense homesickness grabs me painfully and unexpectedly. Suddenly I am longing for the familiar. The temple I am going to loses its attraction and becomes almost ominous, horribly foreign, threatening, a struggle. I think of the pub on the corner where Roy and I sometimes met on a Saturday night. I never liked it. It was packed and pretentious. We rarely found a seat. Yet we went on meeting there in those early months. Or lunch with colleagues in a wine bar near the university. I am nostalgic for bland quiche and coleslaw with sharp dressing out of a jar, for a slab of yellow cheese and a little pond of pickle with a ploughman's lunch, a glass of not quite cool enough white wine. Have I really left all that? Forever? The word means very little. Was it, is it, my intention not to return? Was I really not going to hedge my bets or build in the option of return, with honour? Was I leaving the job, the place, the people? Sure, I had wanted to set it all firmly behind me. And yet, how could I not return?

I discussed my plans with no one. And they were hardly plans. A decision crystallised in my mind and grew: that was enough. In the days that followed nothing changed. I drank coffee with Clare and Kirsty, my allies in the department, and we were bitter, as usual, about the selfish ambition of others. But I said nothing about the sparkling crystal in my mind. I never said, well, not for much longer. Soon it will all be behind me. They never said, Eleanor, we envy you. Or, Eleanor, you're crazy.

Because there was nothing to tell them yet. I had to rein in my sense of expectation, and it was September before the next signal came. I recognised it at once. A chance meeting, a chance conversation. A British Council employee talking about the Far East, exchanges, visiting lecturers. I wasn't interested in an exchange, I said, but who should I contact about going there to teach? He gave me a name.

'Red, Red Wine' plays me to the Tibetan temple. Within a few weeks it was all arranged, but I waited until the new year before I quietly started to prepare. I quietly planned new lectures. I bought clothes. I resigned quietly. Quietly I drew attention to the fact that I would not be around to mark exam papers. I told my students. And quietly I told Roy.

A hush seemed to fill those months. Was it quietness or cowardice? Was it because I was afraid someone might try to dissuade me? Eleanor, what are you doing? You can't just throw in your job... What do you know about China? What happens after you've given your lectures? What then? Yes, okay, great to go there for a term, but to walk out on everything?

I had rehearsed it all so thoroughly I could not face hearing it flung back at me. A few days before I had met the man from the British Council, talking in a noisy, crowded room with glasses in our hands, Roy and I had gone to visit my mother. It was a Saturday afternoon, sunny, and we sat in the garden. She had seemed oddly serene. It would soon be a year since my father's death, and she had slowed to a pace that I scarcely recognised. She let me make tea and bring a tray out to the garden. I noticed, almost with shock, that she wasn't wearing stockings. Her bare legs, knotted with varicose veins, were stretched out to the sun. I hadn't seen her for more than a month. I resented the fact that since my father's death it was harder, not easier, to be with her, and I had never discussed the reason for this with Roy, who was, as always, charming.

We didn't drive straight home afterwards, but instead walked by the canal, as I had done with my father. He always went for a walk on Sunday afternoons, rain or shine, and sometimes insisted that I or George, or both of us, came with him. My mother never accompanied him. As far as I was aware, she was never asked.

It was late afternoon. There were a few people, some with dogs or children. The path is narrow and most of the time we had to walk single file. Roy stopped to watch a pair of coots, slipped his arm around me as I stood by his side, and, without preamble, said, 'Eleanor, what about...' I'd lost count of the number of times he had, directly or indirectly, raised the subject of marriage. This time I said yes. It seemed easier that way. We kissed on the canal bank, each happy for different reasons.

With the end of the year we began to talk about dates. It made sense to wait until summer. I didn't feel I was prevaricating. Nor that I was being cruel. Rather, that I was making it easier to leave. In March I told him. He smiled and took my hand, and said, why don't you wait until after we're married? He said he understood my need for independence, that he wouldn't stand in my way. A week later I tried again. Roy, I've resigned. I'm going away. I'm not going to marry you. Oh come on, love, he said. I know it's important for you to do this China thing now, before other responsibilities get in the way. I don't have a problem with that. We don't need to get married this summer. It can wait till you get back if that's what you want. It's for our families as much as anything, you know. But it would be good to settle a date. I began to wonder if I had lost the connection between the words in my head and the words that I spoke. Was I thinking and hearing something different from what I was saying?

Homesick, resentful at feeling homesick. Eleanor, you can't abandon your past. It follows you. It nags you. It is you. It runs in front of you and waylays you in unexpected places. Especially that. It's there as you round a corner, as you climb the rolling curve of the Great Wall, as you sit by the open window of the Friendship Hotel and stare out into the balmy dark. The past and what you remember are what you are and you should not be surprised at any of the things it does to you. If do not look back is good advice, that is because you do not need to look back. The past is with you. The taxi has arrived at the temple and delivered you and all your baggage. I am where I want to be.

Perhaps this is a good moment for another stab at explanation.

The thought occurs to me, at least. The longer I am in China, over a month now, the more I am taken up with what is going on around me. That's what I want to tell you about. Yet that isn't entirely right, for these probings into the past are running like an undercurrent to everything I do and see. So I am not forcing myself to write about them. They are bubbling naturally to the surface, the words forming themselves independently as I sit here with pen and paper. I should learn to travel like a journalist, with a typewriter under my arm. Although in China writing with a pen on paper is far more appropriate. And it is a satisfying activity.

Where was I? What has bubbled to the surface now? At the gates of the Tibetan temple. I'll pause here, as indeed I did. Through the gates I found myself in a beautiful walled garden with shrubs and flowers and fruit trees spread against the wall. It is a pool, a tank of sunlight. Everything seems to have a translucent quality, as if seen through water. I can't understand what has happened to transform the light, for we are still in the middle of the city. There is a grace, an elegance, an eloquence that was entrancing, so as there were seats spaced along the walkways I sat down for a while transported away from pubs and UB40 and thinking instead, with equal dislocation, of the sort of 'temple of love' imagery that you find in some English poetry. And it was that, I suppose, that led me to Daniel, about whom I've never had much to say to anyone, indeed there was much that could not be said. Daniel discovered an Eleanor that was a great surprise to me. I thought of Dan, for minutes, perhaps only for seconds, and when I opened my eyes I was in a Buddhist temple in Beijing and sitting on the seat beside me, with perhaps a metre between us, was a young Chinese man in jeans and a black T-shirt. He smiled.

I am twenty-three years old. My work has started to go well. I have emerged from a period of a year and a half or so, during which I felt buried in obscurity and uncertainty, unsure of what I was trying to do, unsure of my abilities, unsure of myself. Roy perhaps had something to do with this, with the uncertainty and with the emergence. The effect of meeting him, of falling instantly in love with his slow smile (but not, I gradually realised, with the rest of him) has been a kind of excavation of the ground beneath my feet. I had not wanted to examine it too closely. But as I grew more unsteady I found I needed him more.

There is also the grip of academic life. I've been learning to play the game and find I can do it skilfully enough, although I know my heart isn't in it, and I don't like it. I give papers to my peers in seminars and take potshots at academic egos. My marksmanship improves, but I never learn to disguise the pain when I am the target. I am patronised, of course. I get angry, but I only express this anger to one or two women friends who share it. To Clare and Kirsty, who respond with even more blistering tales of their own experiences. I hate the way I and other women submit to the competitiveness of the male and the clubby comradeship that goes with it. I don't make an issue of this with Roy and push my uneasiness to the back of my mind. I am doing alright. My thesis is nearly finished. There are many hours of checking and confirming to be done, but the argument is there. From time to time the thought slides into my mind that it might become a book.

On my twenty-fourth birthday Roy was away. My parents were expecting me to go home for my birthday. I pleaded the excuse that I was struggling with the final chapters of my thesis, which I knew would impress them. And it was true that I was working very hard, driven now by a deadline and a compelling desire to get it finished. But that was not the real explanation of my reluctance to go home, although I was genuinely worried that any disruption might cut off the flow of adrenalin. When she heard that I wasn't going home, Sally got on the phone. I declined her invitation too. She got George to speak to me. I said I was planning to go out with friends. I sensed his disapproval. He liked Roy, and clearly thought that in his absence I should spend my birthday with my family. Roy and I were not yet living together. When Roy and Sally dropped heavy hints about our plans, our future, I metaphorically looked the other way.

I was still living in the basement flat which I shared with a piano player and her two cats. Julie was even more hard up than I was, and taught a few small children who were dragged to her every week by determined mothers. I got used to the scales and arpeggios that reverberated erratically through the rather damp premises. In fact, I grew to find something rather soothing about them. Roy lived in more desirable quarters nearer the university. He rarely came to Leslie Place. He didn't like the cats or the smell of damp. Although he didn't say so, I don't think he liked the piano teacher or the arpeggios either. At weekends I usually joined him in his roomier space. It was all his own, so we had it to ourselves. We usually had two domestic days together. Roy joined in the planning of meals, the shopping, the cooking. Sometimes we went to see a film. On Friday evenings we had a drink in the crowded pub. On Sundays we read the papers. The rest of the time we worked.

So that night, the night of my birthday, I did indeed go out with friends, and I met Daniel. There were six of us, the only customers in a recently opened tiny bistro in the High Street. It was Daniel's bistro. He owned it and managed it. He had started it with money left him by his father, whom he had not seen since he was nine years old. When Daniel discovered it was my birthday he produced a bottle of Chianti on the house and sat himself down with us. We'd been having a noisy and convivial meal. There was no one else to serve. He drank wine and coffee with us, relaxed but intriguingly separate. Later the cook emerged from the kitchen, wiping his greasy hands, pushing his blond hair back from his face, and taking a glass from another table poured what was left of the wine and lit a cigarette.

I didn't think much about Daniel then. He had a thin, dark face and almost black eyes. He talked with us easily, about the restaurant, about his student days in London, about teaching in a school in Surrey suburbia. At the same time he was attentive to our glasses and our coffee cups, an unobtrusive host. When he stood up to fetch more coffee I realised he was smaller and slighter than he seemed sitting at the table, and that he moved gracefully, with judgement, as if he were aware of just how much energy was required and had no intention of expending more than was necessary.

It was after midnight when we left, and we invited him to come with us, to go on to someone's flat, where we spent another hour or two, drinking more wine and more coffee and listening to Lionel Hampton on the stereo. Daniel sat next to me on the sofa. It was then, with his denim-covered thigh next to mine, that I was invaded, that something seemed to burst in my throat, as if I had taken a breath and could not let it out, and it could only explode. I felt that Daniel must be as aware as I was of this extraordinary sensation. I think I coughed, choked. I heard my heart thumping. But Daniel went on talking. I tried to breathe quietly. The surge of current, which had surely come from him, receded. Soon after, I got up to go home. The others left too and we all went our separate ways. I did not notice Daniel going or the direction he took. I walked home alone through the empty streets. A couple of taxis passed me. Just as I neared my front door a car slowed and I caught a glimpse of a shadowy face turned towards me.

For a day or two I felt quite shaky. I could not get Daniel out of my head, yet I didn't feel I could go back to the bistro, though it would have been easy enough to drop in for a coffee. It was just round the corner from the library where I was spending most of the day. But sometimes you have to believe in fate. The following week I was going up the hill to the library when I saw him on the other side of the street. He crossed on the red light to greet me, as if I were an old friend. He had a bundle of baguettes under his arm. Come and have lunch today, he said. He turned down the corners of his mouth, like Pierrot. We're not busy at lunchtime, *malheureusement*.

I sat down at a small table with a checked tablecloth and a red carnation in a narrow vase. Without asking me what I would like to eat, Daniel put in front of me a plate of lamb that smelled of ginger, and introduced me to Pete, the cook. Both English, they had met in Edinburgh at Festival time. Pete, a newly graduated chef, was without a job. Daniel ditched his. Pete stood beside Daniel in his white knotted apron, wiping his hands as he had done when I'd first seen him. He looked younger than Daniel, his face sweaty and his hair curling damply on his forehead. They were of similar height though Pete had broader shoulders and both his hair and his skin were pale. Beside him, Daniel's hair looked even blacker and his skin more olive.

I ate my food and drank a glass of wine, also put in front of me without asking. There were a few other customers. Daniel served them, yet was able to make me feel at the centre of his activity. I was impressed at the way he managed this, for there was no sign that the others felt neglected while my needs seemed his chief concern. I should have returned to the library. Instead I drank coffee and read the paper that Daniel provided, as the other customers left and Pete and Daniel finished in the kitchen. They stayed open all afternoon. A middle-aged American came in and asked for Earl Grey tea and shortbread. A woman came in with two Marks and Spencer shopping bags and had a mineral water.

Daniel sat with me. He explained that Pete took a break in the afternoon, before starting to cook for the evening. He nodded towards the man and the woman, each at their separate tables. It's hardly worth staying open through the afternoon, he said, but you always hope that having come in for a cup of tea, if you're nice to them they'll return for a meal.

There was nothing I could do. I could not take myself away, back to the books and papers I had left on the library table. Daniel talked easily about how he and Pete had got the bistro going, borrowing more money, working all night, setting up the kitchen themselves, painting the walls, making curtains on a sewing machine they found in a skip. I didn't think I was in love. I didn't think that was possible. I told Daniel about Roy. That was settled. Having done that, I sat without a thought in my head except to remain in Daniel's company for as long as I could, to watch his mobile mouth, the corners turning up or down, his deep, black-coffee eyes.

I didn't tell Roy about Daniel.

And so it all unfolded. Slowly, surely. I could not detach myself. I was exhilarated, I was frightened, I was spellbound. I was not in control. Whatever Daniel suggested I accepted. But it wasn't a sudden whirlwind of passion. It all took time. That afternoon did not end with Eleanor in Daniel's bed. It wasn't like that at all. We got there slowly, not only because Roy returned and I had to account for myself, but because of the magic in the process itself.

6

I ABANDONED YOU in the Tibetan temple. Let me return there, to the garden with the sculptured fruit trees and crisp vegetation watered and cared for, red, white and yellow, jewels in a tank of light. I watch people pass. It is something I value about travelling alone. You can watch as you like, when you like. Your attention can wander and search. There is nobody there to insist that you look or listen or attend to what catches their notice. But I am not quite alone. There is a young man in jeans and a black T-shirt sitting at the other end of my bench, his hands on his knees. He looks Chinese, yet there is something about him which seems to be not Chinese. He smiles again, and this time I smile back.

I try to identify the people who pass me. Some Chinese, a group of Japanese tourists marched along by their team leader with a megaphone in her hand, a couple I guess are German. The Japanese stop every few paces to take photographs of each other. They stand smiling in front of blossoming trees and curved buildings, masking their colour and grace. I get up from my seat and carry on walking. Yong He Gong, the palace of peace and harmony. It has a confident but not over-bold splendour. Once an imperial palace, built in the seventeenth century in the reign of Kang Xi, in a time when a palace could be built on a whim, a fancy in an emperor's eye when he got up in the morning. But this palace is on a scale which I can understand. It became one of the residences of the third Qing Dynasty Emperor.

I am not used to the clarity of the sunlight here. It seems to have dispersed the dust. Perhaps it is simply the power of the encrusted colour on each building. The arched gateways, the halls and temples, red, gold, green, blue. Bronze lions sit on their haunches, curly-maned and open-mouthed. Fire smoulders in bronze cauldrons. People come up and light splints in the coals before setting them upright to burn slowly with a wisp of smoke. Dozens of smoke wisps coil upwards. A monk presides, watchfully, almost suspiciously. I find his shaven head and saffron robe forbidding, the face controlled as if to hide what might be latent aggression. I move away before raising my camera to take a photograph, as I feel instinctively that he might lunge at me and wrest the camera from my hands. And maybe it is offensive of me to be recording his actions. Nevertheless, I continue to put my camera to my eye and click the shutter. Others are doing the same.

Two young girls in white nylon blouses take their splints to the fire. All this is quite recent, you know... it is the man who shared my bench. Not so long ago this place was derelict, he goes on. He speaks English with a slight American accent. Forgive me for interrupting, but I noticed your interest. Are you English? It wasn't the first time I'd been accosted. A woman on a bus had wanted to practise her English. A man had got off his bicycle and walked with me as he asked about medical services in Britain. He was a doctor. I had got used to being stopped and questioned.

I'm from Scotland, I say. He laughs. Ah yes, I know it is different. I've just come back from the United States. I was studying there, at Yale. New Haven, Connecticut, he explained. Do you know it? I shook my head and told him I had never been to the United States. But you've heard of Yale University? he asked. Of course. He seemed relaxed, yet he looked over his shoulder, almost nervously. It's an interesting place. It's an interesting country. I was there for three years, studying. There have been a lot of changes while I've been away.

Now I understand why I had thought there was something not Chinese about him. The jeans, the T-shirt, the sneakers, like hundreds of other young Chinese, except they are all American. He notices my glance. Oh yes, my clothes, they are all American. I brought some Levis back for my wife and little daughter. Everyone wants Levis. But my wife is not here. Last month she got a teaching position in Wuhan, so she is there, and I have not been able to visit her yet. Her parents are looking after my child. You know, it is often like that here. We all have to work, so the older people look after the children. And often we can't choose where we work. He speaks in a practised way, as if used to explaining Chinese peculiarities.

I say I have learned something about how things are since I came to China. I ask him what he studied at Yale. History, he says, western history. My name is Lin Bingshen. In the United States everyone called me Bing. Like Crosby, he laughs. I tell him my name – he has difficulty with Eleanor – and we shake hands. I tell him that I teach English literature. May I walk with you through the pavilions? he asks. I can hardly say no.

Each pavilion has a name. The Hall of the Wheel of Law. The Wanfu Pavilion. The Hall of Yong He Gong, the central hall, houses bronze statues of Ran Deng, Sakyamuni and Maitreya, the past, the present and the future generations of the Buddha. There is a smell of incense, light, unobtrusive, but everywhere. At the altars are offerings of cakes, fruit and sweets, piled high on plates, dusty and unattended mountains. Inside the Wanfu Pavilion a statue of the Maitreya carved in white sandalwood rises eighteen metres above the ground. One hand is lifted, the other waist high, palm towards the ground. Maitreya is swathed in jewels and draperies. He has not yet renounced worldly possessions, not yet stripped himself of material clutter. Behind him are glossy, gilded galleries. I find it difficult to breathe. It isn't the incense, although I can't escape its tantalising scent. Churches sometimes have the same effect, unless they are products of the austere Calvinism of my own upbringing.

I can't get used to it, Bingshen says. I don't believe in all this stuff, but it fascinates me. There seem plenty of people who do believe in it, I say, referring to the taper-burners. They need something, we all need something, Bingshen says, looking over his shoulder again.

In the Hall of the Wheel of Law, Tsongkapa, founder of the Yellow Hat sect of Tibetan Buddhism, smiles benignly into the middle distance. I am not happy with his seeming detachment. He is bronze, not so high as the Maitreya, and sits cross-legged in the lotus position. There seems to me to be little to smile about. I do not like these smiles. Everywhere there are images. A gleaming Green Dalaha, bare-breasted, coquettish, her lotus seat parting her thighs. A golden mandala. A pagoda in gold filigree. A bronze Auspicious Goddess sideways on a horse. Cymbals, horns and chank-shell trumpets. Skull cups and peacock feathers. Silver adds to the intermittent glitter in the dim light.

But there is enough light to see that Lin Bingshen looks at it all through narrowed eyes. We all need something, he repeats. We pause in a dark corner and look where a square of bright sunlight fills and empties as people come and go. He says, so unsure, so insecure. If you believe that yours is the one road, the true road, why so worried that there might be spiritual rivals? Why does it matter if other people are wrong? Do you know the answer to that? I am sure you do. You teach literature. There must be answers in those books. Politics, religion... in history, you cannot separate them, you know. Sometimes people think you can. They are wrong. So why now rebuild the Buddhist temples?

I turn away from another smile, the sinister half-smile and the almost-closed eyes of the Buddha. Why do I find it so disturbing? Why do I retreat from the suggestion of gluttonous inwardness? But I think I find all conspicuous signs of saintliness difficult. I am more likely to linger over the more garish artefacts, the blend of human skulls and silver, of bronze and human thighbones, curious memorials, actual relics of humanity. In Tibet bones not thus preserved were burned while the flesh was ritually fed to the vultures. It was necessary to eliminate all of the body, unless it could have some spiritual function. I can see some logic in that.

Maybe it is for the tourists, Lin Bingshen continues. Now,

China wants tourists. Do you like this? He gestures towards the amalgam of bones and precious metal.

It's intriguing, I reply cautiously.

But gruesome maybe?

I don't think I find it gruesome, not the bits of human bodies. Perhaps it is better to keep the dead with us like this, if you think there is some use in it. In the west, death embarrasses us. We do everything we can to disguise it. But the Buddha – I don't care for him. There's something about his smile.

Look around, Bingshen says. I am not a Buddhist, but you can see that there are many people being drawn back to some kind of religious belief, something that isn't communism, that is beyond economics. Or seems to be. A short distance from here is another temple, a Confucian temple. It used to be one of my favourite places, though I'm not a Confucian either. You should go there too. You'll find an older China there.

He spoke as if he were about to tell a story, but then abruptly said, I have to go now. I would like to invite you to my home, the home of my wife's mother and father where I am staying, where my daughter is. But I cannot.

He takes a step back. We look at each other directly for the first time. He is taller than the average Han Chinese, with a squarer face. I wonder where he comes from, but do not ask, because his face has changed, as if shutters have closed. Perhaps somewhere to the north or west, I speculate. His hair is cropped very short and he has gracefully arched eyebrows. There are lines at the corners of his eyes. I guess he is older than I thought at first, probably more than thirty, perhaps my own age.

He stretches out his hand and I have to reach to take it. You are staying at the Friendship Hotel? Perhaps we will meet again. You know, one day, maybe one day, democracy will come to China, and all kinds of comradeship will be possible. I grip his hand harder. As he lets go he says, there are many things I would like to talk to you about.

I watch him walk out into the sunlight and towards the gate, threading his way easily through knots of people. He is slim and moves gently. He doesn't look back. I think of Daniel.

I follow, but slowly, back through the peaceful, translucent garden, though it too seems removed from the humanity that streams through it with cameras and chatter. Here the Chinese have turned their attention to preserving traditions of Tibet. In Tibet they've battled against them, and the Tibetans have fought back. That is something we might have talked about. As I leave, more buses draw up. It is midday now. Crowds pour in through the temple gates. Bing, like Crosby, has disappeared.

I decide to go in search of the Confucian temple, and cross the road. I stop in the shade of a high crumbling wall to study my map. I've almost missed it. I walk up a narrow, dusty street and find a dingy and unimposing gateway. As I pass through it the morning does not change and the city's din is scarcely any further away, yet something happens. There is a change, almost imperceptible. I look down a long path lined with trees. There are seats under the trees. Only one is occupied. An old man in blue cotton is reading a newspaper. His hair is grey. He wears spectacles. I pass him slowly and he does not raise his eyes, but pushes his spectacles more firmly on his nose and carefully turns a page.

The temple is dilapidated, seedy, hung with dust that stirs as I make my way through. There are no throngs of visitors here. Just a handful of curious individuals, and no Europeans. Everything is grey except for the blue and white of clothing. A man wheels his bicycle out of a narrow doorway, across a courtyard, under an ancient, twisted, knotted tree with pale gouged bark. I feel bathed in peace, and at the same time prickling with the wariness of an intruder. Yet I also feel invisible. No one appears to see me, to register my movements, across courtyards, through doorways.

A door leans half off its hinges. I move cautiously through, and there is a strange collection of musical instruments, penned in by netting, yet not out of reach, though I don't need to touch to discover that they are thickly covered in dust, which lies on each gong and set of cast-iron bells like a snug, protective blanket. There are zithers with broken strings, the snapped ends curled and shrunken. Drums lie in their faded red and gold paint. In the gloom they are dignified yet forlorn, like royalty in exile. Helpless without the sounds that proclaim their life. I stay with the instruments for a while and think of Steve. Does he have such things in his collection? He must know of these, surely. The quilting of dust cuts out any distant sound. The streets have disappeared. Here silence invades every sense. No one else comes in to see this sad collection.

I wander out, slowed down again like everything around me. Into the sunlight, then into another dim hall, which turns out also to be a museum. Here the objects are bronze vessels and ceramic bowls and jugs. There are labels, photographs, depictions of what I guess are burial sites. But the impression remains drab. I peer at the colours of *famille rose* porcelain, but they have a tired look.

Yet this neglect does not depress me. I feel strangely comfortable with it, and moved by it also. I go back to the old, twisted tree and sit for a while in its shade on a seat that creaks and shifts under me. I am not exactly lethargic but feel as if any sense of need of energy or speed has been drawn out of me, as if the only appropriate way of moving is slowly and gracefully. I am wondering – and I don't remember thinking of this before – why I have found it so hard, why almost everyone I know has found it so hard, to avoid speed, or the feeling that in some way speed is necessary and good.

Perhaps it is the inspiration, but as I sit under the twisted tree I recollect the way I did the housework at weekends, charging through task after task. Always compelled to deal with it fast, as if time spent on it could not be acknowledged as real time. I would whip round the furniture with spray polish and cloth, propel the vacuum cleaner from room to room, mop the kitchen floor with rapid strokes, swirl water and cleanser round the bath. And, an extension, push a supermarket trolley briskly up and down the aisles.

Of course I resented the time spent on such chores. Of course I resented Roy's unequal participation, the silent assumption that the care of our living space was my role, and also a task of very little consequence, however necessary. When Roy was domestic, and he was sometimes, he worked with an air of getting through an insignificant if necessary routine. But here, in the courtyard of a Confucian temple in Beijing, it came to me that cleaning was of ritual importance, and should be relished, and accomplished with skill and grace and conviction, not hurried, not despised. Religion had recognised its importance, drawn it into the spiritual, but so far as I know no religion has allowed those who perform the everyday tasks of keeping the home clean to be regarded as signifying more than a means to a practical end.

There is more to see. I find a hall of stones, tablets on which classics of Confucian literature are engraved. For this was not only a temple, but a college, a place of study and scholarship. There are two Chinese men there among the stones, respectable but shabby, middle-aged, peering at the chiselled characters which mean nothing to me. They make excited dashes from pillar to pillar, as if they were playing hide and seek in a petrified forest.

In part of the courtyard there are more stones, taller than me, engraved with the names of all those successful in the civil service examinations. There are several thousand names. These were the survivors, the successful survivors. The examinations were a three-day ordeal. Each candidate was locked into a tiny cubicle for that time and not let out until the examination was completed. The experience killed some, and drove others out of their minds. Once you had begun there was no escape. Even without the turned key it would have been too shameful to give up. Death or insanity was preferable.

I had made choices, though the circumstances were less extreme. Choices from which there is no turning back, in a way locked in a cubicle, walled in. Identified as a high-flyer when I precociously read aloud from *The Wind in the Willows* at the age of five: the choice was made. George was industrious rather than clever. His industry was rewarded and encouraged; industry was more to be trusted than intelligence. Its trajectory was more easily predicted. Pocket money was increased, presents given, as successes were scored. He liked to excel, to be not just good but best, and worked hard for those rewards. In a way I admired him for it. I was 'bright', not better or best, certainly not ever better than George. But I had to ensure, was expected to ensure, that everything I did was a reflection of that brightness. A less than acceptable mark, a careless piece of homework, inattentiveness in class, uncooperativeness at home – these were locked out. And of course, I was 'bright' at the unimportant things – English, history, languages, not maths and science.

I was expected to be bright, but I was only rarely given books, and never poetry or stories. I brought my good marks home from school and knelt on the bedroom floor in front of my doll's house. My father made it for me. This was his weekend occupation, in the shed in the garden, folding his large frame into a small space, wearing his old grey hand-knitted jumper. The sound of the saw and the smell of varnish mingling with the smell of burning leaves. For my birthday is in the autumn, and the doll's house was a birthday present. My father made furniture for it, though I longed for the more sophisticated plastic products that could be bought in toyshops. But he cut and glued tables and chairs and my mother sewed tiny cushions and bedspreads. It was the only tenderness I can remember, this labour, this close attention. For my mother and father did not embrace me. Apart from a pat on the shoulder now and then, my mother only touched me incidentally, when she fastened my buttons or brushed my hair or straightened the sleeve of a cardigan. I think it was for my eighth birthday I was given the doll's house. Look after it, my father said.

Every birthday there was more furniture. With my pocket money I bought tiny cups and saucers for the kitchen, and miniature legs of lamb and bowls of fruit. My father carved a lamp for the bedroom and my mother knitted a little square of rug for the floor. I collected a television set, a telephone, a tray of glasses coloured pink. There was a family to live in the house. Father in a grey suit. I cut out a fragment of newspaper to place between his hands. Mother in a flowered apron, a scrap from the sewing basket that was kept in the dining room cupboard. A little boy in shorts and a little girl in a skirt.

I arranged mama stiffly at the kitchen sink and sat papa down in an armchair. Little boy rode on a minuscule rocking horse. Little girl I placed in the kitchen with her mother. But having achieved the desired arrangement there was not much more I could do. The satisfaction lasted only minutes. I could, and did, move the furniture around. I could make the little boy walk up and down the stairs or sit him in front of the television. I could make the little girl lean out of the open window or go to bed. Mama could answer the telephone. Papa could walk in and out of the front door. And all of this I did, every day when I got home from school, and looked forward to doing as I came along the street.

But after a few minutes I would lose interest. I knew it pleased my parents, to think that I was in my bedroom quietly playing with my doll's house. I recognised the approval, I liked it. When I drifted away and picked up a book, and stretched out on the floor on my stomach to read until tea-time, I let them think that the silence behind my closed door was the silence of absorption in what they had given me.

There was more action in a book. You could do more with the people there than with the tiny stiff puppets who inhabited my little house. There was more noise, more argument. They liked me to be good at reading, yet they were not happy to see me with books, unless they were the schoolbooks on the dining room table, books with sums and maps and stories about Robert the Bruce and Mary Queen of Scots. Reading was a tool. At the margins of its usefulness was the worry that it was also a pleasure, and if it was enjoyed, how could it be beneficial?

They would find me sometimes, curled up in a chair, oblivious to the family activities around me. I would jump up guiltily and try to be a part of what was going on. But there was rarely very much going on that I felt could include me. There were the comings and goings of George and his friends. But I had no place with them, although sometimes I hovered enviously. The alternative to reading was to sit with those other books at the dining room table to avoid being told to find something useful to do. I might bargain for a spell of television watching. On occasion I would ask my mother to let me bake scones or volunteer to help my father in the garden. The response was often, there isn't time just now. I'm too busy. You can do it another day. You'll just make a mess and I've the tea to get.

And if my aimlessness became too noticeable, or if the silence from behind the closed door of my room lasted for too long, I'd be reminded of my homework, or sent to the shops, or asked to polish the candlesticks or feed the cat. I won prizes at school and brought home books with inscribed bookplates. These were passed round visiting relatives and friends. Was Eleanor going to be a teacher? My mother said she thought so, and sometimes added, I was going to be a teacher. My father said, it's early days. Sometimes the question was directed at me. Do you want to be a teacher, Eleanor? It was easiest to say yes, and there was some truth in it. Yet early on I was bothered by a discrepancy. Somewhere I realised that reading *Macbeth* at the dining room table with a jotter beside me was closely related to spending a summer afternoon in the garden, half-hidden by the rhododendrons, devouring *The Thirty-nine Steps*. Somewhere I realised that it wasn't quite right that one should be encouraged and the other frowned on.

I was good at history, and geography too. I liked maps. I liked the brown clusters of mountains. My father would have liked me to study geography. That was a good and serious subject for a girl. It was useful. George was going to be a lawyer. I was only a girl, and therefore the rigours of the legal profession were not appropriate. But geography was alright. I would become a teacher of geography, in a school like the academy I attended, with a long tradition, aspiring to, if not attaining, decency and good order. Until in the course of time I married and had children, their grandchildren, whom I would care for, having done my bit, made my mark in a small way, earned my living performing a task that everyone recognised as purposeful.

I think my mother must have enjoyed her English lessons at school, though she never said so, for she visited the library regularly, to choose historical fiction and detective stories, which she read slowly. It was a weakness my father was prepared to indulge, though she did not often read when he was in the room and perhaps he was not aware of its extent. It was tacitly assumed that reading books, especially novels, was not an acceptable activity in front of other people, not quite good manners. I sensed – what was it? – embarrassment I think. Even the magazines, neatly ensconced in a magazine rack, were rarely brought out in the evenings, when my father sat and smoked his pipe, and read the paper (not the same as a book), or watched comedy programmes at which he rarely laughed.

I am writing this in my now familiar dusty room. It is very quiet. There are occasional footsteps in the corridor, but no one knocks on my door. After an hour or so in the Confucian temple I was hungry and thirsty, but I decided to walk to Jingshan Qianjie, where I thought I could get a bus that would take me to the west of the city, to the Friendship Hotel. It was hot, and my steps stirred up grit from the pavement. It was as if I were moving in my own self-created cloud, like a horse or a camel crossing the desert. But I wanted to walk, needed to walk, which I did slowly, still under the influence of the temple peace. Perhaps the cloud came from the temple. In half an hour or so I'd reached the busy main street that runs north of Beihai Park and found a bus whose driver nodded and smiled at my scrap of paper and its Chinese characters.

I was too late for lunch. I bought a bottle of beer and a box of biscuits at the counter. I drank the beer in my dark little room. Afterwards I went outside and fell asleep on the parched grass. There was no sign of Steve this evening. I don't know where he is. I ate my supper alone and went to my room and sat down with my pad and pen. I want his arms around me.

7

DANIEL. THERE IS more to tell. But I find it difficult to write about Daniel, not just because if I am to be at all honest it means writing about physical intimacies which in retrospect may seem more silly than sexy, but because I am nagged by a need to justify his presence in my life. And there is something else. Writing about Daniel means exposing my own blindness.

Just being in the same room, aware of him. Aware of him aware of me. It wasn't entirely a physical sensation, although I did feel as if the surface of my skin had risen above my flesh. Walking along the street together, our arms touching from time to time. Side by side in the cinema. Holding hands in the dark. Sometimes he took my wrist between his thumb and forefinger. The brush – casual? accidental? – of thighs on a sofa. His lean, dark shoulders. He was thin, narrow-chested. Kisses, tentative, teasing, then probing, explosive.

It was a subtle but mutual seduction. With whom did the power lie? Sometimes I held him as if I thought he would vanish into nothing. In between I climbed into Roy's bed on Saturday nights, not minding, but not looking for or finding pleasure. I discovered there had never been much joy, but also that I couldn't blame Roy for that. While the next night, perhaps, Daniel and I folded together on the sofa in his crumbling rented flat off Easter Road, his fingers imperceptibly searching for uncovered skin, but not, yet, uncovering skin.

The smells of damp and sex mingle. We proceed with

wonderful slowness, unimaginable slowness. Think of taking a deep breath and letting it out by imperceptible degrees. Think of slow-motion swimming in warm, velvety water. Think of every inch of the body wrapped in cool, comforting silk. The conventional pattern of preliminaries was shattered. Daniel did not dive for the obvious places. He lingered at the back of my neck, smoothed the knobs of my ankles. I loved it, loved my own body, loved and explored his slight limbs.

You can't communicate this kind of thing, can you? Because just as there is no way I can be sure that the colour I see as green is the same as the colour others see, each individual will read her own version of ecstasy into what I write. It will not be the same as mine. All I can say is that I felt so palpitatingly transformed that I could not believe that Roy was unaware, that my vibrant physicality did not fill every space in his flat. But Roy was just as usual, good-natured, hard working, breaking out of his usual preoccupations in his normal way, to enquire benignly of my wellbeing, or kiss absently or vigorously as the mood took him.

On Sunday mornings I woke in Roy's bed. We had breakfast together over the Sunday papers, silent, inertly companionable. I felt quite comfortable with him. I felt no need to talk. I did not feel guilty.

I worked undeterred at my thesis. I was asked to teach first-year classes and spent hours on preparation. Daniel had a business to run. The bistro was closed on Mondays, when sometimes but not always, for there was no routine in the affair, he would cook me a meal in the gaunt kitchen of his flat. I did not like his flat, chilly and damp and untidy. Nothing like Roy's. But although I was conscious of its discomforts it scarcely mattered. It was on a Monday night that our relationship was finally consummated, between courses. After the steak and taking the leftover bistro chocolate mousse and the rest of the wine to bed. The signal was a smile across the plates, the corners of the mouth tilted upwards, a glimpse of teeth, eyelids dropping almost obscuring the dark pupils.

When I woke it was to find Daniel's breath moving down my spine. I lay quite still, on the margin of consciousness, and allowed myself to be flooded by his attentions. He seemed to ask for so little.

If I wasn't at my own flat the piano player thought I was with Roy. If Roy phoned and I wasn't there he was rarely curious as to my whereabouts. Infidelity did not seem to come within the realm of his thoughts.

I lay in the bath and Daniel brought me tea and a towel warmed in front of the gas fire. He wrapped it round me and held my warm, wet body against him. And then I went and sat in the library and took notes, and home to my typewriter and the next chapter, assembling my footnotes and references. Biting my lip over a phrase, a paragraph. Trawling the dictionary and the thesaurus.

And I was blind. A week would pass when we did not meet and Daniel made no contact. I did not ask why. The demands of the bistro were sufficient reason, but also it was as if I were entrapped in a delicate spell which I did not want to break. I didn't think about the fact that I met none of Daniel's friends, that after that first lunch it was rarely suggested I should go to the bistro. I learnt that Pete had had a party to which I was not invited. I set aside the mild pang of hurt and puzzlement. Everything could be explained by the closeted nature of my relationship with Daniel and my official alliance with Roy. It was understood. Daniel did not query it – it did not seem to bother him.

I did not really believe in Daniel. Or is that hindsight? I knew it could not last. I was afraid of investing my future on the basis of such an intensity of pleasure. I did not ask questions, perhaps because I guessed that I would get evasions rather than answers. Yet such lack of faith did not make me wary. I was not inclined to give up the domestic safety offered by Roy. I did not want to lose Daniel.

Roy and I were both blind. I wonder now, memory eroded by time, by Daniel, by this vast country, what I would have done if a choice had been forced on me. But it wasn't. Roy didn't know.

Of course, I did lose Daniel. Perhaps it's already obvious why. All I need to say is that one September evening (we had known each other nearly a year), in the week after the Festival ended when an autumnal sadness always engulfs the city which was perhaps why I felt so powerful a need for Daniel's company, I went to the bistro. It was after eleven. There were two men at one of the tables, one rather older than the other, who seemed almost startled when I walked in. The smile of the older one, leaning back in his chair with his hand on his glass, disappeared.

At first I sat at a table. Then, when no one came through, I went to the bead curtain that divided the dining room from the kitchen and looked through. Pete and Daniel had their backs to me. Daniel's fingers were on the back of Pete's neck, entwined in his blond hair. They hadn't heard me. I stood, frozen, staring. They were the same height, both wearing pale Levis, their heads inclined towards each other, one so dark, the other fair. As I stared they broke apart, sensing a presence, and turned, synchronised, like dancers, and bestowed on me identical looks, of irony emerging from mutual absorption.

Eleanor, said Daniel, what brings you here?

Have a glass of wine, said Pete. We were discussing tomorrow's menu.

We thought venison for a change. What do you think? Pete does a great pot roasted haunch.

We're thinking of moving a little upmarket, after a better class of clientele. Halibut rather than haddock.

I couldn't move or speak. Pete picked up a half empty bottle of red wine and poured some into a glass, which he handed to me, smiling.

Have a seat, he said. We won't be long.

Relax, said Daniel. I raised the glass to my lips. I can still remember the taste – it was a rich, fruitcake wine and I felt slightly nauseous. I put the glass down on the table, among the clutter of knives and remnants. I remember leaving. I don't remember speaking. I walked back through the restaurant. The two men were still at their table. I didn't see Daniel again.

I walked down the hill through the melancholy autumn night. There were no stars. Daniel didn't phone, I didn't phone. There were never any explanations. I didn't seek them. There followed months of secret, numbing pain, and Roy as oblivious as ever.

It's self-indulgence, this allowing it all to resurface again. Things have changed. I am not convinced that such memories have much value. Maybe it no longer matters if I never recapture that intoxicating blend of comfort and excitement. Maybe it's irrelevant that its source was a man whose sensitivity towards women was, as I now see it, an incontrovertible part of his preference for men. But I can't be unaware of the irony, that what we've all been taught to want, to expect, was found by me with Daniel. I can't blame my parents, or my peers, or my teachers, for such expectations. And there is little to be gained from blaming culture and the images and icons it offers us. I have turned my back on all that, temporarily at least, yet now I find myself comforted by Steve's burly arms and know that I am reassured by his interest, however brief it is. I lie close to him and reflect on the Chinese, not an overtly sensual people. They reserve, I suppose, their touching for the refinements of the bedchamber. Though I am told that after dark in Beihai necking couples are not uncommon. The youngsters have nowhere to go. I think of Lin Bingshen, and his three-year absence from his wife.

Well. I have written it down, or some of it at least, my secret life. Roy never knew of Daniel, never, so far as I am aware, suspected the covert joy I was experiencing, never registered my transformation. How can the outside remain the same, when the inside sings and shouts? How could he not see? But perhaps I am misjudging him, and what seems to me now to be lack of imagination if not lack of interest was in fact a fine-tuned respect for my own apparently unadventurous requirements. I don't think so.

I don't feel sorry for Roy. He will, no doubt, achieve great things.

8

THE TRAIN CRAWLS. We are passing, so slowly I can see the dulled features on their faces, people, peasants I suppose I should say, working in the fields. We have come perhaps two hundred miles south, and they are harvesting here. I have seen one small tractor, hardly bigger than a lawnmower. I have seen dozens of men and women in the fields with sickles, their eyes shadowed by hats. Knots of labourers work in tiny fields, corridors of wheat and maize carved out of hillsides, offcuts and corners of land that at home would be crowded with thistles and willow herb. In these spaces a few stalks grow, a few heads of grain ripen. Each stalk is cut, each grain is precious.

I watch oxen employed at the threshing, plodding round and round. Nothing moves fast. The train seems to have an ox's pace. I do not feel that I am travelling, rather, the scenes on either side of the compartment are passing like a slowed down film, with a deliberateness that suggests it is all for my benefit, so that I have time to see, to notice.

What am I thinking about during this journey that will go on for nearly twenty-four hours? The truth is my thoughts won't settle. There is Steve. I said goodbye to him, for he'll be gone by the time I get back to Beijing. So I think of him and wonder at myself. And I think of Bingshen, who came to the Friendship Hotel. I bought him a beer. I am not sorry to have said goodbye to Steve yet feel disrupted by our parting. He kissed me on the platform. A friendly, straightforward kiss. I've been trying to remember if anyone has ever said goodbye to me before at a railway station. I don't think so. A strange, irrelevant speculation.

I was glad to have him there, for he knows his way around and that always helps in China. If I had been alone I would have been anxious about getting on the right train. But he ushers me first into the foreigners' waiting room, where there are a few other Europeans and a handful of Chinese military men in uniform, high-ranking officers, Steve tells me. Lesser ranks would not be allowed to make use of this rather gaunt but quite comfortable facility. The station is a fusion of cathedral and department store, lofty, majestic, with huge moving staircases in the central area that take you up to the departure platforms.

After a while Steve escorts me to the escalator and accompanies me up to the higher level. We emerge into another spacious but much less crowded concourse. Steve talks his way onto the platform, which isn't allowed but the girl at the gate is won over by his strangeness and his unexpected fluency, though when I look back I see her turning her attention from the line of people passing through to watch Steve with a little frown.

He finds the right coach and the right seat, a soft sleeper, the easy way to travel in China. We pass coaches crammed with people and baggage, striped plastic holdalls piled everywhere, rolls of bedding, bundles, baskets of food. I have brought some food myself, on Steve's advice. A ham sandwich made with bread and meat bought at the Friendship Store, biscuits and dried fruit. I also have a plastic flask on a strap, full of cold boiled water. Steve sits opposite me for a moment and unscrews the cap from a smaller flask which he has produced from his pocket. I never travel without it, he says. It contains diplomatic whisky which he has obtained through his embassy contacts. We each take a swig.

He has put my case on the rack, checked out my travelling companion, a middle-aged Chinese who eyes Steve's flask with interest. As I step back out onto the platform to say goodbye, two fair-haired, blue-eyed men bustle into the compartment. Steve kisses me as if on the doorstep of a nice home, as if I were going off to work for the day, and steps back.

Have a great trip, he says, raising his hand in salute. Send me a postcard. You'll like Xian. The postcard will go to Vancouver, where his wife will no doubt read it.

Thanks for everything, Steve. The hand is raised again as he begins to move off down the platform. I watch him go, head and shoulders taller than the throng he purposefully pushes through. He had become an anchor in the confusions of Beijing. In a few days time he would be flying back to Vancouver, to Alice, to Rick and Danny and Kate and the labrador. Thanks for everything. I step back on the train.

The train begins to pant and steam and lurch. It moves through a grey undistinguished city. Anchorless now, I think. The Chinese man lights a cigarette and stares out of the window. One of the blue-eyed men opposite catches my eye and smiles. On a little table beside me is a flask of hot water, a lidded cup and packets of tea. Every hour or so the attendant appears and tops up the flask.

Even in open country the train moves slowly. In the fields small figures bend with their sickles, dipping from the waist, their legs a little apart. Two women on a dirt track brace laden baskets on carrying poles across their shoulders. They look up as we pass, but there is little interest in their glance. The train means nothing to them. There is no sense of distance in their lives, no belief that there can be somewhere else. Or is this my western imagination at work? For I see trucks also, with the look of naked practicality that old vehicles have, loaded up with produce, wisps of greenery hanging over the sides, bumping along the road, heading presumably for the nearest town, the nearest free market. I have heard stories of the money they are making, first freighting on bicycles the vegetables they grow, then saving enough to buy a share in an almost clapped-out truck, then becoming sole proprietor of a serviceable vehicle and bringing home a fridge and a television set.

Yet most of the population will never go beyond some nearby small centre. Nor will they encounter those, like myself, travelling from another country, although they will see pictures of people like us, in magazines, on a TV screen somewhere. The train continues its irrelevant passage through the fields, the track laid down on earth that until then had for thousands of years been scraped and clawed and coaxed into nourishing growth, relentlessly dug and ploughed, trampled by the hooves of oxen and the bare feet of farmers, fed with human excrement, watered when there was water, parched when there was none. Narrow strips of ripening maize grow beside the track. I can almost count the feathered ears.

The two men opposite are speaking some Slavic language. West is waste, I am thinking now. If I had to choose a single feature that distinguishes west from east it would be waste. Waste is the measure of a successful market economy. We must all buy more than we use and throw away so that we can buy again. As the train edges through mile after mile of unchanging landscape the thought takes hold of me. All around I see the actions of careful husbandry, and think of the food we eat. I have long since consumed my ham sandwich. It is late afternoon now, and the train left Beijing at eight in the morning.

I close my eyes and rehearse an average day's consumption. Fruit juice and healthful muesli for breakfast. My mother's voice – you must eat a good breakfast. Porridge and eggs put in front me as a child. Coffee and biscuits halfway through the morning. A modest lunch of salad, bread and cheese. Tea and scones at four. Later, red meat and vegetables and sometimes more than one course. And then the extras. The packet of crisps with a drink at the pub, the little something before going to bed. But it's what we don't eat that signifies. The leftovers that fester in the fridge and then get thrown away. The remnants on the plate that go into the bin. The food that's bought out of whim and greed, and grows stale or rotten before it can be consumed. The treats and minor indulgences that we persuade ourselves we deserve, that will make us feel better, cheer us up, help us through the day.

Every week Roy and I humped bulging bin bags down the stair, to join the clusters of pregnant sacks already gathered in the street, to be taken away and dumped. Every week someone had added an old chair, an abandoned mattress, or boxes in which new objects had been brought home, to the mass. Not wasteland but land of waste.

I remember Daniel and Pete in the bistro kitchen. There was a kind of glee in the way food was thrown away. Trimmings from vegetables, heaps of rice and potatoes that weight-conscious customers spurned, chicken bones with shredded hunks of meat still clinging to them. Once I watched Pete straining bones and vegetables, whole onions and carrots and turnips, out of a large pot of stock, and dump them, still steaming, into the bucket. He threw away with the same enthusiasm as he cooked.

The Chinese are careful with their food. Careful in its nurture. Careful in its preparation. Careful in the way it is presented, with a sense of colour and proportion. Vegetables are arranged to look like a fish, carrots cut in the shape of lobsters. Pale green and strips of orange are elegantly combined. At first I thought there was a gross disparity between the labour of the peasant in the field, who at the end of the day would eat his bowl of rice, and the dedication and display that created a banquet. But perhaps they reflect the same attitude of infinite care towards food. Food is precious. It deserves the best treatment. And yet, I reminded myself, the Dowager Empress Tzu-Hsi had vast, multi-course meals prepared for her every day of which she sampled a tiny fragment, just as she had thousands of silk robes which she never wore. What happened to the food that was carried solemnly back to the kitchen? Did it feed the eunuchs and the kitchen maids, the administrators and civil servants, the cooks themselves, the grooms and the guards? Or was it decreed that they should all eat according to their station? Was the banquet of the Empress each day thrown to the dogs?

When Lin Bingshen came to the Friendship Hotel, we walked together on the grass. He told me that he was waiting to hear if there was a job for him at the university before he left to visit his wife. It made no difference that he had not seen his wife for three years – he had to be in Beijing. They might want to interview him again, ask him some more questions. We walked round and round the Friendship Hotel.

I am full of hope, he said. It's a good time to have returned to China. I could have stayed in the US, maybe even my wife and child could have come. But I want to be here. I don't want to be away from my country when change begins to grow. I don't want to miss the fun.

But he knew he was suspect. Everyone who had been out of the country was suspect.

He laughed. They're keeping an eye on me. I shouldn't spend too much time here.

Don't take risks, I say.

Things are going to change, I'm sure of it.

You sound very confident.

My generation is confident. We are the lucky ones. Our parents were the ones who suffered, in the cultural revolution. My father, for example. Now he is a teacher, in the north, in a village near Jilin. But he was a brilliant young lecturer here in Beijing. People remember him. He could come back now, but he doesn't want to. His health is not good. My mother is dead. I have an uncle. He was in detention for three years. Now he doesn't even like me to visit him, because I've been abroad. He thinks I'm dangerous. He's afraid because the authorities are watching me that they will start paying attention to him, too. And maybe he's right to feel afraid, but I know I am privileged. I will try to use my position, my influence, my knowledge. And my friends feel the same way.

What are you going to do with your influence? I asked.

Our goal is democracy, of course. That is the only way forward for China. And democracy means getting rid of the old men. The old men are strangling our country, but their grip is getting slack, slowly their fingers are being prised away from power. It may take a long time, but we will get there. We know how to be patient. I am sure we will get there.

Lin Bingshen, I said, why are you talking to me?

I want people, foreigners, to know what we are doing. One

thing I learnt in the United States – people know nothing about China. It is important that they know what we are attempting. I want them to understand that there will be a new China. And to help us. To bear witness. Just in case. Just in case the old men tighten their grip again.

Ah, I said, so you are perhaps not so optimistic as you pretend.

We have to hope. We have to be confident. There is no other way. There can't be change without will. There can't be will without hope.

He grinned. The dimple I had noticed before quivered in his cheek. When he left he gave me an address and shook my hand. Write to me, Eleanor, he said. I will think of you in Scotland, and you think of me, of all of us, the young generation pulling away the fingers of the old men.

I did not like to tell him that Scotland might not be where a letter would find me. What use would my staying in China be to him?

The train rolls on, so slowly. The two Europeans attempt conversation in halting English. Earlier they had pointed out the coal fields we edged through. The younger looking of the two leant forward, his blue eyes intense, his hair thinning. The other kept getting up, moving about restlessly, in and out of the compartment, up and down the corridor, smoking, looking at me under hooded eyes. The middle-aged Chinese remained silent.

Foreign experts. Mining engineers, they explained, from Poland. The younger one did most of the talking. The other's mouth was set moodily, sardonically it seemed to me, as he reached into his pocket for his cigarettes. Where do I come from? Am I a tourist or a foreign expert like themselves? I tried to explain but I was not sure how much they understood.

You go to Xian? I nodded. We also. We stay in Renmin Hotel. Very big hotel, they tell us. I told them I was staying at the same hotel, then wished I hadn't.

We inspect mines. To help Chinese. Foreign experts. Cooperation. The younger man laughed. He enunciated each syllable separately

71

and slowly and smiled broadly at each success. I can-not speak good Eng-lish. He leant forward, hands on his knees.

In my country, much trouble, he said, his smile vanishing.

I assumed this was a cue for a political discussion and was wary. He went on, you hear of Chernobyl? Much trouble. Very scaring. We think maybe the Russians do it to scare us. Listen – maybe they want it to happen.

Surely not, I said. It's done them, the Russians, more harm than you.

The wind blew it all to us, he said, shaking his head. We cannot drink milk, eat fresh vegetables. The Russians never like us. You know? For hundreds of years. He took cigarettes from his pocket and offered me one. I was aware of the Chinese in the corner, his eyes closed, emitting from time to time a wisp of a snore.

It got to other countries too, I said, including Scotland, where I come from.

He shook his head again. But not like Poland. It is warfare. Listen – we want to be free of Russia, Russian power, Russian politics. Russia is always greedy for Poland. After the war... the Americans, and your Churchill. Gave Poland to the Russians. They don't like us but they want our country. Our country is... is... He struggled for the right word, screwing up his eyes.

Important? I suggested.

More. More. He held up his hands. Another word... Russia needs Poland. Listen – needs. But we don't need Russia. We don't want Russia. So they send nuclear poison, to make us quiet. To make us cause no trouble. We cause trouble, you see. We are always trouble. Other people, always trying to... He opened his mouth wide and snapped it shut.

The train trundled on. He leant back, drawing on his cigarette. We were still passing huge slag heaps and towering winding gear. The sky was as grey as the landscape.

You like China? He asked.

Yes, I said. But I didn't feel I could elaborate, explain. I was not sure I could make myself understood.

The food... ach, terrible.

There was silence for a while, and he stared gloomily out of the window. Then he turned back to me, grinning.

I am... sick for Poland. For home. I don't like this country. It is too difficult here. Listen – two weeks, we are here two weeks. He gestured towards the window. Look... coal mines. The coal is the same. But nothing else. Now we have holiday, they take us to places, to Xian, to Shanghai, to Houzhou. I want to go home to Poland. I don't want these places. In Beijing they take us to the palace, the city of the emperor. Emperors – who cares? They take us to tombs and temples and the Great Wall. You have seen those places? You like them? I want to go home. No more rice, no more strange animals in the food, no more walls.

By the time he had finished talking the grin had faded and he sat back in his seat, lapsing into an expression of unveiled misery. I could think of nothing to say that might cheer him up. I looked down at the book open on my lap. And then he began to talk again, as if the conversation had never stopped, and I raised my eyes to give him my attention although I wanted to read.

They tell us what to do, what to think, where to go. Listen – It's not right. But I can't say it's not right – that's big trouble. Very big trouble. The Russians are old-fashioned. Yes? I try to think of the words. Tell me if I am wrong. Old-fashioned. Poland must be a modern country. Russian ideas are too old. Marxist ideas. Old. Like Chinese ideas. They are not for now, not for us. Our country is not the same as Russia. We are modern. We want new ideas, like the west. We are all interested in the west. Why do they send us here? The Chinese can teach us nothing. They think we can teach them, but... He shrugged.

New ideas? I wonder, but cannot respond. I am thinking, free markets, competition, winners and losers. Social control, social tyranny. It's all been around for a long time. I cannot engage with it. I can only listen, to the Pole, to Lin Bingshen, to Steve who took me to the street markets where the traders competed to sell western-style clothes, jackets, dresses, т-shirts, who told me, it will end in tears.

Now the Pole and I both stare out of the window. The colours swim. Yellow-red earth, yellow wheat, dry, brittle corn stalks. It is the earth itself that predominates, different, intrusive. Earth villages, made of mud bricks, earth roads, earth reaching up through closely-planted crops. But then we come to hills. I see them in the distance first, hazy, greyish-green, hardly distinguishable from the greyish distant sky. Gradually they gain in shape and substance, more precisely green cones, their slopes so smooth, they are hardly natural. They look like the consequence of careful artifice.

It is late afternoon and I am looking west towards a sun that hangs lower and lower in the sky and disperses its light briefly before it sets. The Poles disappear to the restaurant car. When they return the older one continues his pacing and the younger sits opposite me again and complains about the food. Nevertheless, I too shall eat soon. But for the moment I cannot take my eyes off the ranks of darkening green cone-shaped hills, defying credibility. The train – or is it my imagination? – has picked up speed a little. Whiffs of smoke pass the window.

The Pole anxiously reminds me that if I don't eat soon I'll miss my chance. You have another sandwich maybe? Better with a sandwich.

I shake my head. No. No more supplies. Which is not entirely true but I meanly suspect that his need for more adequate nourishment might prompt me to offer him what I have. No, I'll go and eat, I say with a smile.

Not good, he warns. Not good.

In the corridor his companion smokes at an open window. He nods as I pass, but I feel that he is watching me as I make my way along the rocking train. At the end of the carriage the Chinese man from our compartment is drinking tea with the attendant, probably in need of a change from his western fellow travellers.

Dinner is noodles with a dark spicy sauce and an omelette shredded on top. There is no choice. The dish is put in front of me without words or ceremony. I find it tasty. It's peasant food.

The soup that follows is not so nice. A few scraps of greasy pork and cabbage float unappetisingly in liquid shaken by the moving train, but I dip into it for form's sake. There are a few other people, but no conversation, only the sounds of eating, which are considerable. Noodles and soup are sucked up noisily and quickly. Across from me a man finishes a plateful, asks for more, and finishes that before I am halfway through. I try not to watch him eat, although why I don't know, aside from the distant habits of my upbringing. No such inhibitions operate among the Chinese. I feel islanded in isolation, and want to avoid doing anything to attract attention to myself, although it would make little difference. I am too solid an uneastern presence. But I try to contain my movements and keep my elbows against my sides. It changes nothing, of course. What I do or don't do is irrelevant. It's simply what I am, the exterior of what I am, that matters.

9

THE SUN VANISHED suddenly. It is quite dark outside. The bunks have been folded down. Above me my Chinese fellow traveller snores. His preparations for sleep were elaborate and noisy, and involved a long session of coughing, clearing his throat and spitting. I don't know where we are exactly, just that we are south of the great railway junction at Taiyuan. We've been travelling for more than twelve hours. On the map I traced the route of the railway line, following the course of the Fen River, tributary of the huge Huang He, the Yellow River. When I wake tomorrow, assuming I sleep, we'll be nearly at Xian.

The Poles spent an hour or so rolling dice. Now they are in their bunks, drinking vodka from a half bottle which they pass up and down. They offered it to me but I declined. I am propped up against the end of the seat with a cotton blanket drawn over my knee where my writing pad rests.

I look back at what I have written. I was on the subject of lying. It was easy to think of marriage as a lie. Wasn't that how I explained my hostility to the idea? It wasn't ideological, although that was what George thought. We'd argued once, sparked off by his engagement to Sally. He'd come to the flat in Leslie Place to tell me. Luckily the piano player was out, so there was no intrusive presence. He brought a bottle of fizzy wine. I was touched. This wasn't like George. We weren't close, George and I. I was touched that he should come specially to tell me, and that he wanted to share his celebration with me. Though I think it was a kind of rehearsal for the moment when he would tell mother and father.

Like Roy, George was up and coming, doing well. Sally was in public relations. She dressed in suits and crisp shirts and had a bright, staccato voice. I'd only met her twice and hardly knew her, yet of course I had to congratulate George on his proposed commitment to a contract of which I did not approve. But after a drink or two I intimated something of my difficulty.

George, I said, I think you're crazy, but congratulations all the same.

What do you mean? He reacted sharply. Don't you like Sally? I promise you, when you get to know her better you'll understand she's just what I need.

I'm sure Sally's marvellous, I said. What I meant, but didn't add, was that Sally was very attractive, very presentable, slim, poised, went regularly to a hairdresser, was highly appropriate as the partner of a man whose legal career would no doubt take off. No, it's not Sally. It's marriage. I have doubts, that's all.

Don't you think all this anti-marriage stuff is a bit childish? George said condescendingly. These so-called doubts, they don't really mean anything, do they?

The doubts are real.

Why? What's your problem?

The role models are hardly encouraging, I said, with what I hoped would come across as irony, but it was probably lost on him. He didn't have much of an ear for irony. I could see he didn't understand.

Role models?

Our parents, George. I poured myself another glass of wine.

What have they got to do with it? I don't plan to model my marriage on theirs, if that's what you're on about.

Not exactly. I was into tricky territory now. George and I had never talked about our parents. I had no idea how he saw them.

What then? George persisted.

The pause that followed was probably not as long as it felt.

I could hear my father's voice, not raised, but a monotone of deathly sobriety. Not the words, but that was hardly necessary. And my mother looking down, and when I did see her face there was a blank, anaesthetised expression. She was used to it. The endless, toneless rant, the instructions, the criticism. It was always polite. He did not lose his temper. Even as a child I sometimes wished he would.

Has it ever occurred to you that our father is a bully? I said.

Don't talk such bollocks. He's scarcely ever raised his voice. Even when I kicked a ball through the shed window, even when I bunked off school that afternoon with Robbie Johnstone.

No, that's not his style, I said.

So what are you talking about?

I tried another tack. It seems to me that for marriage to work it requires at least one of the two to be numb, chloroformed. How often does father say something pleasant to mother? Such conversation as there is may be neutral, at best, but pleasant? And she copes by not responding, except in an automatic, pre-programmed way. She knows what it's okay to say, and what will set him off. She's not stupid, although he treats her as if she is. Have you never noticed? No, probably not. Sometimes I wonder what or where mother really is. What's going on inside her head. And then I find I'm asking the same question about him. Who is he? Okay, he's a local government official and a church-goer, a respected figure in the community and all that, and he's mother's husband and our father. But who is he really?

I don't see what this has got to do with me and Sally.

No, I don't suppose you do. But you obviously think it's important to tell them about your engagement. I'm sure you're planning a proper wedding. So why? Do you want their approval? Do you want them to like Sally and accept her into the family? Does that matter to you? Why? Because you respect them as individuals? Because you love them? And if they approve, does that mean they see you and Sally as fitting into the mould of marriage that they themselves occupy? Is that what you want? Is that the kind of marriage you're going to have? Wouldn't it be better if they didn't approve?

And so I went on. Poor George visibly flinched and poured out what was left of the wine into his glass. I enlarged on my theme. Marriage, or at least our parents' marriage, was grotesque. What were they playing at? What did they think was going on? What did George think was going on? What kind of life did he think mother had?

She's quite happy, George said.

I laughed. Happy? Is that what happiness is? I hope to God you and Sally can do better than that.

She's never said anything to me...

That's the point, George. She doesn't say anything to anyone. Do you think that when she meets her mates for a coffee in the High Street she tells them her marriage is a lie, that her husband is a bastard? She's so practised at disguise she doesn't see it herself – that's what I reckon.

A lie? What are you on about? You mean that father is messing about with other women? That's bollocks.

Of course I don't mean that. I mean...

I don't understand what you're saying.

George had had enough. He saw, perhaps, that I was about to enlarge on things he didn't want to hear. He got to his feet. I said, I know you don't. At the door I gave him a kiss, knowing it would make him feel uncomfortable.

I sat down with the empty bottle and empty glasses, churning with frustration. I had been on the point of release. But at the same time I regretted that I'd said so much. George did not want to know. It did not suit him to know. He had no resentment against our parents bubbling in his soul. He was well down the road to where he wanted to go. Their approbation kept them happy and out of his hair, and they seemed unaware of his detachment.

He had always managed to find ways of keeping them reasonably satisfied with his progress, seemed to know instinctively what they wanted him to do, wanted him to say. He also learned how to lie convincingly. I'm spending Saturday night with Neil. We're working on our history, got an essay to do next week. I'd see him and his friends after school messing around by the canal. I'm going to Stuart's to borrow a couple of books. I'm just going to the library. I'm helping backstage with the school play. In his last term at school he was seeing a girl called Linda.

Could I have done the same? I sometimes tried, never with conviction. Part of me longed to flout the rules, come in at one in the morning, banging the door and leaving the lights blazing. But if I was ten minutes later than eleven there they would be in their two armchairs.

You're late.

I'm sorry – it's only ten past.

We agreed eleven. Which was hardly correct – I was told eleven.

Your mother worries.

But my mother sat with her eyes looking down at her hands, which slowly twisted each other on her lap. She said nothing. Neither of them moved from their chairs until I had left the room. From my bedroom I heard the familiar sounds of milk bottles placed on the front step and doors being locked.

How can children be fair to their parents? How can they know the real story of what goes on between them? How can they estimate happiness or misery? They can't. That dawned on me, I guess, at about this same time, the time of George's marriage. Before I'd met Roy, before I'd met any man who really engaged my interest. I turned the corner from their unfairness to me into my unfairness to them. It seemed that that was the way it had to be, and I was deeply depressed. But surely my father's rigid convictions, his almost wordless insistence on the way things should be – that wasn't the way it had to be? I observed the wedding of my brother, our parents, Sally's parents, bleakly.

My mother hesitantly consulted me on what she should wear. The reception was to be in a hotel in Edinburgh's southside. Sally's father was a dentist. I offered to go shopping with her, a suggestion I regretted immediately, as to my surprise she agreed.

I persuaded her to try on a dark red dress – I had never seen her look better. But she wouldn't buy it. We trudged on through more shops, had a cup of tea, looked at hats. Finally she said, there's that nice little dress shop in the High Street. I think I'll just go there. I'm sure they'll have something suitable. She bought a pale grey suit with buttons up to the neck. She stood next to my father in his dark grey suit. It was June and the sun shone. Sally's mother wore turquoise and her father a pink shirt and multicoloured tie.

I don't think George ever forgave me for that night at Leslie Place. I think he was shocked, shocked at my hostility, shocked that I didn't react more soothingly and conventionally to his news, shocked that I didn't appear more grateful for his gesture in bringing it to me. At one point in the conversation he asked me if all this anti-marriage nonsense meant that I didn't intend to marry.

Of course I don't, was my reply, but I knew I sounded like a rebellious teenager.

You'll soon change your mind – if you ever meet a man who'll have you.

And now? Is all this a delayed adolescence kicking out? My earlier attempt now seems so tame, so comfortable almost.

I didn't rise to George's bait. He settled back in his chair, glass in one hand, the other gesturing in a manner I was sure he had practised for the benefit of clients. It suggested a kind of relaxed wisdom. Having failed to get a rise out of me he carried on.

Oh, you'll change your mind. Any woman I've met who has said she didn't intend to marry has ended up spliced and domesticated.

This time I snorted. And how many is that? Come on George, you're only twenty-five. And domesticated! Are you really going into marriage with such neanderthal ideas? Even if I do marry, it won't be comfortable domesticity I'll be after. And Sally doesn't look to me like the domestic type either.

She wants security and she wants children. Like most women. You don't know Sally.

And you don't know women. You want Sally to turn into a doormat? Like mother?

Mother's not a doormat.

Isn't she?

I desperately wanted him to show signs of discomfort. But he slipped easily into diversion.

You know mother and father want to see us both settled. You'll disappoint them. I hope you don't talk like this to them.

Of course I don't.

Don't you think all this is a bit immature?

Rushing into marriage is hardly mature.

I'm not rushing into marriage. I've known Sally for nearly a year. I've given it a lot of thought. We've discussed it all at length.

I bloody well hope you have.

There was silence for a while. George leaning back in his chair, his straight sandy hair pushed back from his forehead, his features arranged, it seemed to me, in an expression of smug amusement which disguised any irritation.

You'll grow out of it, he said. You'll learn to be more considerate of others.

I'd like other people to be considerate of me, to recognise that I've a right to live my own life.

I heard the voice of a truculent adolescent again. But I meant it, or at least I meant that I wanted to make my life my own and not slip into a groove dug by someone else, or dug by previous generations of others. George drained his glass and rested his fingertips on the arm of his chair. His clear grey eyes made him look both honest and bland, an asset, no doubt, in his chosen profession. To him, my recalcitrance was obviously just a speck of rebellion in the eye of progress. An irritant, but nothing to get worked up about. He had in fact got more worked up than he usually allowed himself, but perhaps that was the wine, or the heightened state that his engagement had possibly brought about.

I longed to convince myself that I had needled him, and

couldn't leave it alone. So you're getting married so as to avoid disappointing our parents?

Don't be ridiculous, Eleanor. Of course I'm not. But I do care what they think.

I laughed. When George was pompous it always made me laugh, and he never knew why I was laughing. I laughed, and said, congratulations, George, sincere congratulations. I mean that. And give my love to Sally.

I wasn't in any hurry to introduce Roy to my parents or to George. I knew they would jump to conclusions. Roy was so much the kind of man they would want me to get together with. But eventually I took Roy to Linlithgow on the train – we didn't yet have a car – and we walked up the hill at the back of the station to the bungalow I had grown up in. It was a Saturday afternoon. There were swans on the canal. My father sat in his armchair. He would normally have been working in the garden, but clearly considered that not appropriate for the occasion. Mother brought in tea. She had made a fruit cake.

It's too dry, my father said, leaving his piece crumbled on his plate. You'd have done better to have bought one from Crawfords.

Roy offered to wash up but mother wouldn't even let him carry the tray through to the kitchen. We went down to the roofless palace and walked round the loch. Roy had never been there. A water vole slid across our path and disappeared in the reeds. Nice place to grow up, he said.

Eventually I had to tell my parents that Roy and I were buying a flat. I made no mention of marriage. George told me they were very distressed, but the impression that I got was that my mother blurred the distinction between cohabitation and wedlock. Or perhaps saw the joint purchase of a flat as the first step towards an inevitable marriage. Something was sufficiently consoling for it not to be an issue.

My father reacted differently. We were sitting at the table eating meat loaf. You are very foolish and very selfish, he said. As usual, my mother said nothing to mitigate his pronouncement.

He didn't enlarge on it. He didn't elaborate on what made my intentions foolish and selfish. I said nothing, looked across the table at a large man, his shoulders slightly hunched as if he couldn't otherwise fit into the same scale as the rest of us, his thick hair fading from blond into grey, and I remember that he seemed to be at a great distance from me. I would have had to shout to make him hear me.

George and Sally reassured them. She's finished the teenage rebellion thing, they said. It's just a matter of time.

And they were right, really. Now it seems almost funny. They all knew better.

10

I WENT ON writing. As you can see, from time to time the train jerked my hand across the page. The Poles finished the vodka and settled at last into sleep or the semblance of sleep, the younger one below, the silent one above. I had the uncomfortable sensation that his eyes were not closed, that he was looking down at me over the edge of the bunk. In the black window I saw only my own face staring back.

I put away my notebook and went down the hushed corridor to the washroom. At this end there was a European-style toilet which reeked of disinfectant but did not function very well. From the tap came a trickle of cold water. I had a perfunctory wash but could not quite bring myself to clean my teeth, cursing but not overcoming my western fastidiousness. I made my way back along the rocking train.

In the compartment the air quivered with a thin snore. I wanted to take off my clothes, which felt sticky and grimy, but I'd noticed that the men had retired in their shirts and trousers and even if they were all asleep then there could have been embarrassment in the morning if I had stripped to my underwear. So I pulled down the blind and slid between the coarse but clean sheets in the khaki trousers and red T-shirt I'd put on in the morning in the Friendship Hotel. It seemed weeks ago. My head rested on a hard little pillow. A grey cotton blanket covered the sheet. And I slept, at least for a little while.

When I roused myself and raised the blind a few inches, it

was to look out at brilliant sunshine. The railway line passed close to little villages. People, animals, bikes were moving about. The fields were already busy, the oxen already tramping their ponderous round to thresh a heap of grain, men prodding with sticks, women carrying baskets. A small boy in a flapping shirt ran in the dust and waved.

While I am writing the Poles come to life and start to scramble together their belongings. They are unshaven, which makes them look bad tempered, but they both say good morning, and so does the Chinese, in English. The Poles have a lengthy discussion in Polish, which I interpret as a debate about breakfast. As they then go off, followed by the Chinese, it seems they made a decision to look for it. In their absence I put on a clean T-shirt and make myself tidy. With my hair combed and a splash of cologne I feel better, and sit patiently in my seat, staring out of the window, writing, and waiting for Xian.

The younger Pole returns. Breakfast – ach, bad, very bad, he says. My friend likes to eat too much. He sits on the edge of the seat and watches the passing green landscape. Then he asks me if I am married. I hold up my ringless hands and shake my head.

Why not?

I don't want to marry, I say.

Or maybe no one wants to marry you, he laughs. He slaps his hand on his knee. I joke, he adds. Why not? Why you don't want to marry?

It doesn't appeal to me.

Ah, women's lib, he almost shouts, his eyes gleeful as if it is a huge joke.

I shrug, possibly frown. I'm a feminist, I say. I know I sound very prim.

Feminist? I hear the question mark, but am not sure if it means he doesn't understand the word or the idea.

Women should have the same chances as men. I don't think they get that in marriage. Not that I can see, anyway.

Ah, women's lib, he says again. My wife, she has everything

the same as me. Everything. We don't need women's lib in Poland.

Well, I say, I suppose you can say it's an old idea, but the practice is pretty new, if not the theory.

I don't think he understands me, so I ask him if he has any children.

Yes, one boy. He holds up a finger. One is enough.

Who looks after him?

He goes to school. Listen – my wife is better, women can take care of children better. Sometimes I bring him from school, sometimes my wife. She works in a hospital. When she works at night I bring the boy from school, so she can sleep, you know?

Who cleans your house? What a hypocrite I am, I am thinking. Lies of inference.

It is a small... small... not house, but in a big building.

Flat, apartment.

Yes, yes. Apartment. Two rooms. Not much. Not much to clean. Easy.

Well, I can't pursue this. What's the point? And anyway, my mind has begun to travel on a different if perhaps parallel route. What a hopeless idealist I am (so George would have said, did say I expect, and so Roy would say if I gave him the chance) to feel that in some way it is important to live without lies. Yet here I am, in a train trundling through a bright oriental morning, in conversation with a Pole, of about my age I guess, pleasant enough, yet I can't confront him, just as I couldn't confront Roy. Cowardice. And unfair, I admit it.

Is this what I'm expected to explain? Why didn't I give Roy a chance? Why was it that Eleanor Dickinson, on the whole a woman who behaves with decency and some thought for others, with such unfairness, with such deceit (the word is apt) abandoned Roy? Abandoned in effect her mother, her brother, her friends, her colleagues, her students. To none of them did she say anything, not so much as a hint or a clue as to what she was planning.

Explaining why I left, which is I suppose what I am trying to do in these pages, is not the same as explaining why I behaved badly. It was cowardice partly, I know that. Bad behaviour often is, isn't it? The things we do – or don't do – that hurt people most, often arise from the urge to run away from, not the truth itself but the need to present the truth to others. We can rationalise. I could say I didn't want to hurt Roy with words, that it would have made things worse if I had tried to justify my actions. But of course, I know that's not true and I also know I have hurt him far more by withdrawing my words from him, by not telling him what I proposed to do, than if I had forewarned him. No. It's myself I am trying to protect. Because the truth, laid out for the benefit of others, is painful for me. I can face it alone, I persuade myself, carry through its demands, but to be forced to see it in different circumstances, through another's eyes, is infinitely harder. I can face reality – I think – but to explain it, justify, handle another's differing perceptions, that's what I ran from.

How would Roy have seen it? Well, idealism I guess. In other words, lack of realism. But I don't accept the antithesis. He would have found it difficult to believe I was unhappy, even after my father's death, because I never said I was. He shared my life. He had no sense that things weren't right because I took care not to convey that, and yet felt that he ought to be aware. Idealism, again. The person you live with ought to know these things. And he thought he would know, I'm sure. So it couldn't be unhappiness, not real unhappiness, nothing that couldn't be sorted out. Perhaps I was temporarily discouraged, knocked off kilter. Nothing that time won't heal, Roy would have said, no doubt adding that bereavement was a bad time to make sudden decisions.

Perhaps this time the conversation would have had a new edge to it. Roy would have noted a chink in my armour. Nell, he might have said, you've made your point. You don't need to prove something to your father any more. Let's get married. Let's have a family. You won't need to give up work, not if you don't want to. You know that's not an issue. But if you do want to, no problem. I can support a family. We'll do whatever you want, arrange to have the kid looked after, whatever. I don't want you to give up your career. I'm proud of you. But you're not getting any younger. Let's not wait too long, eh? The longer you wait the more difficult it'll be. You know the statistics. I don't want you taking any risks. And think how pleased your mother would be.

Am I getting things wrong here? Wasn't this the conversation we did have? It's not a 'what if' – it happened. Or something like it. And I agreed. I said yes, when he again suggested marriage. He was right, I thought, there was no need any more to take this stand against my father. Yes, I said. Why not? As long as there's no big fuss. Why not? He didn't seem surprised. He knew all along that in the end I would agree. He took my hand and said, we'll sort out the details...

Roy could be tender, concerned. It could have been different. I could have resisted, as I had done before, tried to explain. He would have come and sat beside me on the sofa and put his arm around me. He would have been reasonable. I don't want to put pressure on you, Nell, he would have said. It's just that I don't see why you're making such an issue of it. And what could I have said in reply? I don't want a child, Roy, so why get married? But that would have been another lie. To be truthful I would have had to say, I don't want your child, Roy. Why not Roy's child? Because some instinct was telling me that Roy's need of a child was quite distinct from his need for me. It had nothing to do with me. He wasn't interested in what it would involve, in spite of his concern. He simply wanted there to be a child. And how could I tell him that he was the problem?

Wordlessly, secretly, I applied a test and Roy failed. It is not an uncommon phenomenon, but it wasn't fair. Poor Roy had no idea what the test was, or that he failed it. It's not even on my part a simple refusal to pander to his egocentric idea of propagation, his perfectly understandable need to mirror himself in his offspring. It is something much harder to define – or perhaps it is more simple than I am making out. Perhaps it is a lack of curiosity, a lack of interest, a relegation of the physiological, of the inner workings of gestation and childbirth to a lesser sphere.

So Roy absorbs himself in the study of rituals, many of them surrounding childbirth, and neglects what is really going on. Rituals, no doubt, are full of interest. I share his interest. After all, literature too is about rituals. Story-telling is itself a ritual. We used to talk about that sometimes, and we would both get caught up in the excitement of exchanging ideas, exploring intellectual possibilities together. I can see him in a green shirt he had, the sleeves rolled up, his swivel chair turned away from the window as he talked to me, sitting with my knees drawn up in the big lumpy armchair which was in his study because it was too ungainly for the living room (the lounge). Pushing his hand through his hair as he talked about the role of the story-teller in tribal societies, the preserver of the past, of tradition, of tribal identity. He smiled, his generous but sceptical smile, when I maintained that the writers I read and taught were story-tellers too.

That's what I said to my students. Novelists, poets – they're story-tellers. They have a function, a traditional function. Humankind needs stories. Some of them thought I was demeaning literature by saying this, reducing art to the level of mundane necessity. Others argued that literature was a luxury. No, I would say, we can't live without stories. I still believe that. In running away from my safe employment in a department of literature I haven't run away from stories. But I myself was in the wrong story. Now I'm becoming aware of a different one, meandering, slow, inconsequential, like this train, which carries my old story and allows me to glimpse through the moving window, without much comprehension, the stories of others.

A true story? Do I approve of where I find myself? Surely, I haven't escaped the lies, for I have been to bed with a married man, an apparently happily married man who seems to value – I'll avoid the word love – his wife. At least he didn't insult me by producing some tale (story again) of woe and misunderstanding. When Steve talked about his wife and children it was with cheerful affection, and perhaps it was that as much as anything that numbed my moral sense and smoothed the way into his bed.

Would the unknown Alice ever know? Was harm done to her?

The steady rhythm of the train takes us nearer and nearer to Xian. The landscape beyond the window has the brightness of a theatre set. The anxiety of arrival is beginning to take hold.

Why did I do it? Beyond the comfort of warmth and contact – why? It seemed no big deal, to borrow a phrase my students liked to use, when I pointed out the lateness of an essay, for example. It's no big deal, Eleanor, they'd say. They mostly called me Eleanor. You'll get it tomorrow. No big deal to slip between the covers with Steve, naked, warm. No big deal to feel soothed and aroused by his friendly, competent but not especially expert hands. No big deal to respond in kind and accept his entry into a body that had learned to be remote when the occasion required. It had learned from Roy, of course, or discovered from Daniel, a lesson that perhaps I'd been taught all my life, that I'd implicitly colluded in the pressure to divorce my mind from my body. Lies. But if you fully succumb, mind, body, heart and soul, fully submerge yourself, you risk everything. And who can afford that? With Daniel, I risked everything.

There are other kinds of risks. Lin Bingshen and his hopes for the future. Three years away from his wife and child. That's a huge risk, but he didn't seem to see it that way. In other cultures the restriction of political freedom might focus hope on the personal. For Bing the personal was sacrificed to what he saw as more important goals. Wasn't it hard, I'd asked him, to leave your wife and baby daughter, knowing you wouldn't see them for three years? Yes, he smiled, it was hard, but many Chinese students accept that necessity, many families are split when people work in different parts of the country, many fathers and mothers do not see their children for months at a time. That is what it is like here. When he talked of the impulse for democracy, of prising apart the old men's fingers, I felt a lick of fear. There were risks being taken there that I could not fully comprehend. They are hinted at through his sudden departures, the inconsistencies. The first time we walk in the grounds of the Friendship Hotel he is relaxed. The second time he wheels his bike between us and stays only for a few minutes.

The third time – there isn't a third time, for he doesn't come at all. I'll see you tomorrow, he says, and does not come. I don't think much about it, I don't worry. But there is just a hint of unease at the margins of my mind.

Xian comes. It is eight o'clock in the morning. I find myself on the wide platform in the bright light wedged in the midst of a vast slow-moving crowd, its baggage bumping my calves, heading inexorably for the exit gate and the street. If I had wanted to go any other way it would not have been possible. And although I am taller than most of those around me, except the Poles who are ahead of me, exclaiming in Polish, cursing I suspect, I feel crushed into insignificance.

Once off the platform the crowd disperses a little. I see the Poles being met and escorted to a waiting car. I would like to get my bearings, but there's no chance for that, for I am hailed by several hustling taxi drivers. Renmin Hotel? Renmin Hotel? they bark. I nod. One of them seizes my bag and bundles me into his vehicle which noisily sets off down a wide dusty street. I peer through the dirty windows. Which direction? How far? I wonder, could I have walked it, taken a bus? My bag isn't heavy. But it is too late. We turn into a tree-lined street and then through an imposing gateway, up a curving drive. As I get out I see the Poles and their suitcases on the front steps.

The hotel is extraordinary, monumental and hideous, set behind lavish fountains. The taxi driver asks for six yuan, crashes his door shut before he drives off. I carry my bag up the wide steps and enter the cavernous building, which smells of dust. A straggle of hesitant foreigners have clustered at a door which says Chinese International Travel Service in English. The Poles have disappeared. The door opens and a voice says in staccato English that the office will open in half an hour. I have already learnt that that could mean anything. Some of the others disperse. But suddenly I have no energy and no desire to go anywhere. I sit on the floor of the passageway, my bag beside me, and shut my eyes.

It takes about an hour. The door opens. A fraught but fluent English speaker sorts out hotel rooms, train tickets for the next leg of the journey, tour bookings, lost baggage. In front of me are Australians, Americans, a woman I think is German but find out later is Dutch. I lean against the wall, waiting my turn. Nobody smiles. There are no seats. What I'd really like, I'm thinking, is a nice cup of tea, Indian tea, with milk, and digestive biscuits. I remember I have had no breakfast. I have forgotten why I have come to Xian. I have forgotten why I came to China. There is dust everywhere, I can feel it in my nostrils. I have forgotten why I left home.

All I think about is now. A nice cup of tea.

I I

IT IS TOO early. I can't get into my hotel room. But I set off down the wide, tree-lined street with a map and my camera. At a corner, under the trees, there are young men playing snooker and a little further on, older men in blue, squatting on the ground and playing cards. I turn down Bei Dajie and walk to the Bell Tower that straddles a major intersection. Once the bells tolled out the hour. Now it stands solidly, circled by trucks, buses and bikes, an incessant current of traffic that flows without a break. I carry on down Nan Dajie to the south gate of the city, propelled by a need to keep walking, as if it is the only way I can hang on to myself in this alien place.

The sixteenth-century city walls slope into a wide, murky ditch. The walls have a bare, raw look. They don't seem old or weathered. Beneath them are older walls, the fortifications of the ancient city of the T'ang emperors. And before that a much older capital, of the megalomaniac Qin Shihuang. Hungry for power, but most of all hungry for immortality, Qin Shihuang unified China, but probably killed more men through his greed for monumental construction than through conquest. Building is power, and stone in particular embodies that power. Stone, hewn and moved at his command, lifted, hoisted, piled up, would last.

Here near the base of the wall there is a straggle of market stalls and a constant noise of people, bicycle bells and hooting horns. I thought I had got used to attracting attention, but I feel horribly conspicuous. There are fewer foreigners here than in

Beijing. The children and the old stare unselfconsciously. There is much I want to look at, heaps of vegetables I want to identify, haphazardly butchered hunks of meat, streaked and oozing, suspended on hooks, enamelled basins steaming with hot food. By a noodle stall a Mao-capped man hurriedly scoops up the contents of his bowl with his chopsticks, his bike leaning against his hip. Then he is off, swinging his leg over the crossbar and pushing into the flood of traffic. On his way to work, perhaps. I pull out my camera, but I've lost him before I can focus. He's absorbed, without shape in the current. So I swing round and the shutter opens on a stall heaped with cabbages and garlic.

It takes time to focus. And so often the eye is deluded. The camera lies as readily as the tongue. The eye cuts out what it doesn't want to see, or registers only what is pleasing or what confirms existing expectations. Those shadows on the margins of the picture, that blur of movement, that sudden slipping of the mask that opens up a chasm of a face.

I take a road that swings round the outside of the wall and tramp, keeping my eyes open, and wonder, yet again, what am I doing here? I have to go over it all again, not just to make things clear, but to remind myself, to keep in touch with the thread that leads back to Edinburgh. Even when the plane took off the knowledge was there but not the understanding of what I had done. Going to China? Yes. Foreign guest or foreign expert, it hardly matters. Everyone goes to China these days, students, backpackers, businessmen, goodwill delegations, lecturers, tour groups. There is a way I can be labelled. They can't all be running away, I thought confidently, looking about me as the plane climbed. Of course not. My fellow travellers must have good reasons to be going – curiosity was good enough. But I knew that if I had always wanted to go to China (and I can't identify a moment when the desire took shape) it was not out of curiosity, but the need for another world, another – was it possible? – universe.

Adventures in space. In the Easter holidays George and his friend Alistair built a spaceship in George's bedroom. For a week the door was shut against me. I was forbidden to enter, on pain of dire consequences. From time to time they emerged to set off on forays to collect cardboard boxes. One evening they consulted father in low and earnest voices, and the result was money to buy silver spray paint. I was puzzled. Father did not readily hand out cash. There were strict rules about pocket money and spending. The next day George and Alistair came into the house, having bought the paint. George made sure I was present when the canisters were taken out of the paper bag, but I wouldn't give him the satisfaction of showing any interest. I was about ten years old then, I suppose.

Why wasn't I playing with my own friends? I don't know. It could have been because I couldn't bear to be distracted from what was going on behind the closed door, although I never saw it. Even when the spaceship was completed and mother and father were invited in to admire, I was excluded. Not you, stupid, George said. Not for girls. That evening I sat leaning on the window sill of my bedroom. The window was open. My father came out and lit his pipe, paced to the end of the garden, turned, paced back. I liked to see him smoke, which he did not often do inside the house. It broke the sternness of his face. The early daffodils were withering, the tulips were not yet out.

I never questioned the closed door. I never wondered why, when George ushered mother and father into his bedroom to view the results of a week's activity and I was told abruptly to stay out, they themselves did not point out to George his cruelty. And it was cruelty. Girls don't care about spaceships, girls don't know anything about space.

Now I would say it was insecurity. Even at twelve years old, George knew I was cleverer than he was. But I didn't realise that then. How could I, for how could a younger sister be more clever, more anything, than an older brother? It was against the natural order of things. During that week I knocked timidly at the door from time to time, as if compelled. As if in some way I had to enact the role allotted to me by George and Alistair and my parents. Little sister on the margins. Little sister complying with her exclusion, drawing attention to it by knocking on the door, knowing that a voice would roar GO AWAY. And little sister went, first shouting through the door, don't be so mean, George. But even that was collusion. George wanted to hear my complaint.

I plotted to sneak in when he wasn't in the house, but was warned off. I have a secret way of knowing if you go in my room, he said. I thought I might just open the door a crack. I'll know even if you open the door the tiniest bit, he said. But I thought he'd get tired of it all eventually, and I could be patient. I'd just wait. When term started and we were back at school he'd lose interest.

On the last day of the holidays Alistair was round. There were whisperings, conspiratorial putting of heads together. They disappeared into George's room, the door firmly shut as usual. Then noises... ten, nine, eight... BLAST OFF. Roars, thumps, shouts, something that sounded like kicking. It seemed to go on and on, while I sat on my bed and listened. Then I heard George's door open, the sound of the boys' footsteps running down the hall, and a few moments later their voices in the garden. I crept out of my room. George's door opposite was open. Through it I could see a tangle of torn and caved-in cardboard, shreds of silver, brown corrugations. Then the kitchen door banging, running footsteps. Let's burn it, let's burn it! I dodged back. They ran into George's room, scrabbled around, out into the garden again. From my window I saw them with armfuls of crushed cardboard running to the end of the garden where father burnt leaves and garden rubbish. They piled the remnants in a heap. I know where the matches are, George shouted. Then the voice of my mother, what are you doing boys? But it was too late. George had got a box of matches from the shed and was striking one after another, until suddenly there was an orange flare. By the time my mother realised what was happening the bonfire was burning merrily and the two boys were watching in gleeful satisfaction.

I followed my mother into the garden and we watched,

mesmerised by the flames. That night I was sent to my room while George was lectured by my father. If there was more than a lecture George never let on. For the next few days his mood was a mixture of sulks and triumph.

Perhaps home-roosting chickens have sent me here. I should be able to turn to a number of people and say, it's all your fault. But I don't feel that. I replay the events of my childhood in a matter-of-fact kind of way. I wasn't unhappy. I see it all differently now, but can find no one to blame, not even my father, and no purpose, no point, in blaming anyone. Nothing can be done about it now. Why blame parents, siblings? Only in order to dodge responsibility, only to be able to say, it's not my fault. But why this preoccupation with blame? That's easy, isn't it? The inheritance of Calvinism? The terrible acid of guilt, eating away at one's wellbeing. My parents taught me to feel guilty. I think my father had a burden of guilt, for what I don't know, perhaps general rather than particular, which he had to share by seeing everyone else as blameworthy as himself.

The guilt is inherent, not induced. We are born with it; it is not a consequence of our actions. The relationship between cause and effect, sequence and consequence, drowns in the morass of original sin. My mother has shown no sign of guilt or remorse for what she did. When she told me it appeared a simple statement of fact. I pulled the plug, she said, and I didn't at first understand what she meant.

The great, bare, slanting wall seems to shrink my footsteps. Perhaps the need to explain myself has faded not because of distance but because I have no wish to find culprits. The wall once enclosed an ancient city, not the original city, which lay to the east, not the centre of Qin Shihuang's vast empire glued together with blood and terror, but a capsule of the centuries nonetheless, vibrant with a radical existence. This broad road is less crowded. Perhaps that is why I am thinking about myself, and not about the people who have jostled me and stared, whose solemn looks have sometimes melted into smiles of disbelieving amusement.

I have walked as far as the east gate. Its heavy presence

breaks up the traffic and the people trying to funnel through it. I am back in the current now, pinned to the kerb by trucks and buses, awash in cascades of hooting horns and bicycle bells. For a while I make no attempt to move, just watch it all go past. A radical existence. What do I mean? If that is what I am looking for I must be clear about what I mean here. Behind the solid stone of the gate, a hefty, commanding artefact, built three hundred years ago. Around me a river of humanity and the wheels humanity invented, in China as in other places, for the inventive nature of humanity has expressed itself spontaneously throughout the earth.

I feel, in some way I can't describe, in the heart of things, though not within that heart. And isn't 'radical' about heart as much as roots, the source of the blood's flow, the powerhouse? Carts, baskets on backs and carrying poles, slung on shoulders, pushed on bikes, trucks, all laden with produce, with food grown in the countryside, brought to the free markets that sprawl along the streets. Stalls displaying brightly coloured cotton goods, for Xian is a textile town. Food and clothing. The raw materials of survival. That's what I mean by 'radical'. All around me are the raw materials. That's what I feel divorced from in my other life. That's what I'm looking for. That's what we've forgotten. I cannot speak for the human race, only for my little tribe.

I move at last, back across the flow of traffic. I'm in a shadier street now. Trees have been planted, though they look dry and brittle. I am romanticising. Maybe. But I'd like to free my mind to explore these thoughts. Even that is an achievement. I walk past shops that are open to the street. A carpenter is at work, a smell of new wood and shavings clouds the air around him. A bicycle repair shop, oily, little heaps of screws and tools and bike chains on a low bench. The light catches snicks of polished metal. An adolescent boy bends over an upturned bike and spins a wheel. A hi-fi shop. Incongruously gleaming ghetto-blasters stacked on rough shelves in the dusty interior.

Sitting on a low stool on the pavement outside this shop is an old man with a small child leaning against his knee. Something prompts me to smile at them. The old man points to my camera, hanging on its strap around my neck, then to the child. I smile again, raise my camera. He nods, pushes the child a little to the front. The boy's round and serious eyes show alarm and he hides his face in the old man's shoulder. The old man coaxes him to look up. He speaks to him softly. But the boy still clings and shows only one wide eye to the camera's view. The man, too, is solemn and sits stiffly on his little stool, but when the picture is taken he relaxes and smiles and waves a gesture of thanks. He speaks also, but I do not understand him. I move on up the street, but I am troubled by the thought that he might have been expecting an instant picture, or money. I don't look back.

There is a little park tucked against the wall and through the trees in the dappling sunlight I can see a gathering of men in blue cotton. They are squatting on the ground. I cannot make out what is going on – dice, I wonder, or cards? I draw nearer, but hesitantly. No, it is neither. Beside each squatting figure is a bamboo bird cage, on the ground or hung from a tree branch. They've brought their birds out to enjoy the sun. They squat in the grassless dust, smoke, talk a little. I can hear the birds. I shelter behind a tree, like a spy, and watch them. It seems a very private gathering, here in this open place. I have walked, almost, into what feels like an intimate ritual, not for my eyes. Nevertheless I take my photograph.

The rituals at home were centred on my father. But they were low-key rituals, habit, assumptions. Ceremony did not have a place in our household. My father's chair, my father's place at the table, the shape of things around his working day. Breakfast was a meal, not something snatched hastily before school. The table was laid, with butter dish, marmalade pot, milk jug. My mother poured the tea, but did not sit down. You know your father likes everyone together at breakfast, she would say if George or I were late. Yes, we knew. But why? It did not occur to me to ask. He rarely spoke to us. Did George or my mother know or wonder? To enquire, to suggest that my father himself might think about the reasons for doing certain things in certain ways, was to challenge. We were none of us rebellious. My father sat at the breakfast table, nodded at us as we sat down, ate his porridge, read his *Scotsman*.

He was considered a decent man. I think he was respected. Even when I was quite small I recognised the value of that, and I didn't dislike him. He was too distant for that. Met in different circumstances, I expect I would have seen a man of honesty if little imagination, a responsible husband and father, a deservedly valued member of the community. He wasn't a hypocrite, he didn't proclaim his own virtue. He rarely raised his voice. I had heard the fathers of friends shout at their children and their wives, and no one seemed to think it odd. It made me fearful, uncomfortable. When I was older I realised that my father's stern silence had the same effect on my friends, and I myself felt it oppressively.

He required certain things of us. By the time I was fifteen or so I saw this as diminishing my mother. There was expectation, but no praise or admiration. If we failed to make the grade he said so. There was no virtue in neglecting to draw attention to our insufficiencies. I came home with good exam results. I remember thinking how thin my mother looked. She smiled and wiped her hands on her apron. I thought for a moment she was going to kiss me. Your father will be pleased, she said. And indeed when he came in he spoke a gruff well done, without looking at me, and I felt embarrassed, because by then I had learnt the lesson that praise was a sign of weakness, of disorderliness even.

So father was at the centre. He was the heart, the powerhouse, regular and requiring regularity. I am sure he was the same at work in the local government offices – reliable, attending to detail, uncompromising. Younger men were promoted over his head, but he never spoke of it. I learned this from others. At home he never missed a beat, or so it seemed, and never accelerated either.

One afternoon, I was perhaps thirteen or fourteen, I was alone in the house, restless. I wandered from room to room. I remember wishing that we lived in a house with stairs. I drifted into the kitchen, opened cupboard doors, looked in George's room. I often looked in George's room when he was out, although there was little there that really interested me except for his record player, which he had campaigned and saved for. There was a pile of records. I checked to see if there was anything new. A jumble of clothes on a chair. Rugby pictures on a pinboard. Schoolbooks. An empty cigarette packet on the floor. That was careless, it must have fallen out of his pocket. I picked it up.

My mother did not go out much, except to shop or help with the Sunday School. Occasionally she met a friend for tea. So I wasn't often in the house alone for any length of time. I dawdled out of George's room. Next door was my parents' bedroom, the door closed. I opened it. The room was neat and dim. It faced east and onto the street, and net curtains at the window cut out the afternoon light. There was the double bed with a wine-red cover. Three or four newly ironed shirts were folded on it. I moved over to my mother's chest of drawers. She would have said the devil was finding work for idle hands.

I pulled the drawers open, one after the other, unearthing items of underwear, blouses, jumpers, stockings, all with a smell that mingled staleness with lavender. Then I went to her dressing table and opened first a large jewellery box that stood on it. She rarely wore jewellery. There were brooches and necklaces, many of which I'd never seen. Several looked old-fashioned, and I guessed they had belonged to my grandmother. There was a heavy gold locket on a twisted chain and a pebble brooch which I cradled for a while in the palm of my hand, rubbing my thumb over the smooth surface. There was something satisfying about its feel. Then I opened one of the small drawers. There was face powder, lipstick, little containers of hairpins and odd buttons, a half-empty tiny bottle of Chanel No 5. There were jars of face cream and cotton wool. I looked in the mirror and tried to see my mother's face. I frowned in my effort to see it with make-up – but yes, she did wear lipstick sometimes. I saw her in her good coat, with lipstick.

I slid the lid off one of the lipsticks and swivelled it up and down. In the mirror now I saw the bed, large and dark. But my mother and my father were the woman and man who sat at either end of the table at mealtimes, who occupied separate armchairs in the evenings and pursued their separate activities, and even when engaged in the same activity, like watching television, did so separately. There were bedside tables at either side, a little lamp on each. I did not see the bed as a place of union.

I put the lipstick back and pushed the drawer closed. But the lid of the jewellery box was still open. I picked up the pebble brooch again. It had one large chestnut-coloured stone, slightly mottled. I pushed the lid of the box shut and left my parents' room with the brooch still in my hand.

They had married late after a long engagement, for my father had been caught by the last year of the war and had to wait to pursue his education at Glasgow University. He was in his thirties, my mother twenty-nine, before they married. I'd never thought of them as young. I went into my room and lay on my bed with my face against the pillow, listening to the silent house. I had given much thought to sex. I was curious. I had begun to read DH Lawrence. I searched my mind for a picture of my parents that would fit what I had read, but part of me did not want to find it.

I lay for a while in the silent house, then quite suddenly was on my feet again and looking at the mirror in my room. I spent a lot of time looking at the mirror. I was dumpy, broad-faced. I longed to be slim. I longed to banish the freckles that bloomed every summer. I wanted to be like Judy, with whom I walked to school every day, whose boyishness was emphasised by her short-cropped hair and quick movements. My hair, which I now roughly pushed back from my face, was another source of despair, for it was thick and unruly and my mother was always telling me to brush it, as if brushing alone would cure its wildness. The changes in my body only made me feel larger and more awkward. I did not want breasts and rounder hips. I remember raking my hands through my thick hair and thinking, no one will ever want me, no one will ever think I'm beautiful, and underneath, unarticulated, was a chorus: it isn't fair, it isn't fair. No one will ever want Eleanor, dumpy, freckled, unkempt Eleanor. Tidy yourself up, my father would say. You can't go out like that.

But I discovered before very long that people did want Eleanor, that boys would kiss and fumble, that men would watch and wolf whistle. And in a few years, hands would unfasten buttons and dislodge zips, and nervousness and curiosity and excitement would twine and knot with distaste and acceptance of the inevitable. And perhaps if I am truthful – but I can't be truthful, can I? it would be like claiming immortality – but if I were to try to be truthful I might admit that the distaste did not disappear. Until I met Daniel, who made all that had happened before seem entirely without grace.

Well, there's a turn-up for the books. That's what I was thinking, walking up a street in Xian lined with dry, bone-like trees. A lie unearthed. For if it is true, can it be Roy's fault? Is Roy's well-mannered preoccupation with himself really the cause of my dissatisfaction? It could be, after all, within myself that the causes are to be found. Yet if Daniel released me from the hereditary grip, why not Roy? And am I really admitting that it took a man to set me free?

My father was at the centre. No, I'm not being as inconsequential as it seems. My father was at the centre. As he grew older George began to join him there, never fully of course, for a son can never share a position with a father. But he moved inexorably nearer to the bull's eye. And I understood from earliest consciousness that I would never have a place within even the outer circle. And if with Roy I moved inside the outer circle, I accepted or at least did not challenge, that my place was not at the centre, that Roy, armoured and secure, chose to occupy that place alone. Only with Daniel. Only Daniel, who gave himself so convincingly to my pleasure, made me feel at the heart of something – but it wasn't his centre. Is it just sex I'm talking about here? Just sex? Just?

I slip away from the men and the caged birds. They sing regardless, their calls and whistles more penetrating than the traffic. There were no women there. And no younger men. It was a pastime for older men, squatted in the dust under the wall, exchanging few words as I observed them, absorbed by their imprisoned feathered friends. Roy felt no need to shut the door of the cage because it never occurred to him that his bird might fly. My mother sprung her cage, but perhaps it is too late. I don't believe there's anywhere she wants to go. Perhaps there never was.

I still have the pebble brooch – I brought it with me. Was it never missed? I have worn it once or twice, here in China. I hope it did belong to my grandmother. I never dared to wear it at home, in case it was recognised and my tiny crime revealed. But here I am safe, it is safe, a piece of memory, even though I cannot myself reach into it.

12

I AM TIRED. I'm sitting just out of reach of the fountain's spray drinking pale, scented tea. I have just written a postcard home, my first in five weeks. A banal message on a poor quality card that showed a square, ruggedly patterned bronze *ting*. I did not say I was in Xian, the legacy of a mad emperor who could not bear to die. (After all, that's hardly a fault. The prospect of death is one most of us would fortify ourselves against if we were able.) I said that I was well, the sun was shining, and China, I wrote, is very interesting.

Which is all true. I am well. I haven't thought much about how I feel, but now that I do, I realise that I am well. And the sun beats down through air that is clearer than in Beijing. The sky is a real blue, unhazed by dust and Gobi sand. The fountain sparkles. And indeed, China is full of endless interest. On the other side of the fountain tourists board a minibus. They have nothing to do with me. They are a million miles away. Yet I have no doubt that they too find China interesting and will return home with their pictures and invite their friends to slide-shows.

In my walk around the city I saw only one European face, that of a young woman on a bike, her blonde hair tied back in a ponytail with a straw hat perched on top. I watched her as she stopped to buy strawberries from a street stall, and wondered who she was, what she is doing in Xian. The minibus departs, skirts the fountain, tyres crunching on the gravel, down the drive, through the gate, with a cargo of yuan-stuffed pockets, I make believe, to be offloaded at the Friendship Store. No doubt I too will make my way to the Friendship Store and look for things on which to spend my dwindling money.

I am tired. It's not just the walking or the heat. It's the thinking. Is my mother happy now? How much has her daughter's flight disturbed her liberation? George is probably angry. It will be hard for him to find appropriate words to explain his sister's defection, and it is second nature for him to spin as well as narrate the facts. Sally. I'd forgotten about Sally. Sally is unlikely to be generous in her view of me. I will at best be foolish, rash, inconsiderate. At worst, cruel, destined for disaster. Victimising my mother. Or perhaps having to be rescued. At any rate, I'll be back with my tail between my legs, no doubt George and Sally will agree in the privacy of their bedroom as a prelude to embraces. But no, I won't let my mind dwell on that particular scene. Instead, Roy. I wonder if he is embracing someone else now? It's only been a few weeks... but who could blame him? Though it's hard to imagine. Do I want to imagine it? Would I rather that only I will do, other women flavourless in comparison? But the thought doesn't convince or reassure me. I don't feel less uncertain, but I feel unmoved. I search for crumbs of regret. But it does not matter to me whether Roy at this very moment has another in the bed we shared. That at least for now, at least at this moment as I sit with my notebook and drink my tea screened by the fountain's spray, unremarked as far as I can tell by anyone, is the fragile truth.

Yet the fountain is not screen enough, for through the mist of water the grotesque and incongruous building looms. I want to laugh at it, it is so grossly outrageous, yet what good does it do, to laugh at a building? Buildings do not yield to laughter. Even some interiors can resist a human presence and response. Our interior was commanded by Roy, as my father commanded the interior of the family home. I submitted. I colluded in that captaincy. If I had not done so perhaps I would not have fled.

I need to sleep. Tomorrow I will take my turn on a tour bus, heading for the wondrous grave of clay soldiers.

13

TWO WONDROUS GRAVES, though one, a huge, green, artificial hill of earth, lies undisturbed. It teems with tales of riches guarded with death-dealing devices. There is no doubt that it is sinister, humping upwards, containing the remains of mad Qin Shihuang, but it is the other grave that amazes, the earth-clogged tomb of thousands of sculpted warriors.

Space is not wasted, food is not wasted, but human life is, though you may believe that, like excrement, it is recycled. Life is precarious. Every visitor to the east notices. The commentators agree. Life is precarious, life is cheap. Quantity devalues. You don't need to set foot in the arenas of war and violence to be aware of it. You don't need acquaintance with tyranny, slavery, genocide, mass neglect, napalm, bombs, starvation, to learn that human lives are going cheap.

Overproduction. The teeming streets. The solid throng at the railway station, moving slowly like a river of mud, in the midst of which I hold my breath against panic, for I am at the mercy of several thousand human beings, and if a few should die, trampled, suffocated, what matter? How do you estimate the loss? One significant individual, European, light-brown hair unevenly bleached by the sun, blue-grey eyes, five foot six, intelligent, a first-class honours degree, a promising career (abandoned), a respected teacher, sensitive, caring, thirty-three years old (a magic number?) Crushed to death in a huge crowd of Chinese going about their business on the station platform at the city of Xian in Shangxi Province. A locomotive whistles and steams slowly onward.

The packed buses, the bicycles locked together like horned animals, the train's hard-seat carriages where life is carried on, eating, drinking, sleeping, playing, probably praying, although there is no room to move. And on the streets, too, the whole of life. Cooking, eating, washing, cleaning, laundry, sewing with machines on pavement tables, games and pastimes, everything but the sexual act, though I dare say there are quiet places, in the parks at dusk maybe, where men and women denied space of their own contrive to get together.

Like thousands of fish fry, millions of insect larvae, colossal overproduction because most won't live. For the survival of ten a thousand must be produced, and so these creatures battle, exhausted and compelled, and eggs are produced, to be consumed by predators, destroyed by the elements, and young are born to struggle with just as much cost against the same odds, the voracious enemies of whatever kind. Teeming humanity ensures its own survival. The human race will continue, but at the same time death matters less. What luxury, to fear death, to elevate it. Yet we all do that, not only emperors. It isn't only the privileged who give a meaning to death. It is the essence of the human condition.

I was not encouraged to reflect on immortality. There was no room for that kind of sentiment. But here of all places human beings have been preoccupied by it, an undisguised preoccupation, unlike that of Christianity. Here, where flesh and blood are expendable, where death resides in intimate proximity to the everyday hours and their tiny activities.

Qin Shihuang built his empire through force of arms, as emperors usually did. In an army, of workers as well as of soldiers, it is numbers that count, not individuals. It is the way a battalion behaves that wins or loses on the battlefield, not the courage or cowardice of one. While in a guerrilla band every fighting soul is worth the sum of action and experience that he or she represents. The carpenter and the bicycle repairer – the university lecturer? – are worth the sum of their own skills and the results they achieve. Add together a million workmen and their individuality is obliterated. Their sum is no more than the section of wall completed, of sepulchre excavated. A massive total if you're an emperor, but where do you see the accomplishment of an individual pair of hands?

Qin Shihuang used thousands for his great work. It is possible that it mattered more than his conquest of China. And here are the soldiers, life-size, protruding from the dry earth. They are fashioned from terracotta, but I see them as corpses. I look at each set of features, each different, each individual, and see them as once alive. For I know that in creating this huge tomb and the thousands of sculpted guards with their horses and their chariots and their weapons to protect it, many died. There were those whom the work itself killed, and those who were put to death because they carried the secret of the emperor's resting place, knew what it would contain and how it would be fortified against intrusion. So these clay men are in effect the dead. I see them as the dead, from the railed walkway that is so thoughtfully provided for the visitor.

Their blank stares have the uncomprehending vision of the dead, their immobile features, their heads that cannot turn and their eyes that cannot weep. There is a knot in my gut as if I were viewing a catacomb of corpses. They are more real than skulls and bones, more fleshly in their configuration, more like life, and infinitely more disturbing. Over their cracked heads a roof has been erected. Tourists in bright clothes, I among them, peer at their stricken limbs. Their rigid stance is no less than one expects of soldiers, permanently at attention, always at the ready. The earth is removed gently. Lingering crumbs are brushed away with soft brushes. The famed Chinese brushwork, not this time creating fluid shapes on silk or paper but caressing the clay features of this ancient army.

Clay features. Oh Roy, why do I think of you, and not of the millions who have nothing to offer, nothing to say to me, to whom I am nothing, although this is where I want to be? I was something to you, I know, even if only a reflection of your clay self. Clay, like you, fashioned before birth, moulded before my mind could take control. Immured before the discovery of space and freedom, so they are there, for ever, beyond the fortifications, in the land of the barbarians. Roy, mother, father, brother, thought I was one of them. But here I am, a tourist like the other tourists, moving slowly round, gazing into the earth at the bearded faces of pretend soldiers. Out of reach. I cannot touch their faces or go beyond the wall.

It was never hard for you to say you loved me. I wish it had been harder. Did you ever notice how hard it was for me, although for a while I think I really loved you? I was always afraid (or is this hindsight, a fear I planted later?), always afraid at your facility. How easily you seemed to love, how readily words dropped from your lips. You could say 'love' with as little thought as you could say 'kinship' or 'field study'. The word was part of your everyday vocabulary. So much of your charm was that readiness. I liked it so much, those first few months. Your smile, the dimple on your left cheek that came and went like an eddy in a pool. (Lin Bingshen has a dimple, surprising, on his smooth olive-ochre skin; I found it reassuring when we first began to speak.) You seemed so open, so responsive.

I was used to caution and lack of curiosity. You charmed them, all my family, won them with your smiling good manners, your neat clothes, your effortless interest in their lives. And when I saw that they had no wish to resist, I realised I was well and truly won also. Or so it seemed. How could I hold out, when they, whose fear of feeling I had absorbed at my mother's knee, yielded so willingly to the first young man I introduced them to. My father's keen eye identified substance and reliability. I was not so much a rebel that I did not want them to approve.

So there you were, quite comfortable, it seemed, as they welcomed in their quiet way the right sort of man for their Eleanor. And their Eleanor knew all along that her need for spontaneity, for warmth and conviction, so strong yet so secret, demanded more. So she staked her soul on a banal refusal to get married, at the same time as she colluded in her family's acceptance of this nice young man. How was he able to speak their language, she wondered, as they worried over litter and teenage drinking?

Rejecting marriage made it alright. It made Roy satisfactory, because in the midst of his constrained existence – not that he thought it constrained, moving onward and upward as it was, with frequent excursions to exotic parts of the world – in the midst of academic and domestic routine I could hang onto a dissent which masked the conformity. Roy did not share in the dissent, modest and unadventurous as it was. But he tolerated it. He may even have been attracted by it, its immaturity a pleasant reminder to him of his adult manhood. I presented no challenge, because in the end I would come round. Roy, fulfilling the older and wiser role that suited him so well, assured the family that Eleanor would grow out of this childish resistance. Instead she grew out of him, grew up enough to run away. That's how I like to think of it.

Sometimes we gave dinner parties. We always discussed the food and wine with some seriousness. He was anxious about my cooking. Though he didn't cook much himself, he took an intense interest in food. I think it was the only time I saw him nervous or short-tempered. He'd fuss with the table setting, taste the wine, polish the glasses. He'd slice lemon and reject imperfect slices. He'd rearrange the cutlery. And I'd be in the kitchen, flustered, stirring a sauce that had knotted into lumps or despondent over a salad that had gone limp or meat that was not tender. For God's sake, Eleanor. Why do you leave everything to the last minute? There was an echo of my father in his voice.

Roy stood in the kitchen doorway with a corkscrew in his hand. Two bottles of claret were already open. We were expecting a visiting professor who could be useful to Roy. Flushed and fretting, I could think of nothing to say and was glad to be busy at the stove so I didn't have to look at him.

Don't forget to warm the plates. And have you made the

salad dressing? And taken the brie out of the fridge? Last time you forgot.

If sheer effort and concentration could remove lumps from sauces, mine would have been as smooth as silk. And I said nothing, and kept my back turned as the door of the fridge was opened and closed. I said nothing, but stored up the evidence, not fully aware of what I was doing. But storing up the evidence because, one day, I would make my case.

And now here I am making my case, though I never made it to Roy himself. I come out of the hangar-like building that shelters the excavation and into the bright heat. There are stalls selling curios and small images of the petrified warriors. But I shake my head when I am accosted and wander on. Making my case. Roy is judged and is banished on the grounds of bad temper when we gave a dinner party. But there were never any real disasters, my cuisine was not as ambitious as he would have liked (I should have paid more attention to Daniel) but always, I thought, acceptable, the lumpy sauces ultimately sufficiently smooth, our guests usually good company. When the door was shut on the professor and his amiable wife, Roy sat down on the sofa with a sigh, poured himself another drink, and said, I'm knackered. I'm off to bed. A lot of work to do in the morning. I'll need to follow up tonight's discussions. Might get a trip to Dar-es-Salaam out of it. And still I said nothing, but gathered dirty glasses and coffee cups on a tray and silently retreated to the kitchen. Like my mother. By the time I got to bed Roy was asleep. And by the time I was back in the kitchen the next day, he was up and dressed and staring keenly at the screen of his word-processor, as if it were the source of all enlightenment.

I took some coffee in to him, in my dressing-gown, unwashed, uncombed. He smiled and said thank you. That went well last night, don't you think, love? he said, without taking his eyes from the screen. That chocolate and orange mousse was rather good. My bare feet on the carpeted floor made no sound as I turned away and the empty space where I had been did not impinge on his consciousness. I heard the faint rattle of plastic as he keyed in another line.

I closed the door of the kitchen and cried into my coffee. I don't often cry. What was the matter with me? A Sunday morning. The papers on the kitchen table along with fragments of last night's feast. I picked up an oatcake and nibbled it through my tears. The brie which I had failed to take out of the fridge in time had oozed gently all night but its present state of perfection did not tempt me. Beside me is a marmalade jar without its lid, and toast crumbs. Sometimes on a Sunday Roy went out for rolls for breakfast, but not this Sunday. I cried harder. Yes, I was childish. I wanted rolls for breakfast and Roy had not brought them for me. I didn't ask for much, I thought, not much.

I never asked for enough, and now I am asking for everything. Escape. Freedom. My money will run out soon. It would last longer if I chose to travel the hard way, crammed against the sweaty bodies of the Chinese peasantry and proletariat, breathing the fumes of the food and the live chickens and cats that travelled with them. I could join the brigade of dollar-a-day Americans and traverse Asia with rice and noodles to fill my stomach. I could pretend. If I don't pretend I'll have to go home. And if I go home I'll have to pretend.

Eleanor, I'm beginning to think you're a fool. They won't have you back, you know. You've burnt your bridges. They won't have you back. So what are you going to do? How are you going to live? With your mother in Linlithgow, where old school companions will be met in the supermarket or pushing prams in the High Street, coming out of the chemist with huge parcels of disposable nappies? And what are you doing now, Eleanor? Still at the university? No?

Nothing, just nothing. Living at home, reading novels. I hear you went to China. How exciting. That must have been awfully interesting. Yes. Awfully interesting. And here I am, home again. Living with my mother, in the same house I lived in for more or less two decades, with the school I attended almost within sight, and the High Street and the church, and the cinema long since closed down, and the new supermarket. And the empty palace and the loch where people wander on Sunday afternoons.

My mother is worried. What could have possessed Eleanor? To leave her job, leave her lovely flat, leave her hus... to leave the man who was going to marry her, such a nice young man, doing so well. Nice young man, doing so well. The refrain comes easily. You're alright, Roy. They'll never blame you, and indeed they shouldn't.

Warriors, weapons, horses. I am surrounded. Found accidentally by a peasant seeking water. What riches have sprung out of his well! A fountain of soldiery, who will never retreat, never turn tail and flee. Their eyes are beautiful, open, almond-shaped, alert. The lids will never pucker, neither age, nor sand, nor arrows will blunt their sight. Upright and open-eyed. And if your limbs crack, if a hand goes astray or a thigh crumbles, craftsmen will set to work and make a man of you again.

I have lost... something. But perhaps we come into the world with a sense of loss and it is that feeling that there is something to be found, some treasure, that supports our steps, that makes us go on living. Are all lives and all stories about searching? Is that what my mother was doing when she pulled the plug? Without a sense of loss, surely we would be poorer.

14

I WENT TO have dinner in the hotel's echoing dining room. I had sat for a while in the last of the sunshine, writing. At last I am beginning to say what I want to say, even if the result is confusion. Today, with the terracotta soldiers, I felt confused, but I seem to have a better idea of what needs to be set down.

I sit at a round table, by myself. The room is half full, I suppose, a few oriental faces but mostly western. I ask for a beer. A girl brings me a large bottle, and then several dishes of food which are placed in a semi-circle around me, fish, cabbage, chicken, tiny meat balls, rice. I begin to eat. Then I see coming through the door the two Poles. They wave, and thread their way to my table.

Good evening, good evening, my friend of the train greets me. Good evening, good evening. The other nods, an abrupt dip of the head. Is it... we may sit, yes? With you? Okay?

Of course I smile and gesture, though I am happy enough without company. They sit. The younger one looks curiously at the food in front of me.

Very tired, he says. All day we drive around. With a guide. I think we are everywhere. You go to the warriors? Wonderful. Listen – I take many photographs. To show my wife. Tomas, too. Many photos. With a Russian camera.

He grins. Even Tomas smiles. They order beer.

The beer is not bad, says Tomas. I am surprised. I'd assumed he spoke no English. He bites his lip. When the beer comes he pours a glassful and downs it. Very tired, very thirsty, he says. He looks at me, straight in the eye, a knowing look, a complicit look, and smiles.

Within minutes they have both finished their beer and order more. I begin to eat again. When their food comes, another array of small bowls set out again in a semi-circle, they at once tuck in with more enthusiasm than their previous criticisms would have suggested. The clash of dishes resounds through the large space. Attempts at conversation stop as they struggle with chopsticks. Tomas stolidly manipulates compacted grains of rice and with concentration gets them into his mouth. He frowns, and brandishes his chopsticks in the air. Stupid, stupid, he mutters resentfully.

My name, says his companion, when he has finished eating, is Jochanan. This is Tomas.

I'm Eleanor, I say. We all shake hands across the table. It seems a little bizarre, as we have already spent twenty-four hours in each others' company.

Glad to meet you, glad to meet you, says Jochanan, as if we had not spoken on the train. Tomas nods. He has begun to turn over bits of food with his chopsticks and examine them with apparent suspicion. Jochanan surveys the scattering of leftovers in the bowls and tries to spear fragments with a single chopsticks. I have started to eat like the Chinese and pick up my bowl to scoop up the rice. I shamelessly stretch across the table to grab some delicacy with my chopsticks and convey it directly into my mouth. My parents would have been appalled.

But why not? I am thinking as I reach for a piece of chicken. It certainly doesn't matter a damn what the Poles think. After a while, a large white bowl of soup is put in front of us. It is slightly murky, with unidentifiable vegetables floating in it. Jochanan peers into it and shakes his head. Instead of sampling the soup he picks up a glutinous wedge of rice in his fingers and pops it into his mouth. I want never to see rice again, he says.

Tomas calls for more beer. As they drink they become more voluble, but in Polish. I can't help wondering if they are talking about me. Tomas is looking at me. His eyes are a darker blue than Jochanan's, his brow heavier, his shoulders broader. He fills my glass from his bottle. I would like to go but am not sure how to accomplish it gracefully. The two of them seem alien in these surroundings, in a way that is different from the other tourists scattered round the dining room. There is a kind of resignation about them, as if they know they are being used but are equally aware that they can do nothing about it. As if they are not only suspicious of everything Chinese, but suspicious of being what they are and where they are. They have not chosen to come to Xian. They have been sent. They take it for granted that whatever they have been told, the real reasons for their visit are quite different.

Their conversation is now animated. I am about to stand up when Jochanan breaks off to address me again. He makes a vague but expansive gesture. Politics, you know. We talk politics.

He goes on, apparently inconsequentially, I want to do my job, look after my wife and my child. We are told. Do this, go there. Go to China, they say. I don't like to be away from Poland. My wife. Tomas, he is different. He likes a holiday from home. Tomas is smoking, and a sardonic smile curves round his cigarette. I realise now that he understands perfectly well what is being said. Listen, Jochanan continues, things not so good in Poland. We have Chernobyl. Problems. Sometimes we go to buy food and there isn't enough. My wife waits and waits, to buy coffee, to buy fruit. But better, much better than China. I don't like this country. Tomas doesn't care, but I don't like it.

Tomas silently pours more beer into my glass, although I protest. The beer, says Jochanan, the beer is okay. German beer. They make it in China, now the Chinese make it. What about Scotland. Good beer? What about whisky? Scotch whisky. You drink a lot of whisky in Scotland? Polish beer is good. Polish vodka. You want some vodka? We have vodka upstairs.

Tomas leans forward, his breath on my face. Why, he asks, why you come to China?

What can I say? What do I say? One is not supposed to tell

the truth in these situations. But I reply carefully, slowly, I have always wanted to visit China.

Tomas crushes out his cigarette with a look of disbelief. Jochanan's eyes widen.

Very strange, he says. China is very... very... not modern. Perhaps you like old things? I like the warriors, yes, but temples, palaces, old buildings... He shakes his head. In Poland I like old things. History is okay. But listen – we must have more than history, more than the past.

He believes in the future, Tomas says abruptly, as if belief in the future were the ultimate expression of a naive faith. One day he will grow up.

Yes, yes, the future. But not here, not in China. China is too... too...

Backward, I say, without thinking.

Backward! Jochanan seizes the word and nods vigorously. Backward. Backward, yes. Not modern. And the people... too many. How can they live? But what can you do? I do not understand. Yes, they are learning. People like us come and tell them. But the mines, the coal. We come, we tell them what is modern. We sell them new equipment, of course. But we know it can't make China modern.

You're the experts, I say. The irony is lost.

Experts, yes, foreign experts.

I nod, smile, drink my beer of which I have already had more than I want. Tomas tips back his chair, his hands in his pockets, stares at the ceiling, then towards the door, then through half-closed eyes at me. I feel he is waiting for something. I get to my feet before he can fill my glass again. Jochanan stands up too, but he makes no move beyond that. He is being a gentleman. Tomas watches.

Goodnight, goodnight, says Jochanan.

I go to the hotel's broad and imposing entrance and look out into the night. It is quite dark now beyond the pool of yellow light cast by the building. I can hear the fountains. I walk slowly to the rim of darkness and the fountain scatters drops of water on me. The air holds the heat in layers and as soon as I am beyond the influence of the building I feel myself walking through strata of warmth. The spray catches the light from the hotel.

There are few people about and no one pays any attention to me as I move aimlessly, skirting the fountains, catching a heavy scent from the shrubs and flowers. I am under the trees, deeper in darkness. But relaxed, quite contented, I realise, my mind moving slowly, free from the ache of pressure which was such a constant presence in my working life that I could not imagine being without it.

And it is only now that I am aware that it has gone. I take a lungful of scented air. That anxiety, that knot of worry that could sometimes ravel into panic, sitting constantly in one's head and guts like an evil goblin. It has melted away. There was always something that had not been finished, a problem unsolved. A colleague with whom confrontation was unavoidable, a student insisting on attention and argument. But, I remind myself almost with indignation, I liked, loved I often said, my job. Surely that was so. Did not teaching excite and satisfy me? Was I not, as they say, dedicated? Did I not care genuinely about my students, their abilities, their achievements, their welfare? Do I not want them to do well? But you left all that, Eleanor. No, no, I argue, it was the goblin I ran from, not the role itself. That was fine, that was what I wanted, a licence to explore words in all their diversity of meaning and nuance and arrangement in the company of those who shared my wonder and curiosity. Ah, but how many were there, really, to share? And was not that wonder eroded by competitive colleagues, demanding students, mindless administrative duties, tedious meetings, petty rivalries... I pause under the trees. I could go on, but I want to banish all this from my mind. It has come upon me unawares, just at the moment that I noticed it had gone.

Alone in the dark in a strange land, but not in any way nervous. Since arriving at Beijing airport in the sleepy early hours I've never for a moment felt unsafe, except on a bicycle in the Beijing highway torrent. So when I hear a sound nearby, that is not the hum of the fountains or a voice carrying through the warm air, I pay no attention. It hardly penetrates my consciousness. I continue my slow meandering pace, breathing easily, savouring the smell of hot earth and heavy blooms. I am beginning to get the hang of it, to loosen some of the bonds.

I drift nearer the hotel. Now I catch pleasant, comfortable sounds. Voices, a car starting and moving away, the crunch of gravel. I move away again, in a different direction, my back to the lights and water. Now, again, there is a different sound, very close. I think, someone else is enjoying a night wander. Instinctively I look around and there is a shape under the trees, a shape that seems familiar, and now moves towards me and is only a few feet away when I recognise it. Tomas.

He pauses, then says hello, quietly but deliberately. Then, even more deliberately, as if forcing his tongue, beautiful tonight. I do not want to have a conversation with Tomas, but cannot move away from him. I step back and he steps forward. I wonder, briefly, if he is referring to the evening, the garden, or to me, whose features he probably can't make out. I can't make out his features. I feel mildly irritated. I sense, but cannot see, his sardonic smile.

Tomas steps closer. There's a ripple of nervousness. Why should I be nervous? This is only the rather sullen Pole in whose company I spent nearly twenty-four hours in a train, who drinks beer and smokes, whose friend likes to chat, who shared my table at dinner. Who has been watching me, clearly – but why shouldn't he? I begin to walk away. He walks beside me. We reach the drive near the gate onto the street. The street is quiet. I'm about to turn towards the hotel but he puts his hand on my arm and steers me across the drive.

I'm ready to go in, I say, lightly.

Oh no, he says. Too early. Beautiful tonight.

So we are on the grass again, and among the small slender trees, further from the reassuring sounds that radiate from the building. I know what is coming, and yet can't anticipate, can't say don't do it, can't turn away. Something compels me to walk calmly at the side of this man although he has now become repugnant. He says, beautiful, again, as if it is the only English word he knows. He lingers on the word, soothingly. I am thinking, why don't I dodge round him? Why do I politely remain, as if denying all that my senses tell me?

He takes cigarettes from his shirt pocket and offers them to me. I shake my head. He takes one and lights it. Poor Jochanan, he says. He misses so much. Well, I say, I think I'll go back. Tomas throws his cigarette on the ground and grips me by the upper arms. His hold is firm but not painful. An alien mouth descends and clamps on mine. I do not think of it as a kiss. I do not struggle. I am holding my breath. I am totally still. There is a beating in my ears. Perhaps my lack of response will deter him. It seems like minutes, but it can only be seconds. Everything is suspended. I feel blank, nothing, not even anger. No instinct, no indignation, comes to my aid. My mouth, his grip on my arms, nothing.

I feel his tongue. Now I react. Now I clench my teeth and lips together. Oh, but he doesn't like that. He pushes me against a ragged tree, which jars my backbone. His left hand tightens on my arm. He pulls his head away and puts his right hand over my mouth. I think he is going to slap me but he just presses his hot palm against my lips. It smells of cigarette smoke. He says, do you want to fight me? Do it, then. Fight me. He takes his hand from my mouth and clamps it on my forehead, shoving my head painfully against the tree trunk. He kisses me again. Every muscle is tensed against him. But I don't believe what's happening, I don't believe he can persist when my whole body shrieks rejection.

My teeth seem to be bruising the inside of my mouth. Then he pulls back. Women are so stupid, he says. You walk out here in the woods, in the dark. Then you play games. With a sudden movement, he tugs at the front of my shirt. Now at last my paralysis evaporates and I wrench against his relaxed grip and deliver a rather feeble kick on his shin. I run a few yards, and in moments I am back on the main drive and there's the sweeping, brightly lit frontage of the hotel. He's not going to follow me. I slow to a walk and run my hands through my hair. A button's gone from my shirt. There is silence behind me and I walk towards the light.

I am angry but, it seems, not frightened. He won't follow me. I am reluctant to enter the magic circle of light and sound, and instead of making straight for the broad steps that lead to the hotel's wide glass doors I skirt the fountain on the wet paving stones within range of the spray. I let the water drops cool and calm me. The sound of water envelops me. My shirt is getting wet.

This time there is nothing to warn me. This time I am approached by stealth and grabbed roughly from behind. He says something in Polish. If I let out a cry – and perhaps I do, I am not sure – it is drowned by the sound of fountains. His hand covers my mouth again, and again I smell cigarette smoke. This time I struggle, kick backwards, but my foot slips on the wet paving and it throws us both off balance. Surely someone will see us. I have fallen painfully to my knees and he is on top of me, straddling me, his arms wrapped round me in a fierce clutch.

I could be a million miles away, looking at this extraordinary scene from a great distance. A million miles away, beyond my own body, my own being. At the same time I think, I must have skinned my knees, they hurt, and my arms feel bruised from his grip. His breath grates noisily and unevenly. He moves his hand. I know what he's doing, he's tugging at his trouser zip, but it gives me a chance, and for the second time I wrench myself away, get to my feet, stumble, and walk, a little unsteadily, to the hotel steps.

I go through the glass doors. There are one or two people about, a few curious glances. I want to run but don't let myself. I can't go into the lift. Up two flights of stairs, my legs trembling, along the hall, rooting in my bag for my key, which I can't fit into the lock because my hand shakes. I rest my forehead against the door and take a deep breath. Come on, Eleanor. It happens all the time. With my head still against the door I open my eyes and see the torn, slightly bloodied knees of my trousers. I fell off my bike once when I was ten. My knees looked just like that.

The key goes into the lock, the door is opened, and flung shut. In the mirror of the gaunt wardrobe I see a wild-haired creature. I tear off my clothes. The nakedness in the mirror is untouched, except for two scraped knees. I fill the greyish bath and allow warm water to cover me.

15

IT'S ODD, ISN'T it? Whatever disgust and outrage I felt was tempered by a kind of acceptance. My pulse surges unevenly, I feel sick. But resigned. As if the experience of assault is part of the female condition. He wasn't planning to stop. It was anger that drove him rather than lust, and I think that was what scared me. Lust is easier to understand.

I slept leadenly. In the morning I got out of bed and did everything as usual. I put on clean clothes. I avoided breakfast. I shouldered my camera and walked out of the hotel into the bright sunshine. I walked past the fountains, showering their light-capturing spray, past the flowerbed vivid with colour, and the shrubs and trees shining with a recent watering. Down the drive, keeping clear of two tour buses coming up to collect their passengers, but not hurrying. I refuse to hurry. And out into the street.

It is early. The tai-chi practitioners are still at work. I am absorbed by their slow inward movements, their balance, their purposeful reaching into space. There are two, a man and a woman facing each other, neither of them young, each with a staff, making wide, contained gestures. They appear not to be aware of each other, yet their movements are synchronised. I watch them for a while. They are so within themselves. I walk on for a bit. There is a man alone, his movements fluid, slow, as if at any chosen moment he could freeze and remain motionless for ever. His eyes are open, but looking in, not out. While I am watching he stops. He does not look at me or at any other passer-by, but picks up his briefcase, placed carefully beside his bicycle, and wheels off into the traffic. I look back, and see the others, the man and the woman, walking away from me, side by side, not speaking.

I find the Drum Tower. Beyond it are the narrow streets of the Moslem quarter and the mosque, with its lovely and incongruous merging of Chinese curly roofs and curved gateways and meticulous courtyards, with the call of the muezzin and the murmur of prayer. I buy a ticket at the entrance. Three men with brown, lined faces sit in a row and watch me. Their faces are narrow, the lines etched, it seems, by years of heat and skin scoured by the dust of the deserts to the west. But they may never have been near the desert. There have been Moslems in Xian for hundreds of years.

The mosque is a refuge, my refuge. Open, airy, sunny. But I am being watched. There is nothing predatory in the faces of the three men, but they are watching. Not here, I am not being hunted here. Tomas, no doubt, will quickly forget his little escapade, me, my face. Who and what I am were nothing. That was part of what was sickening, that and the fact that he read in my face something that wasn't there. Or perhaps not. Perhaps that was irrelevant. The irrelevance of messages, the omission of identity, the ghastly dislocation of the body from the mind and from feeling. Under the gaze of the seated, dark men, I try to smile at male importunities and to banish the word rape from my consciousness. Tomas had been silent, awkward, angry. It occurred to me to feel sorry for him. I do not like these watchful eyes. I do not like the way they seem not to speak to each other, yet communicate through my presence, European, fair-haired. Tomas had watched, his eyes half-hidden by his sullen eyelids. I remember the way he watched me on the train, in the hotel. I feel no threat now, but the three dark men deflect the sense of security that I breathe within the walls of this bright, friendly place of worship.

Islam is no more generous to women than Calvinism, I

remind myself. If there is anything in the three pairs of eyes it is disapproval, not danger. They wish me no harm, though they may wish me not present. My legs in trousers, my arms bare, my head uncovered. My single entrance perhaps more intrusive than if I'd been one of several women. The interiors are cool and dark, the colours muted. Nothing more than arrows of sunlight are admitted.

I am resentful, tears at the back of my throat, but also numb. My heavy sleep seems to have blanketed me, blunted my perceptions. I move like a sleepwalker, putting one foot in front of the other without volition. I am out of sight of the three men now, but they will still be there when I emerge. Tomas is still there.

It is absurd, absurd. It can't have happened. But what did happen? It was nothing. I have skinned knees – so what? I discovered a bruise on my shoulder this morning which hurts if I prod it. Whatever it might have been, it wasn't rape. What does it matter? It happened, only hours ago, and is with me now, but it will fade. The knot inside me which wants to dissolve in tears will go away. I'll think of Steve. It's only days since he held me. Or Roy, kindly stretching his lean and handsome body beside mine, undemanding, uninsistent. Or Daniel, nurturing desire. Tomas has no place with them, damn him.

But of course I can't expel him. There is no one to talk to. All I can do is write it down, knowing that he could break in on me at any time. Suppose something like this had happened at home, within the environment of familiar streets, a whistle away from familiar people? Would I be talking now? Would I have sought out friends, made a complaint – to whom? I don't know. Numbness cancels judgment. I may be, now, seeking refuge in silence (but writing breaks the silence, and I am trying to speak through my pen on paper as best I can). Silence, a kind of simulation, a pretence. As if by silence I can make it not have happened, undo the actions of the past. Well... I know it's a common response. Nothing happened. Nothing happened.

I am a practised dissembler. The silence to my parents, the

silence to Roy. Letting them believe that I accepted it all, their ways, their views. Pretending most of all to myself, until I could do it no longer. Arch dissembler. The cruellest lies are told in silence. Roy's voice. Why didn't you talk to me about this, Nell?

I don't know why I climbed Caerketton that June night, whether it was accident I found a universe placed in brilliance, or whether that was what I was looking for. Perhaps some corner of consciousness in my mind read the sky and told me, tonight's the night. Tonight you have to do something. Tonight you will experience something wonderful. I feel, now, helpless. I think back to that decision on a cold spring day, an ordinary day on which I was going about my ordinary business. Carrying out accepted and acceptable tasks, travelling well-known routes, giving a passing metaphorical nod to familiar sights. That decision could equally have been the reaction to some tiny, incidental, now forgotten stimulus, some little hiccup in the pattern of things, a reflex, unconscious and uncontrolled, as the result of the weeks, months, years of deliberation.

A current, guiding my hand, taking me now back out into the sunlight, raising my camera and adjusting the focus to capture three men, now with their backs to me, their heads inclined towards each other. The heavy features of Tomas crowd them out, and a vision of the glasses of beer he poured voraciously down his throat which reappear as a cluster of empty glasses on the table before him but were of course only a single glass with the bottles removed as soon as they were poured. How could I know it, when I stepped out into that warm, redolent evening, that I was obeying some urge, some invisible compulsion, that led me to assault? Surely I understood those hooded, staring eyes.

The great epics are all about compulsion, about obeying some external fate, interior dharma, whatever. This compulsion is you, part of your heartbeat and the rhythm of your consciousness – and conscience. And it is also larger, stronger, further-reaching than a single individual can ever be. The great heroes reach in to their inner selves, and out, beyond, to these illimitable forces.

Heroic action is full of such striving, but they teach acceptance, these stories, resignation. Acceptance of challenge, resignation to being simply human, unsimply human I should say. It is the balance that is so captivating, of resignation and rebellion. These heroes (rarely heroines), guided by instinct rather than reason. (Reason gives us Hamlet, and he, I guess, is no hero.)

What I'm trying to say is, what I'm trying to ask is, do I trust my own instinct? But the problem goes back a step further. Can I read my own instinct? Do I understand its message? I did not want to mistrust Tomas, in spite of all the signals. If women must learn to mistrust men, the polite figments of social concourse would disintegrate, or revert to the complex networks of artificialities of previous ages. Something told me I should not damage the fragile veneer. Only in extremity did a more primitive instinct come to my rescue.

Well. Perhaps it was all fated, the will of Allah. Perhaps at that moment acceptance was required, not resistance. Perhaps I should have let Tomas tear off my clothes and rape me on my knees on the wet paving stones by the fountains of the Renmin Hotel, Xian, Shannxi Province, China, Asia, the World, the Universe. Perhaps this was destined to be the experience that would change my life. Send me back to my native heath to re-embrace Scotland and my heritage? Turn me away from the mysterious and threatening east where I had no business to be? After all, whatever I find in the Orient, it is unlikely to include a means of earning a living. I have no more lectures to give. Nor is the love of my life likely to walk towards me along a dusty Xian street.

Back to Scotland, humbled, contrite. Please, it was all a mistake. I apologise. Forgive me. When I was in China I was attacked by a foreign expert. Dangerous place, hooligans, brigands, no respect for women, terrible experience. Sinister orientals. Lies, mostly, but how welcome to the ears of those I'd left behind. I would settle back into my comfortable seat, still warm, and resume the self-fragmenting existence of lecturer and teacher in an environment of petty contention and uncreative rivalry. And

Roy and my mother and George would say, I told you so.

In the end the books themselves, my solace, let me down, and will let me down again, I have no doubt. But I must go on trying to tell this story. I was not happy. (There were times when I was not happy.) I went about my business with spirit and conviction, I'm sure – I hope – I did. Faced each day, most days at least, for there were some lapses into discouragement, positively. People found me cheerful, constructive, helpful. I know they did. I did not complain, or only occasionally. Others complained. Others built up day by day poisoned portraits of colleagues, delineations of adverse circumstances, injustices.

I had a few allies, all women of course. Clare used to say that the best thing for us would be a male secretary, to shift the image of women existing to provide a service. Typing, sex, what's the difference? I thought this might be interesting, but would change nothing. A male secretary would probably treat us just as our male colleagues did. Clare would fulminate about male exploitation. Spit in their faces, I would say. Tell the bastards no. And I'd laugh, which made it all not very serious, and anyway they all knew I would never do that.

I wasn't serious enough for Clare. Her sweeping hair glowed like her grey-green lamps of eyes. Clare is fiercely beautiful. Men are afraid of her. They avoid her. Even her students, who were fired by her but were too nervous to venture close. As if her creamy skin were marble-hard. Where were the softness and sympathy they were entitled to expect from a woman? Well, they got it from me. They queued up at my door. I was nice to them, I listened, I smiled, I soothed, I encouraged.

Clare was right. It was real enough, the exploitation. Bill had a term's sabbatical? Which lady would take on his classes? John off to a conference? Which lady would do his exam marking? The ladies didn't say no because they had to prove themselves. They had to demonstrate all that the men took for granted. And the men, setting forth their academic conquests like battle spoils, honouring the name of equality, failing to see, or pretending the failure to see, the insidious operation of double standards. Clare smouldered.

Clare challenged them. They were clever enough to sidestep. Others colluded. I colluded. I winced sometimes at Clare's anger. I have no doubt that in the pub the men murmured, confidingly, perhaps even sympathetically, about Clare's lack of stability.

Eleanor accepted, never resisted except in her head, all that came her way. Because she had to prove herself. Roy was soothing. At the end of the day he'd pour a gin and tonic. You can handle it, he'd say. Complacent faith. And he'd settle himself at his green screen as Eleanor, gin by her side, in a sea of books, explained she had two extra classes to teach because John was spending a term in Canada. You can handle it. And perhaps before the keys started to rattle, he'd turn back to her as a pleasant afterthought and bend down to kiss her cheek. You'll cope, you always do.

Eleanor should have screamed. Why did I never scream? Eleanor now lingers in a Chinese mosque in all its wonderful incongruity, her mind suffused with sunlight and assault, remembering. She wanders among serpentine architecture watched by the men of Islam in robes that suggest tribesmen of the desert plains. Tomas is beside her. Roy trails behind. You can handle it. They are still watching her, she feels, as she passes through the gateway. As soon as they are at her back a chill comes over her, although the street is hot. Three pairs of male eyes on her thick, sun-bleached hair, on her hips encased in close-fitting trousers, on the swing of her shoulders as she walks away. And other eyes, which she cannot quite locate, but feels.

Out in the narrow crooked streets she dallies among stalls and open-fronted shops. They are hung like Christmas trees with bright cotton clothes, toys, mobiles that spin lethargically in the hot air. She buys a mobile, a little carnival of birds and fishes in yellow, red and orange. She buys it thinking that to have such a thing makes little sense. It implies a space to hang it. But she is glad to have it.

On the way back to the hotel she stops at the Friendship Store and buys a pack of cards. She knows she is putting off the inevitable return to the hotel. She tries to reprise the conversation of the night before, as the three of them sat together in the dining room. They were flying to Shanghai. They had to get up early for the plane. Was that today, tomorrow? She is tired. Jochanan had mentioned their last evening. Tonight, last night? She plods along the dusty street, trying to force a memory. They might have gone, whisked away in a taxi to the airport before she was up. I'd rather go by train, Jochanan had said, stabbing a piece of pork with a chopstick. He didn't trust the Chinese in the air. He'd heard stories.

She turns in through the gates of the hotel and walks slowly up the drive. There are the fountains, and the building's ghastly façade. Three or four people are sitting in the sun. A black car is parked at the entrance. There seems to be someone inside it, but she cannot make out a face. Two young men with rucksacks are standing on the steps, one with a bush hat pulled over his eyes. She has plenty of time to look at all of them.

If she asked at the desk, would they tell her if the Polish mining engineers had left? Would she be able to make herself understood? Would she understand the reply?

Back in her room she lies on the bed. She hears footsteps on the soft earth scattered with leaves and twigs. She smells the evening scent of flowering trees. She feels Tomas's hands pulling at her clothes, his hard mouth. She is rasped by his breath, the smell of beer. She closes her eyes but is unable to contest these thoughts. She searches wildly for another image. Daniel is faint, unsteady as a reflection in water. Roy is on the other side of a door, a keyboard rattling. Steve is walking away. She gets up and at a small table by the window lays out cards from the pack she bought and plays a game of patience, letting each card flick from her thumb with a little snap.

In the evening Eleanor enters the dining room. She pauses before finding a table at the outer edge, against a wall, where she can scan the rest of the room. No. They are not there. She eats her meal alone, without much appetite. She has a book with her, but does not read. It lies unopen beside her bowl. She has nearly finished eating when a tall, blonde woman in a pale blue denim dress approaches her table.

Is this free? She asks in English. Eleanor nods. The woman's pale denim collar is open and shows the low-necked white T-shirt she's wearing underneath. The skirt of her dress is full and gathered. She sits down and lights a cigarette.

Do you mind? she asks. She speaks English with a slight accent. Eleanor shakes her head. The blonde woman smokes thoughtfully and silently for a few minutes. She has a look of distant amusement, and seems quite at home. Eleanor wants to write. But something keeps her sitting opposite her silent companion.

16

SINCE I LAST wrote I have begun to feel less remote from myself. This last couple of days I have been watching myself from a distance. At times what I have seen has been a small figure on the horizon, indistinct, almost unrecognisable. I suppose it is me, that woman, with hair that needs cutting which she has now tied back with a scrap of ribbon. I have thrown away the trousers that I wore that night, stuffed in the little wicker basket provided in the bedroom. I found a spare button for the shirt and sewed it on. It's been washed and crisply ironed by the hotel staff.

I have been telling myself that most women at some time or other, in some way or other, have experienced what I experienced. Unwanted attentions, a kiss, a grope, a fumble. I wonder if men feel the same anger, the same tearful helplessness, the same horrified estrangement from their bodies, if women or other men handle them importunately. And what about children? I make an effort to exclude that speculation. And generalisation doesn't help either. It does you little good, gets nowhere, leads to no truth or moral. Push it all to the far reaches of your mind, I say. Beyond the boundaries if you can. Don't think about it. Don't let it drive you or dismay you.

So. Let me tell you about Petra. Petra is the blonde woman who came and sat at my table, who smoked silently and reflectively before she spoke. Tall, big-boned, her broad haunches disguised that night by her full skirt but outlined in all their glory the next day when she appeared in sleek, cream-coloured trousers. She is from Amsterdam. Her English is excellent. We have been talking. I find her extraordinary. She uncannily embodies what I have been trying to tell you, tell myself, in the way she speaks, her command of my language, her cool apprehension of the possible.

Her food was set in front of her. I thought I was ready to go, but even before she started talking I knew I wouldn't. She ate a little, then lit another cigarette, with the little dishes in a semi-circle around her, gracefully and unhurriedly raising the cigarette to her lips, dragging in a lungful of smoke, lowering her hand, breathing the smoke onto her food. She smoked it right down to the filter, then put it out with studied deliberation and pushed the ashtray to the edge of the table. There were nicotine stains on her strong, tapered fingers. She picked up her chopsticks again and took some rice and cabbage.

It's a foul habit, she said. I am sorry to inflict it on you. She ate straight from the serving bowls, sampling small amounts from each. Not bad, not bad.

I agreed, although looking at what remained in the dishes around me I could not remember what I had eaten.

I have been to too many banquets, she said. Everywhere I go there is another banquet. You can get tired of banquets. And I like simple food. But I think I would like some fish. She turned and gestured. I would like some fish, she said, when the waitress approached. She spoke quietly as if making a casual but self-evident comment. The waitress frowned and shook her head. Petra drew the shape of a fish on the tablecloth. The waitress looked doubtful. Petra made swimming motions with her hands. The waitress nodded and smiled. Five minutes later a large dish containing a whole fish was set before her. Petra began to pick at it with her chopsticks.

It's excellent. You must have some. It's really very good.

So I tasted some of Petra's fish, and it is good, crisp and spicy. We had no idea what kind of fish it was. Where does it come from? I wondered. We are a long way from the sea, or even a lake.

Doesn't matter, Petra said. She waved her hand vaguely. Eat it. Enjoy it. Who knows when you will get another fish like it?

I tried a little more. Petra explained that she was on an official visit on behalf of the city of Amsterdam. This is her second visit to China. Last year she came with a delegation that included the mayor of Amsterdam. Now she had to come to arrange a return visit from a Chinese delegation. After a week of negotiations in Beijing, she was taken on a tour. All was arranged – there was no choice involved.

I had left the pack of cards laid out on the little table. I was going to go back and play another game. I thought it could be a diversion. There was a long evening in front of me. We ate early as the restaurant closed at seven.

We could still drink, however, in the little plastic-seated bar. Come on, Petra said, I'll buy you a brandy. We took our glasses outside and sat on a seat by the fountain. It was only twenty-four hours ago. The water glittered and fell softly. The warm light from the hotel poured out. Last night, I was thinking, surely it doesn't exist? For a second I was tempted. For a second I wanted to tell Petra about what had happened. But the moment passed, and it was with something like relief that I realised that I'd missed my chance. Perhaps I thought that if I remained silent it would indeed cease to exist. Have you been to Shanghai, Houzhou, Canton, she was asking. And at my negative reply, she went on. You must go. You must see the south of China. It's very different. Next time I shall go west. Kashghar. And Tibet of course. Maybe next year. There was something reassuring about her certainty. There is a sense of control. Here is a woman, I thought, who would never allow things just to happen to her.

Her voice had a satisfactory quality, quiet but with a rough edge, probably from smoking. She had a dry rattle of a cough. She talked about her life in Amsterdam. I saw her majestically cycling from her canal-side flat to her place of work in the mayor's office. The tall, narrow buildings, shoulder to shoulder, as if holding each other up. A few months earlier there had been an international writers' conference in Amsterdam and she had looked after delegates from China. They'd had no money. She took them to museums and art galleries and paid their entrance.

They stared politely at paintings by Rembrandt. There was a ripple of response when she showed them round the Historisch Museum and pointed out the blue and white porcelain imported from China. She bought them coffee. Each evening they went to a different Chinese restaurant that had been persuaded to offer a free meal to the distinguished poets and novelists from China.

Such pride, such humiliation. Petra spoke into the dark. It wasn't just the language that made it difficult for them to mix with the other delegates – we provided an interpreter. It was the fact that they had no money in their pockets. They couldn't buy a drink at the bar or go out on the town in the evening. They could only eat if someone else organised them a meal. So the interpreter and I took them to Chinese restaurants where they could not communicate properly with the Cantonese speaking proprietor. Then on their last night they came to my apartment. They drank a lot of genever and argued with the interpreter. I had cooked not Chinese food but Indonesian food. It's more traditionally Dutch, you know! They ate hardly anything. But as they left they were so... polite, but more than polite. Warm. They shook my hand and invited me to visit, promised to come back, said they loved Amsterdam.

Petra laughed. Of course, I will almost certainly never see them again. She took a mouthful of brandy and looked back at the hotel. What a hideous building! But it amuses me.

In the dark, with the light spilling out of the windows and a hint of murmuring voices, it looked less aggressive. Petra asked me where I was from.

Scotland, I said.

Ah, she said. Scotland. I liked Edinburgh. I liked its hills. I was there on business. Just for two days. Not much time to look around, but I liked what I saw. The sea appears when you don't expect it. You can fly from Amsterdam, direct. Very easy. Easy the other way, too, of course. Here's my card – you can visit me. I plan to go again. To Edinburgh, for the Festival, you know, and to the Highlands. Definitely the Highlands. It's exciting, you know, for me to see mountains. The mountains in China.

Incredible. I need to go to the top of one. So what do you do in Scotland?

I sipped my brandy before I answered. It wasn't very good brandy. Rough, abrading the back of the throat. Petra was busy with another cigarette. She perhaps didn't notice the pause before I replied. In that pause I was thinking, shall I tell the truth? Or take the easy option? The brandy perhaps made me reckless.

I used to be a lecturer in English literature, I said. But I've left my job. I've left Scotland. I decided I'd had enough. So I left, and came to China.

That is interesting. That is very interesting. I also know of people, at home, who have done something like that. People who have been very unhappy as part of the establishment, but who are not... not rebels, exactly. They also have left good jobs. But I know no one who has come to China. Why China? Usually it is the alternative lifestyle, the little farm in the country. You know the kind of thing. Or for the real rebels, dropping out, drugs... Though with us drugs are no big deal. But China. That's brave. And what next?

I don't know, I said feebly.

Can you teach here? Perhaps you can teach. You have to make a living, I suppose. Most of us have to make a living. Petra is brisk. I get the feeling that she is used to organising other people's lives.

Yes. I have to make a living. I've given some lectures. I arranged that before I came. But now I just want to be here.

As I was speaking it occurred to me that it was odd Steve never asked what I was doing in China, why I had come, what my plans were. I was just another 'foreign expert'. Beijing was full of them. They came and went. In fact, he expressed little curiosity in anything to do with me. He asked few questions. He talked readily of his own life, but I felt no need to supply him with information, to talk of Roy, of Edinburgh. I suppose that was what made it alright. If it was alright. I was displaced, without a context, without reality. Like many people who found their way to Beijing. He could take me to his bed without taking on board a past, a future – or even a present. So I did not need to impinge on his marriage, on the other life at home. Maybe that's alright, I reflected, if other lives are thousands of miles away. Distance makes some kind of difference to the way things appear. It helps to banish, refuse admission to, certain kinds of reality. But I've brought all my realities with me. Steve never noticed. Or never acknowledged – but it was all there. I looked around me, almost as if I expected to see a heap of messily packed and shapeless baggage to be shouldered again when I left my seat.

I did get up, but to get more brandies, not to leave. I was enjoying Petra's company. I felt protected. I walked, unfearful, into the building and to the bar. It was nearly eight o'clock. It would close soon.

Well, don't worry, Petra said when I returned. It is good that you have come here. You can't run away from things here in China, there is too much confronting you. I mean, you can leave your past behind, sure, but you can't get away from what really matters. It's all around you.

I wondered if she had read my thoughts.

All the richness of the past, she went on. Thousands of years that you can't escape. And a life that for many has not changed. Have you seen the men and women in the fields, cutting grain with little curved sickles? The oxen tramping out the chaff? They've been doing that since the Bronze Age. There, in front of your eyes, as if time and progress and modernity are all meaningless. And maybe they are. We are terribly ignorant, don't you think? We do not know how to live any more. I would not exchange my Amsterdam apartment for anything. I love it. It's modern, beautifully designed, full of elegant, comfortable furniture. Things I have chosen. I earn a good salary. I live well. I indulge my taste for pictures, good wine, good music, the best seats at the theatre. But I am aware of what we have lost. It's important. I am not romantic and I have no illusions. I wouldn't give up my job. I have power, responsibility. I go all over the place, expenses paid. I like the way I live. I like to be strong and independent. I don't want to be a peasant and live close to the earth. Not for me. I am quite content not to have a relationship with the earth. I don't want to be a wife and mother. But these are all things I want to understand. I want to know what I am missing. I want to know enough to make an intelligent choice.

She paused long enough to take a drag from her cigarette.

I can learn a lot from China. Everyone can learn here.

Her clarity and confidence were almost too much for me. I had blundered into China, carelessly, impulsively. I heard the voices echo across the oceans. Eleanor, careless, impulsive. And no doubt adding, rash and immature and without thought for others.

Uncannily, Petra continued. Sometimes you have to be selfish. My life is selfish. I know it. So what? I don't lose any sleep over it. That's what you say, isn't it? Don't lose any sleep. She dropped her cigarette to the ground, crushed it with her heel, and drank more brandy.

Many women find it difficult to lead selfish lives. I don't have that problem. She laughed. But people should be aware of what they are doing. Spending time somewhere else, somewhere like China, helps.

Yes, I said. You discover something about the dimensions of your life, coming here. You also discover that there's not much you can do. I'm running away, I know I'm running away. But it's not a real escape. It's all there waiting for my return. Even if I never go back, it's waiting. But I'll have to go back. I pretend sometimes that it's all behind me, all over, obliterated. But I know that's not true. I'll have to go back.

The important thing is to know what you are doing, Petra said, slowly, casually. Running away is alright, if you know you are running, if you have chosen to run.

Well. I think I chose to run. I was smiling. It was a kind of endorsement. It was what I wanted to hear.

I suppose you are running from a man? When women run, there is usually a man.

I laughed. That's part of it, I said. The man I've been living with for several years. I said I would marry him but I knew that I couldn't. A man, a job, a way of life. Assumptions, expectations. Family. My father died, that was part of it. That helped to make it possible. I'm thirty-three. At what point does it become too late? I felt that if I stayed much longer I could only be what everyone wanted me to be. I would not be able to refuse to get married, but anyway that's such a tiny corner of territory to stake a claim to. It hardly seems important now.

It's never too late, said Petra. I'm forty next birthday. But fifty, sixty. Why should it ever be too late? It's hard to be confident if you allow yourself to think that anything's too late. Confidence is essential. And men, they weaken, they... there is a better word...

Undermine?

Thank you. Yes. Men undermine women's confidence. It is an instinct with them, they can't help it. So often I've seen it. And if it doesn't work – and it doesn't work with me – off they go. Her laugh was gruff with cigarette smoke.

What about having children?

Yes. Children. That is the crux for some women, I agree. But you have to go beyond that. You can relate to children without giving birth to them, you know. And lots of men find that impossible. Unless to exploit them. For men exploitation, too, is almost an instinct, I believe. They have to prove their power, and how easy to force a child, especially if they cannot force a woman. I'm not talking about sex necessarily. I'm talking about seeing women and children as reflections of themselves.

I did not want the conversation to bring me back to Tomas, so I said, do you not think that one day, when it is too late, you might want to have a child?

Of course. But it isn't going to inhibit my life now. Now, I have decided. Later, I may wish I had a husband, a child. Who knows? I'll deal with that when I come to it. I may say, Petra, you've made some wrong decisions. But too bad. When I say it's never too late, I mean for change, for shaping your life. It's never too late not to submit. It's never too late to take another direction. She looked at her glowing cigarette. Or to give up smoking.

We both laughed. The fountain's play filled the silence that followed.

You can always jump off the train, Petra went on. Especially as it's usually going very slowly and round and round the same track. You can always jump, even if you get bruised when you land. And, you know, usually you can jump back on again, if you want.

I put my hand to my shoulder. There are worse things than bruises, I said.

Sure.

We had one more brandy, sipping as we walked round the fountain just out of reach of the spray. The taste and smell and roughness of the brandy mingled with the sensations of the dark.

I couldn't sleep that night. I lay on the bed. Brandy is not such a good idea, I reminded myself. There were images rather than thoughts in my mind, images that merged and split and reformed. George and Sally and their children in a frozen tableau, as if posing for a photograph. My mother at the table, up and down, carrying a tray, hardly still. Tomas's thick hands. My father as I saw him last, his tall body masked under hospital sheets and tied to tubes and wires, his breathing shallow and fragile. Petra's pale blue denim skirt and substantial body. Lin Bingshen walking round and round the grounds of the Friendship Hotel in Beijing, pushing his fingers through his short-cropped hair, his dimple coming and going as he talked. Daniel's eyelids dropping over his eyes like half moons as his face rose above me. The rolled sleeves of Steve's checked shirt. Roy, with his collar turned up and his briefcase, at a windy corner of the university.

My money would not last for ever. Another day or two in Xian, and I would go on to the next place.

17

I AM STILL struggling. Talking with Petra has made things more, not less, complicated. I can't think of this any more as an adventure, an indulgence, and therefore exempt from the rules. The rules have caught up with me. No explanations, I said at the beginning. I can't say that now.

She has her explanations ready. I admire her purposefulness, but find it formidable. Knowing what she wants. Mapping her progress. Like Roy. Yet I can't be sure that he wanted me. What I represented, perhaps. An intelligent woman who approved and supported him. A good-looking woman who, without being excessively domestic, could perform more or less adequately certain social functions. The social functions are important for him, part of the smooth incline that leads upwards and onwards. The confidence that the way would be smooth, so long as he did the right thing at the right time, amazed and charmed me. It was part of the attraction, why I'm not sure. Was it because it conformed with my parents' view of the world? That you get what you deserve? That, putting it crudely, the poor are poor because they're lazy, the rich because they are clever and careful and work hard? And if you're decent and industrious you'll be somewhere in between, which is a perfectly acceptable place to be. They would have been happy for me to be somewhere in between. They were familiar with that territory.

Roy fitted into their picture. It wasn't hard to avoid the topic of marriage, because everything about him seemed to suggest a safe, solid, suitable partnership. And we, I, colluded in this. From time to time, when Roy was not present, they'd take me on one side and talk to me as if I were a naughty child. It was not just that I was being silly and unreasonable; it was hurtful to them. I should understand that, and understanding it, should put it right. They deserved not to be hurt by their daughter. Am I a naughty child? Naughtier now than before? With no tall, stern father to reprimand me.

One October weekend I went home. Father had bronchitis, though he was up and dressed by the time I arrived that Saturday lunchtime. I'd come in the train (Roy must have needed the car) and walked up from the station. The roofless palace was outlined against an intense blue sky and there were boats on the loch, leaning in the brisk wind. In the ten minute walk to the house I was thinking, I like this place.

Father didn't hold with staying in bed. He'd retired recently, at last and reluctantly. There'd been a farewell do, which my mother attended. There were people my father worked with who had never met her. I imagined her using her handbag as a kind of shield, while my father accepted a book of photographs of West Lothian and a crystal decanter and glasses. As a child I had occasionally gone to the local government offices and they had always seemed rather like school, musty, drab and smelling of disinfectant. They had probably changed. Everything else had changed, as I had heard my father say often. He was the last of the old guard to go. His boss was a young woman with smooth shoulder-length hair. He was resigned to the chaos that would follow his departure. So he was there at the door, dressed but with his eyes liquid and uneasy, and bursting into spasms of agonised coughing. He had started to redecorate the kitchen when he became ill. There was half a wall of cream and blue wallpaper. I could see how painful it was for both, to be forced to tolerate an unfinished job.

There was fish for lunch. Mother had made a special trip to the fish shop in the High Street, walking because she had never learnt to drive and father was too ill to go out. She had come back up the hill with her shopping bag of messages. As we sat down to haddock baked in cheese sauce, a dish my mother hoped would tempt my father's flagging appetite, I began to say that if she had phoned I could have done her shopping for her, saved her the trip. But I realised that this journey had filled a morning and given it a purpose. What would she have been doing otherwise? Cleaning the already spotless carpet, perhaps, or polishing the gleaming silver.

Father ate only half his haddock, slowly and silently. But I understood that even so the journey had been, for mother, worthwhile, and gave her something to talk about in the face of his silence.

Mother sat in her synthetic navy dress (purchased at the High Street shop where she was known – Good morning Mrs Dickinson, yes we had something in just last week which I'm sure would suit, now it also comes in a sage green but the navy is nice, very nice, and practical) and a grey cardigan and urged him to eat. On his plate was a piece of haddock under a slick of sauce, two boiled potatoes with a sprinkling of dried parsley, and boiled carrots. Each little island of food occupied its own neat area. When father ate he did not disturb this neatness. He was wearing a lovat green Shetland sweater over a pale checked shirt, and no tie. His off-duty clothes. His face was almost white. His hair was thinner, but sleeked down exactly as it had always been since my earliest perceptions. He sliced his knife carefully through a potato. Took fish tidily onto his fork. But every few minutes he put down his knife and fork and took a rasping breath, as if he found it impossible to eat and breathe at the same time. Mother would stop eating and watch anxiously and not take another mouthful until he began to eat again.

She didn't sit still for more than five minutes at a time. It had always been like that. We were sitting in the dining room. When I visited now I was treated as a guest. Family meals had always been in the kitchen, except on Sundays. A white tablecloth and napkins. But mother wouldn't stay put. When the vegetables had been served she had to return them to the kitchen to keep hot in the oven. Then she was up to refill the water jug. Then it was, would you like more butter on your potatoes, dear? And without waiting for an answer was away to fetch the butter. Let me do it, I'd say. But she was too quick for me, off and away before I'd got to my feet, and because I knew she would be, there was not much conviction in my offers.

After lunch father went upstairs for a rest. His dismissal of mother's assistance was feeble. When he got to his feet he clutched the edge of the table, his knuckles white, his large frame bent. I did the washing-up. I urged mother to sit down, but she wouldn't. She was incessantly busy round the kitchen, putting things away, wiping surfaces. I did not feel I was helping her, almost that she would have been happier dealing with the dirty dishes in her own way. I braced myself for the inevitable questions.

She began by asking after Roy. I said he was fine but under pressure. He's really sorry he couldn't come today. He's working on graphs for a paper he's giving in Newcastle next week. It's really important. I knew that would please her and I did it deliberately, conjuring up an image of Roy applying himself with dedication to his 'important' work.

Of course I understand how busy he must be, mother said. He's doing so well. But we'd like to see more of him. I think she genuinely meant it. I think she felt reassured by Roy. And I felt a rush of guilt, as I hadn't even suggested that Roy come, and it hadn't occurred to him. He had nodded approvingly when I told him that since my father was ill, I felt I should see him.

It would be nice to see you settled, Eleanor.

But I am settled, I lied.

We could hear father coughing upstairs. I plunged dirty pans into the soapy water. I was glad I could speak with my back to her.

It's not the same. You know very well it's not the same. For father's sake... He's not well. He'd like to know you were settled. You don't understand what a worry it is, when you have a daughter. You want to know she's going to be looked after.

Mother, I don't need to be looked after, not any more than

George does. I've got a good job. You know, security and all that. You don't need to worry.

But that's not everything, not enough.

It's more than lots of people have. And it's what I want, I lied again into the soapy water, angry at the pointlessness of the conversation, the rehearsal yet again of an old chorus.

You've worked hard. Why shouldn't you have a good job? It's no more than you deserve. If other people applied themselves as you have done... You know what father says. People won't do anything for themselves any more.

It's not as simple as that.

You're going to want children, Eleanor. She'd changed tack. Out of the frying pan into the fire. You'll regret it, you know. So much better to have your children when you're young. You're past thirty. Your father and I were late starters, but that was partly the war. Don't leave it too long.

Late starters. I hadn't thought of that.

You've got grandchildren, I said, trying to mask the truculence by running the tap to rinse out a pan. George has done that for you.

It's you I'm thinking of, Eleanor. I know you like your job, but for a woman that's not enough. Think of your Aunt Jessie. A teacher all her life, but no husband, no children. It soured her, you know, you could see that. Of course I'm proud of George's two. But a daughter's children are different, you know. James and Fiona are closer to Sally's parents. I'm not complaining – it's always like that. It was Sally's mother who helped out when Fiona was born and it was Sally's mother who looked after Fiona when Sally was having James. That's what you'd expect. I'd have done it of course, but she wanted her own mother, that's understandable.

I'd never met Roy's mother. It had never been suggested that I go to Devon to visit his parents. I'd seen a photograph of a woman with long grey hair tied back leaning on a garden fork. All Roy's sisters were married, all had children.

I scrubbed at another pan. Mother continued briskly wiping plates.

Your beautiful flat. There's perhaps not enough space for

children, but you and Roy could afford something bigger, I'm sure. It would please your father so much if you settled. Somewhere with a garden, three bedrooms, and a study for Roy, of course. Like George and Sally's house. I know it's large and takes a lot of looking after, but Sally manages wonderfully well. And George is good around the house, practical. He's made himself a very nice study. Have you been there since it was finished? Did it all himself, I don't know how he finds the time, his work keeps him so busy. All the shelving and units for the hi-fi equipment. Father was very impressed. He would have helped of course, but George wanted to do it himself. James had a cold the last time we were there. I wouldn't be surprised if it was James's cold that started off father's bronchitis.

I finished the pans. I cleaned the sink, pushing the cloth round the back of the taps.

It's not like you, Eleanor. You were always such a good little girl. George was a little bit wild sometimes, boys are, but you were so good and quiet, happy with your books. I know sometimes we felt you read too much, but we were proud of you really, you know. It's not a lot to ask. It needn't be a big wedding. Just family, if that's what you want. Think of Roy's career. It can't be good for him, in his position... I don't think you're being fair to him, Eleanor. I really don't.

I knew if I spoke there would be an argument. I knew I had to speak.

Mother, Roy is perfectly happy, I said quietly. It really doesn't make any difference. He's not bothered. He respects my feelings.

Yes, that's all very well. Roy is a very considerate young man. But you can't expect him to indulge you for ever. How can you be sure that he'll stay with you if you're not married? It's very short-sighted of you. You'll only have yourself to blame if he finds someone else.

Marriage is no guarantee of permanence, I muttered. Then, more loudly, it's not just me that's against the idea of marriage. He's not so keen himself. It's our relationship that counts, not whether we're married. We stay together because we've chosen each other. Even as I spoke them the words sounded false, simplistic. As if I were translating something dense and difficult into words that someone unfamiliar with the language would understand.

If you've chosen each other you should get married. That's what marriage means.

I couldn't go on cleaning the sink. I put down the cloth and turned to face her. Yes, I said, marriage means choosing each other, but choosing each other doesn't necessarily mean marriage.

Her mouth tightened. You're being very selfish, Eleanor. You're thinking only of yourself. You weren't like that when you were a little girl. You thought of others when you were little, even your head teacher noticed that. I remember him saying how helpful you were. And it's very immature, especially now with your father ill. Who knows what will happen? He's not young any more. He's worked hard all his life. Worked hard for the family, for you, and never got the recognition he deserved. He never told me that his boss was a woman, thirty years younger. It didn't seem right, seeing her there, not much older than you.

I picked up the cloth again, wiped the draining rack which was now empty. I took a deep breath. None of this was fresh ground. When I turned back to her she had sat down, making no pretence now of being busy round the kitchen. She still had her apron on and a dishcloth in her hand. I noticed her thin legs, under the chair, and her narrow shoulders, turned inwards. No, they weren't young any more.

I said, mother I don't want to hurt you and father. But I must do what is right for me.

You've become very selfish, Eleanor, she repeated. That seems to be what university does for you. Why education should make you selfish I don't know, but it has. You've had much more than I ever had. I didn't go to university, but I'm not any the worse for that.

No, of course you're not, I said, trying to soften my voice. I'm sorry if I seem selfish, but don't blame my education. If I'm selfish, it's me.

She twisted the cloth in her hand. The sound of father coughing came from upstairs. She looked up. She wouldn't be so indelicate as to refer to death, but death was what I was thinking. The coughing continued. Death and selfishness. A long afternoon stretched out in front of us. I knew I couldn't leave yet.

Is there anything I can do while I'm here, I asked brightly. Any job that needs doing? What about shopping? Anything you need?

She shook her head.

What about the garden? Father won't have been able to get into the garden. Is there anything needs doing there?

Again she shook her head. He's well on with the garden. And he likes to do things his own way. He wouldn't thank you if it turned out different. And you like to do things your own way, I thought, or at least in the way that suits him.

The kitchen was immaculate. We went through to the sitting room. Mother picked up her knitting. She knitted jumpers for James and Fiona, as she had knitted jumpers for me and George. I read the *Scotsman* and leafed through magazines. An occasional car passed down the quiet street. Children – there was the sound of roller skates. The clock ticked and struck the hour and half hour. Mother's knitting needles fell silent and her eyes closed. I got up and went to the window. The small square of front garden was clogged with wet leaves. I could have done something about that. I would have enjoyed it. The Michaelmas daisies were turning brown. A strengthening wind was driving greyish clouds across the sky, blotting out some of the blue. I wished I had indicated my intention of going for a walk, even though she would have interpreted that as an escape. Selfishness again. To come and see them, and then go out. I could have gone down to the canal and walked beside the scummy water, looked for coots and moorhens. I could have drifted round the loch, in the company of Saturday afternoon couples and families and dogs.

Half an hour later she woke, knitted a couple of rows, then went into the kitchen. I didn't follow her. She'd be making something for tea. At four o'clock she came in with a tray with teacups and a plate of warm pancakes. I heard a door close and father's footsteps on the stairs.

Did you get some sleep? I asked when he came in, looking frail but freshly washed and combed.

Aye. I dozed a bit. Five minutes mebbe.

Mother returned with the teapot and poured the tea. We ate and drank in silence. Father picked up the *Scotsman*. I went back to *Woman's Own*. The television was turned on for the news. At six o'clock father got up to fetch the sherry decanter. Without asking, he poured sherry for me and mother, and a whisky for himself. There followed another meal. Ham and salad. A plate of bread and butter. Cheese. It grew dark. At eight o'clock I left.

An hour later I arrived home. It had begun to rain as I walked from the station. I let myself in. Roy was seated in front of his green screen. There were dirty dishes in the kitchen. The usual Saturday chores had not been done. The kitchen floor was gritty and the rubbish bin was so full it wouldn't close properly. I went into our handsome sitting room and moved yesterday's newspapers so I could sit down. I was suffused with helplessness. Neither words nor actions would change anything.

I sat in the dark and listened to the rattle and bleep from Roy's study and blusters of rain against the windows. I wondered if my mother was right. It was selfish, of course it was, to ignore the needs of others. I could have said that I had considered her needs, my father's needs, Roy's needs, and rejected them all in favour of my own. Yet that wasn't true either. I could forgive myself, I thought, if it had been true. If I had gone all out to put my needs consistently and purposefully before those of others. I would have had more respect for myself if I'd know what I wanted and had calculatingly set out to achieve it.

My parents would not like to hear me say that. Yet it was what they admired in Roy and encouraged in George. Sally was right for George because it was what she encouraged too. How clever of George to choose her. I sat in the dark staring at the black rain-streaked window and struggled to find some point of contact, some thread that would connect me and them, my mental and emotional wanderings and their understanding. But it was all too tangled. It did not seem possible.

Nor did it seem possible for me to find the end of the thread that would lead to Roy, that would link my needs and his, my vague, restless lack of direction and his clear-sighted, purposeful progress. Roy did not see me as directionless. It suited him to think me content. And why shouldn't I be? Everything was in place for a satisfactory life, or so I had been saying to my mother. Roy, I am sure, thought our relationship secure. He was loyal. For all his travel and conference going, and the opportunities I have no doubt these presented, he had no interest in other women's beds.

Why don't I pull the curtains, I thought inertly. I have much that friends and less fortunate colleagues envy. I should think about all those who live alone or with erosive partners. Alison, for instance, with her alcoholic husband, Clare, vibrantly but unhappily solo. Those with large families and little money, at whose innards the promotion of others gnawed. Of childless women who worked and wanted children. Of women with children crushed by work.

Such meditation arrived always at the same conclusion. There was no one among my acquaintance whom I envied. No one I could point to and say, she's got it right, she is the one I will try to emulate. And the lives of men had no relevance. I could not compare myself with them.

Such conclusions did me no good. In fact, they almost made me feel worse. For to be dissatisfied at the same time as knowing you should be satisfied is a double curse. Curled in the capacious armchair we had bought at an auction near Melrose, I lapsed into an indulgence I didn't normally allow myself. I thought of Daniel. I thought of ecstatic sex as salvation. I though of warmth and mutual sympathy, attentive communication. Was that the missing factor in my life? My skin prickled. The key to understanding, the missing piece of the jigsaw. But no, that was too easy... and too fraught, for where there was Daniel there was also Pete. Impossible to forget the pain of tenderness built on illusion. Daniel's love had transformed me. How could I not have been the only one? Human communication. Not the key. The key could not depend on another individual. The key had to lie outside the vagaries and accidents of human existence. The chance intimacies. For that was Daniel. Intimate, illusory, accidental.

There was no answer there, however comforting, momentarily, until reality caught up and shattered the time warp, such indulgent musings might be. I wondered if Roy ever found himself exploring, if only in his mind, such possibilities. I wondered if I had underestimated him. Perhaps totally misunderstood him.

It could be hours before Roy tore himself away from the keyboard. And I, mistakenly perhaps, would not try to tempt him. There was no value in intrusion, I thought. Nothing to be gained. But I've changed my mind, haven't I? Nothing could be more intrusive than what I'm doing now.

18

NEAR THE SMALL Wild Goose Pagoda I have found some shade. The ground is hard, the grass dry and brittle. Not far away are two white women sitting on a bench. They are wearing white hats. They are of middle age, though I am not sure what that means. One sits with her knees apart and her head back. Under the white hat her hair is grey and her skin pale. Clearly, she has kept out of the sun. The other is sitting forward, turned towards her companion, a compact camera on her lap, talking with some animation. I think they are German, although they are too far away for me to distinguish the language spoken. All I can hear is the tone, the tenor of sound.

The woman who speaks is thin. I can see her thin legs and slim feet in white sandals. Her bare skin is tanned but with that dry, leathery look of over-exposure to the sun. I don't know why I am watching them so closely, or why I am wondering about their lives. How have they come to be in the shady garden of the Small Wild Goose Pagoda? Are there just the two of them? Friends? Relatives? Travelling as part of a group? What tangled threads stretch from the Small Wild Goose Pagoda in Xian to the centre of Europe?

The Pagoda was built twelve hundred years ago. The thin woman shifts on the bench and leans back also, so the two of them now sit side by side, their bodies matching in angle, both looking straight in front of them. They are silent. Inside the Pagoda there were once Buddhist scriptures brought from India.

Four hundred years ago there was an earthquake that toppled its crowning tier.

From the top of the Pagoda I looked down into thickly green gardens. Oblivious of my eyes, a young man pulled off his shirt and carried a basin of water from an open door. He washed with methodical care, soaping his upper arms, his chest. Cupping his hands to lift water to rinse off the soap. With my camera I stilled him.

I am in danger of seeing Xian as a series of framed pictures. The camera gives me purpose as I walk down the wide streets lined with dusty trees. As I watch the women I remove the lens cap, then change my mind. Threading through lanes and through the mingled smells of dust and garlic and urine, I am halted again and again by the random yet exact compositions that present themselves. A black bicycle crisply outlined against a pale wall. A dark doorway edged with flowerpots. Young men playing billiards in a dappled street. Tomas slides into the dusty margins of my mind. Street stalls piled high with cabbages and greens I can't identify. A line of small children in white shirts and red sashes, casting sideways looks at me.

I've tramped and tramped. My feet ache. I can feel the grit in my sandals with each step. I have been to the museum and looked at bronzes and porcelain laid out on lengths of fabric like old and not very clean tablecloths. But I liked the museum. It was open and bright. I have forgotten about food. It is late afternoon now and I have had nothing to eat all day. I have quenched my thirst with sweetish orange drinks bought on street corners. The bottles lie in enamel basins of water which gradually warms. My feet ache more now that I am neither walking nor standing. I slip them out of sandals.

I have been again to the Friendship Store, where it is cool and dim. I wandered from floor to floor, section to section, looking at rows of crude soapstone figures, swathes of garish silk. I bought another pack of cards, because I like the red dragon on the back and the coy, cute women featured on every card. Even the jack and king are women. And I bought a shadow puppet. I have not bought much in China, not through intentions of economy, more as a sense of restraint in acquiring things. There is no reason to – what would I do with them? Part of this journeying is certainly an escape from possessions. But the cards and the shadow puppet appeal to me.

That night in my room I used both packs of cards to play a more complicated game of patience, over and over, until at last I won.

Now I am at Hot Springs. I have come in a bus through fields of vegetables and ripe wheat. Some is being harvested. The bent backs don't straighten as the bus passes, although it is the biggest and noisiest vehicle on the road. There are bikes, carts, barrows, wheels turning in each direction. Steadily, inevitably. I sense less purpose than lack of choice, but perhaps I am imposing again. The bus driver leans on the horn but the smaller traffic pays no attention. The barrow-pushers plod on, the cyclists don't waver. The woman next to me is stealing glances at the clumsy piece of flesh sharing her seat. I feel not just clumsy but somehow unclean. Perhaps it is the patches of sweat on my thighs and armpits, the stickiness of my clothes, the clogging of my pores. She is neat, in faded cotton, and smells, literally, sweet.

Life clings to the sides of the road. There are never more than two or three figures in the fields. On and beside the roads there is a slow, moving mass. Every fifty or hundred metres there is something for sale. Glasses of tea with a cover to keep out the dust. Bottles of pop in tepid water. A woman, sometimes a child, squatting alongside. They do little business, although there are so many people about.

Huaqing. A pool that receives water from hot springs. The trees are thick with green and the buildings touched with bold paint in blue and yellow and red cluster around the water. Behind, hills rise steeply, in particular Li Shan crowned by towers built during the Han Dynasty. Watchful, defensive. On the mountain, I am told, there is a shrine to Nu Wa, the mother of the human race, the creator. But it is not Nu Wa who commands the interest of the people who flock to Huaqing and climb the steep sides of

Li Shan up hundreds of steps built to make it easier.

I have made my pilgrimage, along with a river of men, women and children flowing up the mountainside. There is nothing much to see, only a cave cut into the mountain. It is where Chiang Kai Shek was captured in December 1936. Chiang had taken refuge here at Huaqing, once the summer palace of T'ang emperors, in the days when Chang'an was the imperial capital. Chiang was captured by his own generals, who had made a secret truce with the communists. On that December night he had fled from the palace up the snow-covered mountain. It should have meant the beginning of victory for the communists. There were twelve long years to go.

The flow of people steadily rippled upwards. It was odd, I thought. Here was a memorial to the capture of the arch-enemy, not by one of the heroes of the revolution, not by Mao or Zhou Enlai, but by one of Chiang's own followers. General Zang in the end submitted to punishment at the hands of the leader who had been his prisoner, but who, after polite negotiations with the communists and empty promises, was released. His capture on Li Shan meant very little. I remembered something Lin Bingshen had said. Something very small, maybe insignificant, can become a symbol. Reverence is important for the Chinese. We revere wisdom. We revere places of special meaning. We need now a symbol, a focus, a special meaning. That is the first step for our movement.

Embedded in the crowd I stood a few steps from where Chiang Kai Shek was captured, in the snow, in the early hours of the morning, in his pyjamas. And then I simply turned and made my way down against the upward current. It wasn't Chiang I was thinking of as I descended. I was thinking of Mao Zedong and distance. His march of 5,000 miles. His followers diminished by sickness, exhaustion and enemy attack. His authority. Did he earn a right to absolutism? Does anyone? We shrink from the oriental despot, whether emperor or commissar. But we are taught to admire such dedication, such single-minded purpose. I am entranced, that's the right word, captivated, by the story of Mao's Long March. The suffering gilds the achievement. The death of Mao's wife on the March enlarges his courage, augments his nobility. For his pain is personal and profound. Yet there would be other women. Mao's wife was expendable. He seemed to take a pragmatic view of the value of the female sex.

The Long March still catches the heart. If I have to pin to my sleeve a single answer to why China, it would be the Long March, which I read about first in a battered, dog-eared orange book which I found in a job lot donated to the school library. It represents a level of endurance that reinforces, surely, all that we want to think best in humanity, a merging of the physical and the spiritual, the converse of the self-indulgent existence so many of us occidentals are accustomed to. And the purposefulness, the direction, the goal. How deprived we are.

As I go down, hundreds climb. Old women, holding on to each other. A party of schoolchildren. Soldiers. Young couples. There is a holiday atmosphere. The sun shines. I am the only white face. The other foreign guests linger by the side of the pool and wander among the bright buildings. They have no need to climb the steep mountain to see nothing but a hollow in the rock.

Half way down, I pause and look over the buildings arranged elegantly round the asymmetric lake. I should be thinking about my future. Nagging at me always was this sense of obligation: I must think about my future. I could still be described as a young woman, I suppose. There is a future, in the normal course of things. But how can you think about something that is featureless, colourless? I can see only shapelessness, pallor. There is no scene into which I can project a narrative. I can dream up no face out of the opaque days ahead, although the voice of Bingshen is in my mind. It is like flying through cloud. I can define no possibilities.

It has never been like this before. I wonder if this is what old age is like. You can perhaps think about the day in front of you but you are no longer the central character in your own story. There are quirks of plot, unexpected introductions of new characters. You occupy the closing pages of a chapter, your final chapter, but the prelude to a story that will continue without you. It seems unlikely that I have reached the final chapter. But what I want is a quantum leap into a different story. Yes. I thread my way down against the upward flow. All I can hear is the tramp of feet. That's why I'm here. I'm looking for another story. But even if I find it, how do I break in?

There is more to see and I persevere. I catch the bus to Banpo. Banpo was a neolithic village – I am making a huge vault back in time. The village was built on the banks of the Chan River. The name means 'half slope'. The ground is dry and friable. It is scooped and pitted where houses have been excavated. They had dug a trench, 6,000 years ago, to protect themselves from wild animals and marauders. They made pottery – the relics of a kiln are apparent. They buried their dead with some ceremony, or so the funerary objects in their graves suggest.

The sparse evidence of their lives is assembled in glass cases. They were hunters. They fished in the river. They were gatherers. But they also farmed and kept domestic beasts. They made fish-hooks of bone, tools of stone, cooking pots of clay. They decorated their clay pots. There are geometric patterns, a running deer, fish with mouths agape. I am brought back to endurance again. My Calvinist heritage clasps me with its unrelenting grip. I must return and endure. There was no respite in the effort to survive, at least nothing that stone and bone and clay can tell me of. They spell relentless toil. The river is heavy with silt, the land at times a morass of mud, at times dry and hard. There were floods, probably. Hard work, hazards. The fundamental needs. Food, protection, procreation. Yet there must also have been music, celebration, the telling of stories.

Procreation. Settle down, Eleanor. You read too many books. Too many strange ideas are breeding in your mind. The imagination is dangerous. Real life, Eleanor. Food, protection, shelter, procreation. Don't expect too much from men. They are weak, they are selfish, they have another agenda. Don't expect them to understand. That's a romantic, sentimental idea. It's not that they can't – they don't want to. They're not interested. It's not important to them. But they can father children. Some of them can even look after children. Roy would be a good father, you know that. Never mind the nature of the act that conceives the child, never mind that it may be unmemorable, brief, violent, painful, offhand, unsubtle, unloving. That's not relevant. The end justifies the means. Go home, Eleanor. Let Roy give you a child. In wedlock, of course. It's not too much to ask.

At the water's edge at the foot of Li Shan I thought about drowning. I would not like to drown. I am not a good swimmer, I think I am afraid of the water. But it would be so easy. I knelt down and put my hand in the warm spring water, calm and soothing. It would caress me as it choked the air out of my lungs. Although it frightens me, I find the prospect rather pleasing.

Roy will still be there. Well, perhaps not literally. He'll have finished his exam marking now. Fieldwork beckons. Conferences. But something of him would be there if I were, now, to get on a plane and fly to England, to Scotland. If I were to land at Turnhouse, the plane curving over the Forth, slanting across water and bridges and trees to come down on the long runway with that characteristic upward tilt of the nosecone. I would have told no one. I'd cross the tarmac. Collect my baggage without a glance to the waiters and watchers assembled to meet their friends and relatives and business associates (though I'd reflect that a solitary arrival at an airport, however near to home, is peculiarly lonely). I'd take a taxi to the familiar street in front of the familiar front door. It would be midday, probably. The flat bright and airy. Mrs Macdonald has been and apart from the cluster of dirty dishes in the kitchen all is neat, the dust and the crumbs from the carpet removed. I put down my suitcase. How about a cup of tea? Or coffee? That's more like it. I haven't had a good cup of coffee for weeks. The kettle is where it always is. The jar of coffee is on the shelf. Mugs still hang from their accustomed hooks.

There are carp swimming slowly in the water. It would be easy to drown under the soothing influence of fish. Their beguiling attraction could hypnotise me into death. There must be worse ways of forgetting to stay alive.

Suffering is worth nothing. It is survival that counts. I was fifteen when I began to resent religion and found excuses not to go to church, and turned away from my mother's reproachful looks. It was suffering that killed Christianity for me, although I did not articulate this until later. At fifteen it was instinctive. By the time I left school I could not see what was enriching about suffering. I could not see why those who suffered were, in some way, more Christian that those who didn't. Was there any other religion that had at its very centre such a symbol of cruelty and suffering as Christ on the cross? Was suffering the cornerstone of any other system of belief?

As a student I looked around curiously for someone with whom to test these thoughts. But no. Friends talked about literature and sex, politics and music, the heavy hand of Calvinism. That was alright. But I wanted to find out if anyone else, Christian or otherwise, found the figure of Christ bleeding on the cross repugnant. If anyone else shuddered at the images of Christ's torn body. If anyone else thought, not salvation but cruelty.

Daniel understood. But then, Daniel was a Jew. I watched the carp swim and wondered at their fluid power, as if nothing as crude as muscle could be responsible. And thought of Daniel. Here was a symbol I was happier with, a pair of fish to represent marital harmony; a leaping fish, symbol of successful effort.

The village of Banpo survived for about 750 years. Successful effort. Labels in glass cases, translated into English, told me this, but nothing about what happened to them. Was the village washed away when heavier than usual rains swelled the river? Was it attacked and obliterated? Did drought bring starvation and force departure? How do communities end?

I catch another bus. The roads are still busy. The bikes still stream, in both directions. We overtake a handcart with a pig strapped into it. I am very tired and I sit on the worn seat of the jostling, dust-filled bus, my eyes closing from time to time. Tomas invades my mind again and I try to chase him out with anger. I had been thinking, sadly but comfortingly, of Daniel. If

Daniel is to come now always hand in hand with Tomas...

Tomorrow I have a train to catch. When I get back to the hotel I'll need to pack. Sort out the few of my clothes that are clean and fold them. Put away my Chinese playing cards. Shove a motley collection of tubes and plastic pots into my toilet bag.

When I got to my room I lay on my bed, almost too tired to go and find something to eat. But it is only partial tiredness. I also do not want to risk an interruption to my thoughts. I feel I could be on the brink of some discovery, some decision. It's like panning for gold. There seems to be a glint of something. If I just keep going, scoop another panful of gravel from the riverbed, sift and wash the fragments in my mind, maybe a nugget will miraculously materialise out of the dross.

A sour feeling in my stomach suggested a need for food. I got up and washed my face and put on some make-up, and a skirt, rather crushed but still more presentable than my grubby cotton trousers. I went first to the little bar, reminiscent of the Italian coffee bar I used to go to with some of the girls from school, quaint even then, left over from the fifties, and ordered a gin and tonic. After considerable searching and lengthy conversation some ice was found, for which I was grateful. I enjoyed the sound and sensation of ice cubes in my glass. I'd last had a gin and tonic in our living room, probably sitting on the sofa, or by the window, looking down into the street while Roy talked about his next field trip.

The place was filled with a party of Australians. It wasn't possible to find a seat apart from them. They talked across me. I could only pretend I wasn't there. I tried to concentrate on panning for gold, or more appropriately searching for a lump of jade in a dried-up river bed. It was difficult. At dinner a huge dish of asparagus was put in front me. It was delicious.

19

SURVIVAL. I REACHED Luoyang at four in the morning. The station was totally dark. I had been afraid of missing my stop and hadn't been able to sleep. I'd been waiting tensely with my bag beside me for half an hour before we pulled slowly into Luoyang and trusting neither my pronunciation nor the attendant's understanding uttered the name three times and three times received a nodded affirmative, before I ventured from the train.

I stood on the dark platform as it pulled slowly and hissingly away. The silence after its passing was cavernous – there was surely no one there. I edged my way along the platform and opened a door. There was a dim light shining. I crossed a space and pushed open a second door. I emerged from the station entrance where there were two cars parked and a single street light. Someone was sitting in the driving seat of one of the cars, and he hopped out as soon as he saw me. He approached, speaking French, though it took me a few moments to adjust to the language I was hearing. It was not what I expected. He said he was a taxi driver and would take me to my hotel. He picked up my bag. I could see no one in the other car. No one was on the street. No one else had got off the train. I should have felt at least uneasy but, oddly, I didn't. No image of Tomas interposed itself between me and the man who said he was a taxi driver.

So I followed him, the French-speaking taxi driver, who opened the car door for me. The hotel was only ten minutes drive through the silent streets, a solid, square building facing what seemed to be a narrow strip of park. The taxi driver escorted me in and ceremonially handed me over to a young girl sitting in a dingy office with an unshaded light bulb hanging from the ceiling. Stony-faced and without saying a word, she got to her feet and reached for a key, which she handed to me. It was the taxi driver who showed me the stair and explained that my room was on the *deuxième étage*. I thanked him. He said goodbye with a little wave of his hand. I climbed the stair.

My room is small and grey. I went straight to bed and straight to sleep, waking four hours later feeling, to my surprise, quite refreshed. My window faces the street. I got out of bed and looked out. The daylight is beguiling. It is indeed a park across the way and there are still a few tai chi practitioners going through their morning routine. I found a breakfast of weak tea and sweetish bread and jam.

By midday I was on the banks of the sluggish River Yi. Luoyang, too, had been an imperial capital. Buddhism was making its entry into China. In cliffs rising high from the river bank abundant figures of the Buddha and his disciples were carved in the rock. The work had gone on for about two hundred years: the result, more than 100,000 sculptures. The honey-coloured rock is hard, and many of the carvings have survived, ravaged less by 1,400 years of wind, sun and rain than by western collectors.

From the base of the cliff I looked up to an expanse of pale, pock-marked stone. The cliff walls are crowded with little caves and shrines. There are steps cut into the rock. I climbed from one cave to the next, from carving to carving. Over and over again the secret, benign, complacent, inward smile of the Buddha. On small figures, still jaunty although their features were chipped and worn and some had lost their heads to the western marauders. On huge, overbearing statues, statements of power and the diminishment of humanity. Yet magnificent. If Hindusim was an attraction, I'd thought, it was because gods did not make men and women look small. Gods were only a step away from heroes, heroes mingled with ordinary humanity, gods could change from man to beast and back again to god. But

Buddhism had furnished monoliths to rival anything the western world had to offer.

I sat for a while and nursed my ambivalent admiration. It was very hot now. Along the track below people moved, back and forth, stopping to buy cold drinks from the numerous little stands. They were mostly Chinese. I wondered how many were there out of curiosity, simply, or if there were some who sought some alternative to official belief, some way of getting in touch with a more open world.

Dust and grit had filtered into my sandals, so I took them off and sat with my bare feet against the hot rock, looking up at giant figures towering above me. They were muscular, sinuous, with all the lively liberality of T'ang art. I noticed standing back from the knot of Chinese gazing upwards a lean, tanned young man with a small rucksack slung from one shoulder. As I was watching him he turned and caught my eye, and came towards me.

His grin was friendly. Fantastic, aren't they? His accent was unmistakably southern English. He dropped his rucksack beside me and sat down.

Yes, I said slowly. But I'm not sure I approve of them.

The detail was a feast. Clothes, jewellery, accoutrements, the curling locks of the bodhisattva, whose position on the brink of Nirvana allowed him to retain the signs of worldliness.

Why not? It's not idolatry, you know. Buddhists don't worship these things. They're symbols. Summing up, not a representation.

You seem to know all about it.

I know a bit. But I'm not into it seriously, if that's what you mean. I take a passing interest. I can't take any religion seriously – I mean, not as a way of believing. Look at all the harm religion's done to the world.

I looked at him sideways, curious. His face was thin, his hair cut short and receding a little, his tanned cheeks shaded by a couple of days' growth of beard. He looked as if he'd been on the trail for some time.

I prefer the Hindu gods, I said. They're more fun. You feel they could be companions. Maybe religion is about companionship. I don't think I'd feel comfortable with any of this lot.

You would if you reached Nirvana. That's what it's all about. You'd feel entirely comfortable with yourself, and therefore with everything else.

Maybe. But I'm not tempted.

Well, I'm not going to try and convert you. I don't think I'm tempted either. It's a nice thought, though. Nirvana. I can see the attraction. Sometimes.

He pulled out a tobacco tin and began to roll himself a cigarette, an operation which required some concentration. He didn't seem to be very good at it. He offered the result to me. I shook my head. He searched his pockets for matches and lit the misshapen little tube.

We both looked at the huge stone figures in silence for a while.

Then he said, you're obviously from Scotland. With a group?

No, I'm on my own.

So am I. It didn't start out that way. In India my girlfriend was with me. Now she is into the Buddhist thing. In fact, she spent a while in some Buddhist monastery in Scotland. I forget where. But we were fighting all the time. She left me in Srinagar. It was kind of a relief really. There's nothing like travelling in India to test a relationship. He grinned his wide grin again. It transformed his tight, serious face. I've been in India, Pakistan, Tibet, now China. On the road for four months. Now the money's running out and I'll have to think about going home. The party's nearly over.

Where's home?

London. Well, Surrey. Born in Croydon. But I've been living in Holloway the last couple of years.

Why did you come here?

Do you know the Seven Sisters Road? If you lived there you'd want to get out. But I've always wanted to travel in the east, I guess. My mother was born in India. Used to talk about it, read me Kipling. You know Kipling? Then when I was older I found other stuff to read. I grew up with this vague feeling that one day I would go there. Then when I was a student I had this strange encounter, one of those odd things, and that really started me making plans. I met this strange little guy, sad little guy really. A German Jew. His parents had a shop in Shanghai, he told me. That was where he was born. They sent him back to Germany to school. Round about 1937, I think he said, he was smuggled out of Germany with his aunt. He was about fifteen.

He told me the story of his life. Anyway, eventually he made it back to Shanghai. But then the Japanese turned up. His parents were killed. He hid out, lived off the streets... In the end he got to California, I can't remember how, set up in business, made lots of money, married, divorced, had two kids whom he never saw. I met him in a train in Germany. He'd gone to Germany first but had a ticket to Shanghai. After all these years he was going back.

The funny thing was, I wanted to tell him, don't go. But listening to him made me want to go. Listening to him, things seemed to fall into place and going east became not just something that one day I would do, but something that I was going to start working on, getting together, as of now. So I did. I finished university. Got a second class degree in philosophy. I worked for two years selling computers. Lived in a dump to save money. When I had enough cash I chucked it and got on a plane to Bombay. Elsa, my girlfriend, came too. The problem was, she didn't really want to come. She thought she did. She thought that going to India was the chic thing to do, and that she would spend her time wafting around cool, calm monasteries and throw in the odd spell of meditation. But then she found it was hot and dirty and smelly, and India was full of Indians, and the streets were thick with beggars and men and women without arms and legs, or thin beyond belief... She couldn't hack it. And of course it was all my fault.

That grin again. He'd finished his cigarette and was rolling another. This time he didn't offer it to me, but lit it, hardly pausing in his talk.

So off she went, blaming me to the last. All my fault. So then

I was on my own, but I carried on as planned. It's almost a way of life now. Being on the move. Not having any sort of shape to things. I like it. Don't know what I'm going to do when I get back, but I'll cross that bridge when I come to it.

Do you have to go back? I suppose I hoped that he'd say no, that he had found what I had not.

I guess so. It's the bread, you know. It's running out. I've had months of grot. Packed trains. Sharing beds with bugs and all sorts. There was a place in Pakistan where I discovered in the morning I'd been sleeping on a mattress heaving with maggots. Hitching, not washing for days. Lousy food and not enough of it. I've lost at least a stone, maybe more. And always that uneasy feeling you might be picking up something nasty, dysentery, hepatitis...

He rubbed his thin brown arms. He didn't look as if he could ever have had more flesh on him.

My name's Simon, by the way. Again the grin as he held out his hand. I took it. Eleanor, I said.

So that's my story. What's yours?

I laughed, I'm not sure why. Perhaps it was the thought that Simon must have encountered many people on his travels, telling his tale and expecting reciprocation. The necessary credentials, as it were, to verify the exchange.

So I told him briefly that I'd thrown up a job as lecturer at the University of Edinburgh and left the man I was living with. I offered no reasons or explanations, and he didn't ask any questions. He showed no surprise. He seemed to accept as self-evident that someone in my position would want to leave behind a respectable and promising professional existence, and a promising, if not entirely respectable, relationship. Security was not something to be taken seriously. Like religion. I thought, how young he seems.

It was pleasant, sitting under the sun and talking to Simon, listening to his voice, which mingled a current of Cockney with what I guessed was public school and Oxbridge. It emerged that the latter was correct. He had nowhere to stay in Luoyang, though he wasn't worried. He'd learned the art of talking his way into the hotels reserved for Chinese only, scruffier but a great deal cheaper than those for tourists. There was something strangely beguiling about his conversation, which was perhaps the flood of words that comes from someone who has been starved of speaking his own language. But then I too, in the last few weeks, had grown accustomed to days of virtual silence interrupted by occasional feats of conversation. I felt no particular urge to unburden myself to Simon, but I enjoyed the sound of his voice.

Did you miss Elsa? I asked. I was happy to provide the incentive for him to go on talking.

Yeah, I still do. I cared about her a lot. She was great as a girlfriend in London, really lively and go-ahead. Clever. She was a graphic designer, in advertising. Earned more than I did. It was easy for her to leave because she knew she could walk back into a job, no problem. But I should have known. She didn't have my reasons for coming east, you see. To her it was just an exotic trip, a chance to carry on her flirtation with the Buddhists. She couldn't understand why, when things got rough, we just didn't go home. So we had to part, really.

Now we ambled beside the river, broad, greyish-yellow, its banks crumbling into the sluggish flow. Ahead of us a stark, modern bridge crossed it. Simon seemed happy to talk, without expecting very much from me. I was happy to listen. He returned to the subject of Elsa.

I shouldn't have let her come. I'd planned this trip on my own. I was going to make it on my own. But I liked the thought of her coming, when she started to talk about it. It seemed okay.

So you felt lonely when she left, I said.

There was a pause. Simon stopped walking and stared across the river. I was sorry I had mentioned loneliness. I saw that it might encourage confidences I'd rather steer away from.

Are you lonely? was the unexpected response. He turned to look at me, his expression tense and serious. He had wide, dark blue eyes. It was my turn to study the far bank of the river.

Of course, I said. Sometimes. Isn't everyone?

There are different kinds of loneliness.

Yes, I agreed, wondering where the conversation was travelling.

The worst is being lonely when you're with someone. Knowing that they're not really with you. That you don't really count. Do you know what I mean? His question was eager, hopeful.

Yes, I know what you mean, I said.

Was it that kind of loneliness that made you leave Edinburgh?

Maybe. Partly.

If it was, I understand, he said kindly. I felt infinitely older than this boy, one moment seasoned, laid-back traveller, the next transparently anxious. Anxious to be honest, to be liked, to feel he'd made some kind of significant contact. I smiled, as I might have done to one of my students. It was, I discovered later, a mistake.

We spent the rest of the afternoon in each other's company. We scrambled up and down the cliff and looked at the Buddha until the sight of half-closed eyes and a bland, unregarding smile began to nauseate me. The hardness of the rock did not mitigate the impression of fleshy softness. Simon described to me the lean existence of the Tibetan monks, the hours of mesmeric chanting, the diet of tea and barley meal, the studying of Sanskrit texts printed with woodblocks on thin paper, the disputatious learning. Though of course, he added, the Chinese have got rid of most of that.

All around us streams of visitors climbed in the heat, and descended, and walked back and forth beside the sluggish river. He said again that his money was running out, that soon he would have to return to London. I thought this was a prelude to a request for money, but what came took me completely by surprise. He asked if he could spend the night in my hotel room. He'd sleep on the floor, he said. He wouldn't be a problem. He grinned and added, I could use a bath.

So I agreed. We returned to my hotel, on the way picking up his big rucksack from the CITS office. It was easy to slip him into my room. I sat downstairs and drank a beer while he had a bath and shaved. When he reappeared he looked both cleaner and younger. I bought him a meal. We talked some more about eastern religions. He told me about his family. His parents were teachers, and he had a younger brother in his last year at school. I told him my mother had been trained as a teacher, but had given it up when she married. I thought, he knows more about me than I ever told Steve, and I wondered if it was a good idea.

No one in the hotel paid any attention to us. It wasn't necessary to pretend. We walked up the two flights of stairs together. I unlocked the door of my room and we both entered. I gave Simon a blanket, changed in the bathroom, and went to bed. Without removing his clothes, he wrapped himself up in the blanket and slept on the floor. I couldn't sleep. By the evenness of his breathing, Simon slept like a baby.

All that was the day before yesterday. I'm writing this at the railway station, in daylight this time, while I wait for the train back to Beijing. Yesterday we went first to the White Horse Temple. Simon wanted to go to the zoo, and we did that too, but that came later. The Temple was in a walled compound surrounded by hard-packed earth. It had rained a little in the night, and water stood in puddles on the resistant ground. The exterior of the walls was plain, with no suggestion of the riches that lay within. We paid at the gate and found a maze of temple buildings and courtyards and gardens. There was no one there. The quiet entered our veins, inhibited conversation. We moved from sun to shade to sun again. We stepped through moon gates and sat among flowering trees that I could not name. More Buddhas, in bronze this time, looked down on us. For once I felt tolerant of their inward benignity. Simon took my hand. I was incapable of disengaging it.

The zoo proved to be a tiny cluster of cages in the middle of a large park. There were some small deer in a pen and a lethargic panda sitting beside a pile of wilted bamboo. Much of its fur had fallen out and large patches of scabby skin were visible. It showed no interest in us. Its eyes were opaque and unfocused. As we watched it turned away slowly and lumbered heavily through an open doorway.

I think it's dying, I said.

There was nobody else about, no sign, except for the heap of bamboo, that there was anyone there to feed or care for the animals. As we moved on a grey-haired woman with a little boy approached. They walked slowly and solemnly past the straggle of buildings without a pause and without a glance at the panda's cage.

The park was bordered by a river, where men and boys were fishing from the muddy banks. We watched them for a while. I've never ever fished, Simon said. He again took hold of my hand, almost like a child, and perhaps because of that I still could do nothing to remove it. To do so would be making a big deal of something which was, maybe, nothing.

We walked back to the hotel, past blocks of flats with window boxes. I bought cans of coke. Simon's grin modulated into a sweet, eager smile. I bought him dinner again. I described Edinburgh to him. I painted a picture of a fascinating, beautiful, historic city. Simon takes it for granted that he will stay again in my room. It is not discussed. On the way upstairs he takes my hand again but this time I do disengage, though I also smile. I want to be nice to him, but at the same time suspect that nothing I do really reaches him. Back in my room he puts his arms around me. They feel as hard as the bone inside them, and each rib asserts itself against me. There's nothing importunate about the gesture. I put my hands on his shoulders and push him gently back and there's no resistance. I always liked the comfort of their arms, but this time it seemed too big a price.

Afterwards I thought of Tomas, but not then. Simon made the face of a disappointed boy and gave a little shrug, as if to say, well, it was worth a try. I said, Simon, tomorrow I'm going to Beijing. You're going south. We will probably never see each other again. There's no point.

It'd be nice, though.

On a tin tray were a flask of hot water, two mugs and paper packets of tea. I made tea for both of us and handed a mug to Simon. I sat in a basket chair while he arranged himself cross-legged on the floor. He began to talk again about Elsa but I wasn't really listening. I sipped the hot almost flavourless tea.

That night I slept a bit, waking up frequently to hear Simon's breathing from his blanket on the floor. I woke again in the early morning. There was greyish light filtering through the curtains. Simon was stirring. He got to his feet and dropped the blanket from his body. To my surprise he was naked. He pulled underpants and jeans over his thin white flanks. I lay without moving, pretending sleep. He stuffed his few scattered belongings into his rucksack. He glanced in my direction. I quickly closed my eyes and lay quite still. I heard a muffled step and slight sounds I couldn't quite interpret. I turned a little and opened my eyes enough to see him bent over the chair where I'd left my clothes and bag. Even as I thought, he's leaving me a note, I knew that couldn't possibly be true. I knew exactly what he was doing. I must have made a sound. He glanced in my direction again and this time I deliberately breathed loudly, as if I were coming to consciousness. Through half-closed eyes I saw his shoulders tighten, and then he quickly replaced on the chair what he held in his hand. He swung towards the door, picking up the large and small rucksacks as he went, and softly left the room.

I waited for a few moments, then got up and went to the window. From two floors up I looked down as a figure in jeans and T-shirt, thin, arms darkly tanned, emerged into the early morning light. He paused to ease a second arm through the strap of the large rucksack, ran one hand through his cropped, bristly hair while the other took a firmer grip of the smaller bag, and walked briskly down the street. I watched until he was out of sight. When at last I could bring myself to check, I found my purse open on the chair. A few notes were gone, but I couldn't remember how much had been there. I wondered if Simon was his real name.

Is it an illusion that such encounters have no consequences? I will never see him again. Sex would have been meaningless between us, as it was with Steve, yet I might have gained something from giving and receiving comfort, as I did with Steve. He might have banished Tomas for a night. But only to have replaced him with another spectre, as he made off down the street of a strange city with my money in his pocket.

Well, I found myself thinking, people who live in glass houses shouldn't throw stones.

20

THE SHATTERING OF walls. You think you're breaking through them when in reality you're adding another layer of bricks and strengthening the mortar. You think you've found a gate out, when in fact it's a gate in. A moon gate maybe, round and lovely, or great bronzed doors that swing wide and close again. A hotel room door with a number on it. Whatever it is, why is it that although you may think you're going out, in reality you're going in? And maybe further in, further and further. Deeper and deeper.

I'm going back to Beijing now. I don't know why, except that I have a train ticket that says Beijing in a language I cannot read and a room to go to when I get there. I pack my bag and ask for a taxi. I pay my bill in the currency reserved for tourists.

I am much too early for the train. The station is packed with people. They squat or sit cross-legged or lie with blankets pulled over their heads. It's hard to find a space to wait, but I do eventually, and sit on my bag and bring out my notebook. I am stared at, of course. When I'm finally able to board the train I find I am sharing a compartment with three portly Chinese gentlemen who regard me blankly. I sit down and open the bottle of mineral water I bought before leaving the hotel. I cannot make conversation so I read the label, several times. *Laoshan alkaline mineral water*, it says, *is a pleasant table-water rich in mineral elements, bottled from the spring of the famous mount Laoshan. Its efficacy is generally recognised good for chronic affects of the urinary organs, gastric enteritis, gouty and other troubles of the stomach.*

The train moves slowly northwards. I look out at fields and villages gilded by the evening sun. There are oddly intimate glimpses. Men and women working in the fields, often miles from any sign of habitation. Oxen and mules plodding round and round pulling rollers that threshed the grain. Villages of mud brick houses surrounded by mud walls. Courtyards offering scenes of family life. Children. The scrubbing of tubs of clothes, cooking. At nine o'clock a ploughman is still at work with an ox pulling a single ploughshare. Watching, I can sense the resistance of the baked earth. It turns over reluctantly in the wake of the plough. The tractor-pulled ploughs I have watched in West Lothian seem huge in comparison, slicing easily into soft earth.

The sun sinks rapidly with a last hectic glow, and there is no use any more in staring out of the window. My companions settle down to sleep. One snores. Another coughs and spits throughout the night. I sleep very little, although I am soothed by the train's rhythm and the knowledge that I am being carried through the dark to territory that I know at least a little.

I did have a reason for returning to Beijing. An important reason.

I am used to Chinese station arrivals now. I ease myself into the crowd that pours out of the train and allow it to carry me to the exit, then make purposefully for the cluster of taxis. Back to the Friendship Hotel. It seems almost like home, although I know that Steve has gone. I check all the same. Something might have come up, there might have been some delay. It takes some time for the clerk at the desk to establish... no, very sorry, Mr Carswell is not here now. He left last week. To Canada, I think. I nod. But a small packet is handed to me with my key.

The packet contains a paperback volume of poetry by Tang Wei, translated into English. There is a note tucked inside. *Dear Eleanor, these are the poems by one of the writers I admire the most. His name is Tang Wei, though he is only half Chinese. His mother was the daughter of a Scottish missionary! When you come back to Beijing I will take you to visit him. He is an old man now. I think you would like to meet him. Yours sincerely, Bing.*

I had heard of Tang Wei but had no idea he was still alive. He had been writing in the thirties and forties. I didn't know about his parentage. I go to my room, the same room I occupied before. There is nothing I can do but wait for Bingshen to make contact.

I waited for two days. I read Tang Wei's poems several times. They have precision and grace and a whiplash sting. But I'm restless. I read for half an hour, then get up and pace around my room. I go out for skirmishing walks, not wanting to go too far in case I miss Bingshen. I have a shower, wash my hair, wash my clothes. I check my passport and count my remaining money. There isn't much. I can't make any decisions until Bingshen comes. I can't help it, but there is the expectation that Bingshen and Tang Wei will between them provide an answer.

I eat my meals in the dining room, which is curiously hushed. There are just as many people there, but they seem to be talking in whispers. I've noticed one or two huddled groups in earnest conversation, but pay little attention. On the second day I go out in the afternoon, back to the Forbidden City. It throbs with heat. The pavilions shimmer. The white marble, whiskered with weeds, provides an illusion of coolness. After an hour or so of aimless wandering I leave and go and drink tea in the Beijing Hotel. There are a lot of people in Tiananmen Square, mostly young. Over them all, above the Tiananmen Gate, the Gate of Heavenly Peace, above the entrance used by the emperor, loom the vast features of Mao. When I get back, Bing is waiting for me. I see him at once, in his black T-shirt, jeans and trainers, and fill with pleasure. We shake hands.

We visit Tang Wei tonight, he says, but we must take a bottle of whisky. So we'll go now to the Friendship Store. I have a bicycle for you.

It was a long ride. We stopped on the way to buy *shashlik* on a street corner, chunks of spiced mutton cooked over charcoal on bamboo skewers. I buy the whisky. When we come out of the store it is beginning to get dark. There is another long ride ahead of us. Bing tells me he has been busy, things are hotting up. He shakes his head when I ask him what that means. Maybe later, he says.

Tang Wei speaks very good English, he tells me. He studied medicine at Edinburgh. Because of his mother, I guess – you see, you have a connection. That was way back in the 1930s. Most of his life he has been a communist, a true communist, and he's suffered for it. He is my hero. I am not a communist, not a Marxist, but if Tang Wei's communism had succeeded, then I would be.

We arrived at a dark apartment block. There were no outside lights. Without Bing I would not have found the entrance in a far corner to the ground floor flat that was Tang Wei's home, or noticed the meagre strip of densely-flowering garden near the door. He looks after it himself, Bing said, pointing it out to me. He loves flowers. Every day he spends a little time in his garden. There are no flowers in his poetry, I thought, although there are a few trees with blossom.

A slight but rangy old man came to the door. He greeted Lin Bingshen as if he were a son. Then he stepped back and I saw his lean but very Chinese face perched on the top of a body that belonged on my own hills. He wore shapeless trousers, a neat but frayed white shirt. And this is the visitor from Scotland, he said. His voice was courteous but thin and brittle. It is a great pleasure to meet an expert in English literature – or should I say Scottish? Did Bingshen tell you I lived in Scotland for several years? He shook my hand with both of his and ushered us into the drab, dimly lit apartment. His eyes were tired.

There were two worn armchairs, a wooden stool, a low table, a narrow bed in the corner. There was a makeshift desk heaped with books and papers, and a bookcase crammed with books piled on top of each other. Through a door was what I took to be a kitchen of some kind. I gave him the bottle of whisky, still wrapped in its store paper. Ah, you were well briefed, I see, he said with a sardonic bow. I am most grateful. You must share it with me. I noticed there was already an almost empty glass beside the chair where he had been sitting. He followed my glance. One of my few remaining pleasures, he said with a dry smile. The other is my garden. Did you see my garden? It never ceases to amaze me, how nature continues to flourish in the most adverse circumstances. I derive some comfort from that simple fact.

He pulled the wrapping from the bottle and handed it to Bing. My dear Bingshen, I'll leave it to your youthful fingers to deal with this. You know where the glasses are.

He lowered himself into one of the chairs, stretching out his long legs, then carefully placing one over the knee of the other. I have to be careful what I ask my limbs to do these days, he said. Although his hair was grey the skin of his face was almost smooth, the colour of creamy butterscotch. Bing came back with glasses and poured a generous amount of whisky in each one. We sat, the three of us, like the points of an equilateral triangle, Bing on the stool, so a little lower than myself and Tang Wei.

You have been lecturing here, Bingshen tells me. I am sorry I did not hear you. You have come to China at an interesting time. He stared at the liquid in the glass as if he had only just noticed it. And I think it is about to become a little more interesting.

You must have seen a lot of interesting times, I said.

Indeed. Yes. There was a pause before he continued. So. You are from Edinburgh? I studied medicine in Edinburgh. I stayed with my mother's brother and his family, in Marchmont. Thirlestane Road – a good Scottish name. Do you know it? Yes, of course, you must know it. I made them uneasy, I think, although they were kind. They could not quite believe their sister had married a Chinaman! But there I was. For four years. Every day I walked across the Meadows. I fell in love with a beautiful girl called Elspeth. She became a paediatrician. I wonder where she is now. Dead, perhaps. I came back to China and she wouldn't come with me. There was a war, of course. I don't blame her. The Japanese invaded.

He took a mouthful of whisky. The Japanese killed my father. And ten years later my mother disappeared. I never found out what happened to her. They were confused times. Civil war. I was working in a hospital hundreds of miles away. I was a communist and she wasn't. She tried not to ally herself with any cause except the welfare of the children she taught. He stared into his glass for a long moment. It's something I regret, that I never really knew her. But that is the fate of children, is it not, not to know their parents.

He did not seem to expect a reply.

I was not a fighter, he went on. His smile was self-deprecating, as brittle as his voice. His incongruous, lean, ascetic head was tipped at an angle, and I noticed that his hands were small, too small for his rangy limbs. In contrast to the skin of his face, his hands were almost white, almost translucent. Half a century ago, he went on, his eyes not looking at me, but upwards, or down into his glass. Half a century. Difficult times, but good times in many ways. Optimistic times, hopeful times – such nourishment in hope. Such healing power in optimism. You cannot understand, of course. No, do not argue (I had not intended, either to object or assent), do not argue. You are young, you are of the west. I am not of the west, whatever you may think. Believe me when I tell you, you cannot understand. He seemed quite relaxed, his free hand raised, his fingers graceful. There was a small square of window behind him, with no curtain, so his head was framed by a square of black. The lamp cast a feeble circle of light on his long but frail body.

Difficult times. But of course not so difficult for me as it was for many. I survived. I was doing something useful. I learnt not to let my heart break when I saw people die. And they did die, for such stupid reasons. Today doctors have the luxury of saving a life threatened by disease. Then, it was starvation, septicaemia, burns and gunshot wounds. I married a nurse, a party member of course. We had two children. The first, a daughter, died as an infant. The second, a son, died in jail. I was proud of my son. They took him instead of me, during the Cultural Revolution. Him instead of me. I was the one who published. I was the one who was critical. My wife and I were sent to work in the country, but he was detained. My wife got cancer and I could do nothing for her. A doctor, and helpless. A doctor should be able to look after his family.

His glass was empty. He reached for the bottle, which Bing

had placed on the table. I learned to like whisky in Edinburgh. He held the glass up to the pale light. It is part of my heritage. What a long time ago that was.

He drank a large mouthful, swallowing slowly with the control of a yogi, and smiling at the ceiling. My wife and I, we admired Mao. Supported him. Oh yes. Undoubtedly he was a great man. There can be no question about that. A great man, who accomplished great things. Sometimes I was critical, of course, I would say my say, write an article, publish my poems. But I was tolerated. I did good work in the hospital. Sometimes I was ignored, and I wasn't promoted. I was not happy, but I was not in danger.

I grieved for my daughter, my little Shun, but she was the sacrifice. Then my son. Both children given to the Revolution. Well, well, we thought, my wife and I, others have given more. So my boy grew up clever, goes to university, studies physics. Then comes the Cultural Revolution, the great event. You know what happened then? Of course you do. You are an educated young woman, are you not? He did not join the Red Guard. He rejected the Party. So he was denounced by his fellow students. Of course. What else?

And we – off to collective farms. Not the same one, you understand. My wife goes south, I go west. I didn't mind the work. In fact, I quite enjoyed it. I liked the hills, the earth. I had my health. I was strong. My wife wasn't so strong... China is a very large country.

His dry, ironic tones faded out. Gently, thoughtfully, he tapped his glass.

I wasn't treated so badly. There was no physical abuse, no torture. But I had to work, and it was hard to get books, paper, pens. The food was poor. And my wife and I were not together. It was difficult to write letters. For five years.

Bing sat very still out of the light and I couldn't see his face. He must have heard it before.

They did not tell me she was ill. When they let us go home, we had no home to go to. Our flat had been taken over. We stayed in a kind of shed that a friend let us have. I got back to Beijing first and went to the station every day to look for her. And then when I found her I did not recognise her. She was thin. The flesh of her face had gone, just skin left stretched across her cheek bones, her jaw bones. Her eyes hot and sunken. Her hair quite white. It had been a glossy black when they took her away. It was only the glimmer in her eye that made me realise it was indeed my wife, there with her little bag of things, standing still on the platform as the crowd surged on either side. When I embraced her she moaned. I realised she was in pain. She had been in pain for months. Now I believe that was why they had let us both out. They did not want to deal with her, with her dying. The pain never stopped, there was nothing I could do. I begged at my old hospital, but they would not take her. Too late, they said. Well, they were probably right. And so in a month or two, two months it was, let us be precise, two months, she was dead.

It was not really me he was talking to. He knew it all by heart and the audience scarcely mattered. There was no strain in his smooth voice, though there was weariness. He spoke as if he had conquered pain and was resigned to the endless rehearsal of the tale.

Now my son, my clever handsome son. He was angry at his father, his old-fashioned, old-guard father who clung to the old Party spirit, who could not see how the revolution had become eroded, worthless, who allowed his vision of the future to be clouded by his sense of history, his need to keep faith with something that was dead. My son had no time for any of that. He wanted to be modern. What an irony, do you not think, that my son died for rejecting what I clung to, and my wife and I were punished for trying to be true to what he rejected. I admire his courage. To reject his parents and his peers. An admirable and brave young man. And I don't even know where he died, only that he is, indeed, dead.

Well, it passed, the Cultural Revolution, it passed, as such things do. The wind changed. I was given a government pension. I began to write a little, but I've never been published again. I came here to live alone. One room, no wife, no son, no daughter.

Do I feel sorry for myself? Well, I think I do, a little. I no longer have the strength to resist.

Yet he got to his feet at that moment, unwinding his legs and rising with an unsteady grace, and replenished my glass and Bing's and his own.

I am a man of integrity. I use that word with care. Integrity. I can hang on to that, although I have lost everything else. I will take that with me to the grave. That is why I drink whisky (the dry smile) – it's good for my integrity. Some will twist and turn and deceive themselves and others in order to make life bearable. I drink whisky. It's more honest. I have much to be grateful to Scotland for.

He looked at me, his head slightly tilted, still the hint of a smile. And you, Eleanor, what brings you to China? Apart from the giving of lectures, and we are always grateful for words from the west. To walk on the Great Wall? To admire the ghostly glories of the emperors? To marvel at the march of the People's Republic? If there was mockery in his voice, his eyes seemed to demand an answer.

To be somewhere different, I said, fumbling my words like a nervous schoolgirl. To see things differently.

Eleanor is on a mission, Bingshen said with a laugh.

Ah. A quest, perhaps. A quest in the country of the dragon. Don't forget that dragons breathe fire. Tang Wei sat down again and leant back in his chair, carefully placing one leg over the other. You are a long way from home, he added thoughtfully. A long way from whatever life it is you have left. I'm sure you have not been disappointed. Things are very different here.

When we said goodbye he shook my hand. His grip was cool, delicate but firm. Look after our foreign guest, he said to Bingshen. Guide her well through the dark streets. I fear there are more difficult times ahead.

We cycled back through pockets of warmth that lingered unevenly. It was nearly midnight. Bingshen left me at the gate of the Friendship Hotel. I walked down the long dim corridor to my room through an almost oppressive silence.

21

I WAS ALONE in the flat when my mother telephoned. It was late. A November wind was rattling the windows. She told me my father was in hospital. I still find it hard to believe that he died the way he did, knocked over in the High Street by the flower shop's little Renault van. He was such a big man. The young woman who was driving had been at school with me, I remembered her red hair. They told me that she stood in the road, in the evening dusk, shaking with shock and tears as my father was eased onto a stretcher and into the ambulance. For weeks he lay unconscious.

As soon as I'd put the phone down it rang again. It was George. He said he would pick me up in the car and we would drive to Linlithgow together. It was nearly midnight by the time we got there. Mother came to the door with her apron on and made us tea. We had very little to say to each other. She looked just as she always looked, as if she had long since accepted that there were things she might once have said which she would now never say. She wore a grey skirt and a grey cardigan.

George and I both stayed the night, sleeping in our old rooms, and went to the hospital the next morning. Father lay under a white cotton blanket attached to tubes and machines, his closed eyelids frighteningly still, only the faintest tremor in his throat, an almost undetectable ripple under the skin, indicating that he breathed. Talk to him, the nurse said encouragingly. Sometimes it brings them back. Them. George stood by the door. How could I blame him? Never in all the years of feeling remote from my father had I felt as distant as this. I sat down beside him. It's Eleanor, I said, and George. Mother told us about the accident last night. I'm sure you're going to be fine, you're going to be fine. We're all okay, me and Roy, George and Sally and the kids. You're going to be fine. We'll all come and visit you, someone will come every day, I'll come at weekends, George will come... I didn't look at George.

There was no answering flicker. His large body was an inert lump under the white blanket. The nurse nodded and smiled and went away to attend to someone else. George was still standing. We stayed for half an hour. When we got back to the house, mother was cooking lunch. At first George said he couldn't stay, he had to get back. There were three places set at the table. I said, George! He looked almost ashamed. Mother said nothing, but stood at the cooker, her back to him, and tested the potatoes. So George stayed, and the three of us sat at one end of the dining room table. I'll go up to the hospital this afternoon, mother said. There's a bus at two. I'll take you, said George. No, she said. No, I'd rather get the bus.

She went every afternoon, sitting with him for a couple of hours, going home on the bus. She read the *Scotsman* to him. I got into the habit of phoning every evening. No, no change, she would say, her voice calm, resigned. Apart from her afternoons at the hospital, she carried on just as usual, as far as I could see. She cleaned the house and cooked meals. She read her magazines and carried on with her knitting. The paper was delivered every day, and every day she took it to the hospital and read from it to the shape under the white blanket.

I went to Linlithgow at weekends, George too sometimes. Roy came with me a couple of times, even came to the hospital, where we sat and talked about the need to get everyone in our building to agree to a roof repair while the machines that kept my father alive gently ticked and blipped. It must have been nearly Christmas when I went there alone one weekday when term had ended, and I said, after the nurse had left, father I don't think I can take this much longer. I don't know how mother stands it, coming here every day. You can't expect her to keep it up. Please make up your mind what you're going to do, live or die. You can't continue in this half-alive state, it's just not fair to anyone. Can't you just sort yourself out before Christmas? I surprised myself, half hoped he couldn't hear, and feared that he might. I stared at the hand that lay inert on the hospital blanket, as if it might reach out and silence the box of tricks beside him.

On Christmas Eve mother went to the hospital as usual in the afternoon. She only stayed an hour, it seemed – she had a lot to do to prepare for the next day. I phoned her as usual, at about five o'clock. She said, I didn't stay long. They've put up Christmas decorations, you know. They do try. She didn't say, no change, and I didn't ask. Later that night the telephone went when I was in the bath. Roy broke the news to me that father had died.

Everything carried on. The family assembled for Christmas dinner, cooked by my mother. There was a Christmas tree on the round table by the window. That's where it had always been. Presents were exchanged. The children were subdued and allowed to watch as much television as they wanted. Sally was wonderful, and talked and helped and put her arm around my mother. When George asked mother if she would stay in the house she shut him up and ignored his look of puzzled annoyance. George and Roy slipped out for a walk – I don't think they had ever spent time alone together before. They were out for a long time and I guessed they had found a pub open.

I was in the kitchen taking mince pies out of the oven when my mother said, looking out into the dark garden, there'll be snowdrops in a month. Yes, I said brightly. This year I'd like sweet peas, she went on. He didn't like sweet peas, I don't know why. His likes and dislikes, I could never understand. You couldn't argue with him, you know. A thrawn man, your father. Maybe it was the war that did it, but I never did understand. I should have tried harder. I know that's what he thought. I let him down.

I put the hot baking tray down. She stood there, her shoulders slightly hunched, her face flushed from the hot kitchen, her hands knotted into a tea towel, staring into the black glass. I love the smell of sweet peas, and the colours, she said. My mother always had them in her garden. The more she picked them, for the jug on the dresser, the more they came. I pulled the plug, Eleanor. It couldn't go on. It was what he would have wanted. She turned and looked at me, full in the eyes. She never did that.

I realised that my hands were shaking. I had gone cold as ice, then hot. There was my mother, calm, still, almost smiling. It couldn't go on, she said. I don't think I had ever seen her so still, her eyes so wide and direct. Then, as if a button had been pressed, she was busy again, transferring hot pies to a plate, pouring water into the tea pot, carrying a tray. I heard the front door bang – Roy and George were back. I heard music from the television. I heard one of the children laugh. I slipped out of the kitchen and along the hall to my old room and lay down on my old bed and shut my eyes. He was really dead. He was really no longer there.

I can't have been gone long. No one commented when I returned to the crowded room and took the cup my mother handed to me and crumbled a mince pie. Roy and George were back. Fiona and James were sprawled on the sofa watching *The Wizard of Oz*. Mother sat with one of their Christmas present books on her knee and turned the pages, smiling.

A few days after the funeral Roy and I climbed Cockleroy. We didn't stop off to see my mother, but drove straight through Linlithgow and on by the little road that runs out of the town to the south. The January sunlight was woven with mist. We walked through the trees and out onto the bare green slope where there were a few streaks of snow. I'd suggested it, needed some fresh air and exercise, I said. It wasn't the sort of thing we did, but Roy agreed, trying to be kind, I guess. We didn't talk, saving our breath for the climb, which is steep but not long. From the top we looked down on pools of white mist. The Firth of Forth was blotted out, with the rampart of the Ochils beyond standing clear above it. And beyond that, rimmed by snow, the high heads of Ben Vorlich, Ben Ledi, Ben More and even Ben Lomond, against a blue sky. Nearer, plumes of smoke and a single lick of fire hung apparently motionless above the chimneys of Grangemouth.

Roy and I walked along the ridge to where the rock fell steeply away, and stood side by side. We looked back towards Linlithgow. It seemed to me that we were looking at a town that had settled its relationship with the landscape. The palace, church spires, distillery, viaduct – confident, even if damaged or derelict.

George thinks mother should leave the house, I said. I don't understand why. He seems to think she can't manage on her own, but that's nonsense. She can manage fine.

He's worried about her, Roy said.

Well, maybe. I think he wants to take charge. She's fit, she's not that old. I think... what I think is that she wants a chance to make the house her own.

What do you mean?

I mean, she has lived in her husband's house all these years and now she wants to make it hers. What George should do is help her redecorate, reorganise, put new plants in the garden, choose some new furniture.

Perhaps. But she shouldn't rush things. She shouldn't make any important decisions until she's got over the shock. She's been through a lot, you know.

I thought, more than you realise, but said nothing. We climbed onto an outcrop of rock and watched the smoke belching from the Grangemouth chimneys. I'm glad you brought me up here, Eleanor, Roy said. Wonderful view. Why have you never brought me here before? I should have said, because I never needed to tell you what I need to tell you now. But instead I said, I used to come up here as a teenager. Leave my bike in the trees and climb the hill. This is where I read Byron and DH Lawrence. I had a place just down the slope here, a sort of nest under that rock – see? That was my place. I might have said, our place, but Roy never knew about my faithful childhood companion.

I had come with a purpose, but the purpose had evaporated as we walked. It can't go on, I wanted to say. Things aren't right. He'd put an arm around me and say, you're upset because of your father. I understand. Give it time. You're worried about your mother, I know, but you're right, she'll manage.

So because I knew how he would comfort me, how he would be unable to listen, there was nothing I could do. I couldn't pull the plug. The sun was already low and the sky beginning to blur into a pale apricot colour. We went down the hill again, to where the trees started. A family, mother, father, two children and a black labrador tramped past with a cheerful hello. As the path took us through the more thickly growing trees the sunlight disappeared and it was suddenly colder. There were several cars in the carpark. A man was cleaning mud off his walking boots, a young woman strapping a baby into a buggy, a boy with an action man doll. As we came up to the car Roy put his arm around me. I felt it through the thick material of my jacket. I felt his fingers slip under the edge of the scarf that was wound round my neck, under my hair.

When we called at the house my mother wasn't there. That's a good sign, said Roy. Your mother's stronger than you think. You shouldn't worry about her. I wasn't worrying about her, not at all. I was feeling the start of a strange and unfamiliar current of power running through my veins.

22

I GET A taxi from the station to the Friendship Hotel. I notice armoured cars and soldiers. Within a few days I am travelling again, this time to Tianjin, to give three lectures on the Victorian novel in a packed hall. Afterwards students and teachers crowd round, asking about the possibility of coming to Britain. No one refers to the buzz that runs through the lecture hall, a tingling, a tension. I sense it but can't describe it. It has nothing to do with me. I am approached by students of agriculture, of forestry, veterinary science. They want to go to Scotland. There have been campus demonstrations, but no one talks about them and I feel that for me to do so would be a breach of hospitality.

I return to Beijing. There have been demonstrations there too. On the evening of my return Bing appears, slipping into the dining room as I eat chicken and rice. He politely asks how I am, how I got on, but I notice his hands, clenched into fists, relaxing, clenching again. There are other people sitting at my table. I suggest he comes to my room, which won't do him any good if it is noticed, but he agrees and I buy two bottles of beer to take with us. He sits on the edge of the bed, I on the single narrow chair.

What's going on? I ask.

He shakes his head. I can't really tell you. But it's big, it's going to be big. Have you seen the soldiers?

I nod.

They know it's going to be big. I worry for you, Eleanor.

Maybe you shouldn't be here.

Is it that serious?

Who knows? People say, so long as we are peaceful, there will be no shooting. How can they believe that? Whatever their orders, the soldiers are boys, a lot of them. They get scared. Who knows what will happen?

I think I'll have to go back to Scotland anyway. I don't have much money left. I keep hoping something will turn up... But I'd like to see Tang Wei again.

I don't know, Eleanor...

It wouldn't be dangerous, for him I mean?

Maybe not.

He drinks from his bottle of beer. There is no reason for you to get involved, he said.

Will I get involved if I visit Tang Wei? I feel excited. There's an odd compression of my throat.

You're involved if you see me, Bing says. My wife is here, he adds.

I'd like to meet her.

Maybe you will. Look, tomorrow... If you're going to see Tang Wei it had better be soon. But I don't think I can come with you. Take a taxi.

Bing pulls a little notebook from his back pocket and scribbles in it, tears the sheet out and hands it to me. His address. Show it to the taxi driver.

Thanks. I'll get some whisky.

I guess I'd better go. If I don't see you for a few days, don't worry. And you know, you should see more of China before you leave. You should go to Chengde. It's a nice place, not far on the train. Quiet. There'll be no trouble there.

I open the door of my room. There's no one about, and Bing slips away down the corridor.

So I go in the morning to buy another bottle of whisky. In the dining room at breakfast people are talking about the latest demonstrations in Tiananmen Square. Some of the students are on hunger strike. A million people, they say, demonstrated in support – students, workers, government employees, intellectuals, even members of the police and armed forces, they are saying. In the evening I get into a taxi and show the driver my piece of paper. He speaks to me in Chinese although he knows I can't understand. He seems nervous. There are more troops on the streets. When we get there I recognise the block of flats, and find my way to Tang Wei's door. He seems thinner and older, his voice drier. He is wearing the same clothes as before, and takes my hand in the thin fingers of both of his. He asks me to pour the whisky.

I am glad you are here now, he says. I am glad I have lived until now.

Lin Bingshen thinks I shouldn't be here.

He laughs. That's for you to decide.

What do you think will happen?

Well... well... Tang Wei consults his glass. There is a long silence, then, It is too soon. Nothing is ready, nothing is prepared. But it is beginning and it can't be stopped. It will fail, but it has to happen. Perhaps. All revolutions have to have a beginning. And revolution without failure would not be revolution. His dry, remote smile fades into his glass. I am not sure I understand him.

Is it revolution?

You are right to ask. I think not. But it is rebellion, most certainly, the rebellion of the young, and that's where it has to start. Have you been to Tiananmen?

I shake my head.

You should go, visit, like a tourist. You will hear them sing the 'Internationale' in Chinese. You will be able to tell your grandchildren.

I think my taxi driver was frightened.

He is right to be frightened. It is frightening. They are innocent. They do not understand that they are nothing, nothing in the eyes of the state. And yet they are everything, every single one of them. They carry a heavy burden. China has no future without them.

Bingshen says his wife is here.

Ah. So Suni is back in Beijing. They must be careful, those two.

Do you think they are in danger?

We are all in danger. All of us who believe, who have commitment. I have been in danger all my life. I am used to it. I would not know how to live without it. But for the young people... they do not realise what they have started, that they cannot control events, that history takes over, even before it has happened, even before they recognise that the engine is moving on its tracks.

He pours more whisky into his glass. His hand is shaking a little.

And you, Eleanor you can't have expected anything like this when you set off on your quest for something different. What are you going to do? Are you going to stay and share our fate? There is much more of China for you to see, you should see it while you can. Who knows what will happen now?

That's what Bingshen said. That I should see more of China. He said I should go to Chengde.

Yes. Go to Chengde. It's not far. Five hours only in the train. Through the mountains, the journey the emperors made to escape the heat of Beijing in the summer. Go to Chengde and visit the summer palace and the temples. Beijing will still be here when you return. And whatever is going to happen, it will still be here too.

I was hoping you could tell me more, about what might happen, about what is really going on.

Well, I am a wise old man in many ways, but... He shrugs. Each new generation has to find out things for themselves. Even if I had answers, they would not listen. Why should they? He empties his glass. This time I am quick off the mark and replenish it before he reaches for the bottle. He smiles.

Ah, it is good to have a young woman to fill my glass. He leans his head back and closes his eyes for a moment. He says something in Chinese. Are you familiar with Chinese poetry of the T'ang dynasty? he asks. I have translated some of it myself. There's a poet called Wang Wei who lived in the eighth century, in Shaanxi Province, near Xian. You've been there, I think. 'Yet, friend, there is enough to keep you here.' That's from a poem about an autumn evening – dusk and moonlight and lotus flowers. Perhaps you're looking for something to keep you here, or not here at all, but there, your own country. No lotus flowers, perhaps, but heather, or bluebells? But now, go to Chengde. Bingshen has given you good advice.

Tang Wei's words convert a notion into an imperative. When I went to get my train ticket the queue wasn't as long as usual, and although there were still encampments of travellers, as there had been when I went to Tianjin only the week before, they seemed – or did I imagine this? – subdued. I saw a lot of soldiers around the station, but no weapons.

There weren't many people on the train. But a party of Japanese was already in occupation at the small, seedy hotel. There were no other tourists.

I walked along the dusty main street to the summer palace. It was a faded, melancholy place. I wondered if that was why Tangwei and Bing had wanted me to go there. There were not many people about, a few couples, a few old men in blue cotton, a few children running along the dry, scuffed path. There were remnants of gardens, landscaping. I walked round the artificial lake, paused at little decorative pavilions and pagodas, the misty Rain Tower, the paint burnt away, the wood warped. Melancholy, but oddly peaceful. Once it must have been vibrant with colour, scurrying with life, when the emperor was in residence with his vast entourage. It was here that Lord Macartney had come in 1793, with the intention of negotiating British trade with China, only to be dismissed by the Emperor Qianlong. China had no need of anything Britain could offer. Hunting parties rode through the forested hills. There were archery contests, firework displays, endless feasting, limitless sex. But perhaps in winter it was silent, the water in the lake frozen, an occasional voice rippling in the cold air.

I thought of my mother's face when I told her I was going to China. I could have said I was visiting the far side of the moon. It was one of Eleanor's stories. She'd always spent too much time with her nose in a book. When I told her I was to be giving some lectures it seemed more real. It helped her to explain it, which was the important thing. She came for a walk with me down to the loch and we watched children feeding the ducks. I wanted to ask her if she was alright, but somehow I couldn't. When had she and I last gone for a walk together? I couldn't remember. I pictured George and me on Sunday afternoons with our father, but she was never there.

She walked back up the hill with surprising briskness and we had tea in the kitchen, eating ginger biscuits straight out of the packet.

Beside the lake at Chengde I thought of my mother, and I thought of that Sunday morning with Roy, climbing to the top of Cockleroy and seeing so much of Scotland rolling away from the top of that little hill. I walked back along the burning, dirty street, shaken with ancient trucks that staggered from pothole to pothole, and realised I was missing the Lothian landscape.

That evening I ate in yet another hotel dining room. At first it was almost empty, filled only with the sound of whirring fans. Tinsel decorations were hanging from the ceiling. Then the Japanese tourists arrived and sat in a cluster at the other end of the room, their crowdedness augmenting my isolation. My food was hot and oily, served with glutinous lumps of rice.

Or was I missing Beijing? I felt lonely in Chengde, a long way from anywhere I could locate myself. I had not felt lonely anywhere else, or at least not abandoned, as I felt in this abandoned place. The next day I hired a bicycle and pedalled away from the town. The bikes and lurching trucks thinned out until I was almost the only vehicle on the road. Chengde is ringed with temples, built like the summer palace in the eighteenth century, and all different. They perch in the folds of green hills. A few people are working in the fields. I pedalled slowly, stopping often. Brass roofs glinting under the sun. The largest temple is modelled on the Potala at Lhasa, grime-coated in corners. Small islands of restoration and new paint. Wooden pillars which look as if they might crumble at a touch. There is no one here. I wonder what has happened to the Japanese.

I cycle alongside a field of spinach. Two women are hoeing. They barely glance at me. I find this odd. I am so used to being stared at I wonder if there is something wrong. The Temple of Distant Tranquillity. The Temple of Universal Peace. A twenty-two metre high Buddha with forty-two arms, an eye on each palm. Fanciful excrescences, turrets, mini-pagodas, dragons in gilded copper. And the hills rolling away, erupting in strange rock formations. Toad Rock, the huge oval Hammer-Head, Monk's Hat Hill dark with trees.

Tranquillity. Yes, I can believe that. Freewheeling down from Mount Sumeru, the air is clear, the heat less heavy. I think I know what the problem is. This is an interlude. I want to be back with Lin Bingshen and his wife Suni, whom I've not yet met. I want to be hearing the thin, dry – perhaps mocking? – voice of Tang Wei rooting me in history. I want that blend of innocence, hope and energy, of wisdom and tenacity, that these people offer to the world. It's not here, in melancholy imperial Chengde.

I am hot and thirsty and oddly anxious by the time I get back to the hotel. I drink cold beer, alone in the little cafe that abuts the desolate hotel foyer. I want to be back in Beijing. I ask at the desk if there is any news. The young man looks at me nervously. Very fine, he says, all very fine. The afternoon train, I say, any problems? All very fine, he says again. As he is speaking the Japanese erupt suddenly with their suitcases. His nervousness changes to scorn. They get train, he says. Go back to Beijing too soon. Scared. They are certainly talking non-stop and fussing, checking luggage, tickets. Their leader, a smartly-dressed woman, looks worried and keeps glancing at her watch. As I turn away from the desk she says to me, we leave now. Back to Japan. I think you should not stay. Not safe. My firm say we should go home – special flight to Tokyo tonight.

I smile. It's alright, I say. I'm getting the afternoon train too.

She replies with an approving nod and speaks to the young man at the desk at some length.

And here I am on the train, writing. And wanting to be in Beijing. And feeling homesick for Linlithgow and the loch and the little hills that allow you to see so much of Scotland. It was perhaps not right to climb with Roy to see Scotland. It could only have made it more difficult for him to believe me. But I had climbed that hill as a child. I had biked along those narrow roads, and had walked and biked around the loch. I had taken the roofless palace for granted. I had taken Cockleroy for granted. But when I was there, I knew where I was. Only when I grew up did I find the whole business of space and time baffling.

You never really loved me, Roy. Whatever you said. You never really loved me. If you had, would I now be in a train steaming through the hills to Beijing, where the rebels are on the streets, where the tourists are gathering at the airport to fly home, where Eleanor doesn't understand what she's doing? It's not your fault. It's just the way you are. You are loyal and decent. I wasn't loyal and decent to you. If you knew about Daniel, would you say good riddance? You'll be alright, Roy. You'll make someone a good husband. Not loving, but loyal and decent.

It is getting dark. The train moves very slowly through the endless grey suburbs of Beijing. It comes to a halt. I can see nothing through the window but a dreary expanse of grey buildings veiled by dusk. The Japanese have become silent. Five minutes, ten minutes, fifteen minutes pass. They begin to talk again, at first in whispers, then gradually louder until they are almost chattering again in their normal voices. The train moves forward, with painful slowness, then stops. I peer through the window, but now it is almost completely dark. If anything were happening out there I would not be able to see it. It is silent again in the carriage, and silent beyond, except for the regular escape of steam from the engine.

At last we move again, stop, move again. Two hours later we pull into the station, but even before the carriage doors are opened I sense the difference, the uneasy passage of the train has presaged. There is no milling crowd, no dense surge of humanity towards the exit. A handful of Chinese. No white face other than my own. For the first time I am seriously afraid. Not just nervous. Not just aware of tension as I listen to Bingshen. There are few lights. Our little group spills out of the almost black station.

There are still a few people about with their belongings, but nothing like the usual crowd. The shapes wrapped in blankets hug the outside walls. There are no taxis. The Japanese move away with their group leader, who is speaking to them in a rushed whisper. I watch them for a moment, wondering how they are going to get to the airport. Perhaps everything is organised at their hotel. They disappear down the street, a little band tightly adhering.

Am I going to have to walk to the Friendship Hotel? I cannot understand the silence, and then I'm startled by the sound of an engine. Headlights come towards me. Instinctively, I step back and shrink against the wall of the station building, although at the same time I'm hoping it's a taxi. But I know it can't be, the engine has too heavy, too intrusive a sound.

It is a jeep with four soldiers in it. I can make out their weapons, metal glinting over their shoulders. The jeep slows down, turns, roars away. The silence that follows is terrifying, and yet my mind has not caught up with this. Something is assuming it's all going to be alright. Just be patient. Just wait. There will be a taxi. Or Bingshen will appear with his bicycle. Did I tell him when I was coming back? I can't remember. Then sudden noise, unreal noise, explosive noise. I know what that is, I think. That's gunfire. Then I can smell it. And, I don't think this is my imagination, the sky reddens.

There is a hand on my arm and I almost scream. It is a woman in station uniform.

Where you go? a voice asks.

Friendship Hotel, I say. I knew it was going to be alright. I knew it.

No taxis. Taxis not come now. This man, he can take you on bicycle. I had not seen him, the man in the darkness, although he is wearing a white shirt, the sleeves rolled up. His bare legs are thin.

For money.

I nod. Of course. I can pay.

The man and the woman speak to each other in whispers. Then the woman turns to me again. It's okay. He take you.

He disappears into the dark and returns with a bike. I hoist my bag on my shoulder. The crossbar of his bike has sacking wound round it and I sit sideways on this. We move off. I am aware of every flicker of muscle as he pedals.

I can only trust him. He avoids the main streets. I don't know where we are, where we are going. There is another burst of firing away to our right. I smell his sweat, feel his arms on either side of me, hear his breath, loud and unsteady. It's hard work, pedalling the two of us. From time to time he stops and listens, then pushes on. Then he stops and motions me to get off. We are not far from one of the cloverleaf flyovers that carry the ring road over smaller streets. He takes my hand and pulls me and the bike deep into shadow and then points. Silhouetted along the arch of the flyover, with a lighter sky behind, are tanks. I can make out the outlines of soldiers. Occasionally they move, but there is no noise. The tanks are still. I do not believe any of this.

We have to go under the flyover. Now my guide turns to me and says, how much? I did not realise he could speak English. I offer him three times the normal taxi fare. Is that what my life is worth? he replies. In the darkness I detect irony in his voice, and he cannot see me blush. I offer him ten times the normal taxi fare. I am thinking, it would be so easy for him to knock me on the head, steal my money and leave me. What difference would it make with all that's happening around us? But he doesn't. He nods. He grips the handlebars of the bike. Let's go, he says. No noise. He clamps his hand over his mouth and shakes his head. He wheels his bike and I follow him.

We cling to the shadows. When he stops, I stop. There are sounds I can't interpret, metallic rumblings, occasional voices, the thud of heavy objects. A voice rings out above us, very close. We freeze. Someone tosses away a cigarette and its tiny burning tip falls to our feet. My cyclist puts his foot on it. Then suddenly there is a roar. My guide pulls me under the flyover. There is a smell of dust and urine. Above us the concrete trembles. The tanks are moving. We stay there for what seems like half an hour, but I am not sure. It could have been five minutes. I am beyond any sense of time. My hands are oily with sweat and my shoulder hurts where the straps of my bag are cutting into it. My heart is thumping in my throat and I feel that I can't get air into my lungs.

The rumble has not ceased, the air still vibrates, but we emerge beyond the sheltering concrete. I can see clotted shadows moving, and lights. Now I can hear the slight tick-tick-tick of the bicycle, but my guide's footsteps make no sound and I strain every nerve to be equally silent. Then he stops and pats the crossbar of the bike. I settle myself on it and he slowly pushes off and again I feel submerged in his breath and his sweat. To my astonishment we are soon at the gate of the Friendship Hotel – there is a faint light in the entrance, but no sign of life. I give him money.

By the time I have reached my room and pulled the door closed behind me I am icy cold and shaking. But since then I have slept. This morning, before I sat down to write, I looked in the mirror and saw a pale face with two bumps of cheekbones and lank hair. I went to the shower and washed my hair with the last of the shampoo I'd brought with me. Now I've pulled my hair back from my face and tied it with a piece of pink string that I found in my bag. My lips still look white. I got some breakfast, some bread and jam and tea. There are still a few people about. The telephone is working. I am writing because I have to do something, but really I am waiting. For Bing, for Tang Wei – though why should they think of me? For something to happen. For the telephone to ring. I don't know.

23

ALL DAY I have done nothing, except write, drink tea, walk out into the hotel grounds and listen, walk back. It is late afternoon and a group of French students has just left. This morning some Americans left. Four Canadian actors, two men and two women, are hanging around a cluster of suitcases, breaking away from time to time to try to make contact with their embassy. One of them is at the telephone now. She's replaced the receiver, comes clicking rapidly back on her high heels. She looks excited.

They've organised a coach to go to the airport but we've got to get over to the embassy.

How the hell do we do that?

We catch a bus. The woman on the phone's given me numbers of buses that avoid the centre. She says it should be okay.

Big deal. Anything could happen.

Why don't they send a vehicle for us? Surely they can do that?

I asked. They say there are Canadian nationals all over the city. They can't go and pick them all up.

But we're an official touring group – government money, tax-payers' money...

Aw, shut up, Ted, let's get going. Think of what you'll be able to tell your grandchildren.

The woman picks up her suitcase, hesitates, looks down at her shoes, and kicks them off. She kneels, opens her case and scrabbles around for a moment until she finds a pair of flat sandals. The change accomplished she locks her case and picks it up again. The others watch her without moving, expressionless.

I'm staying, one says.

You're crazy, Ted. There's a plane for us. There may not be another. They've got to look after us. It's their responsibility.

The woman with the suitcase walks to the door and out into the hazy sunlight. The other, younger, woman, blonde hair spread on her back, follows. The first man slings a large camera bag on his shoulder and picks up a suitcase and a Marco Polo Hotel carrier. He hurries out after the two women. Ted remains, biting his lip. He hasn't shaved for a day or two. After a few moments he, too, with a bag in each hand, leaves.

I can scarcely detect the footfalls of the few hotel staff who remain. They seem to melt into the dark corridors. There is a German ceramics expert who chain smokes. He bought me a beer at lunchtime – his name is Kurt. He and I and an English publisher who is interested in translating Chinese fiction sat together. The publisher, Tony, has thin fair hair, round spectacles, a cream-coloured suit and a pink tie. Somehow all these details seem important. He explains to me that his is a small firm, based in Manchester, specialising in oriental books. He mentions names of writers I have not heard of whom he wants to publish in translation. He thinks everything will settle down in a day or two and then he'll be able to complete his deal and go on to Singapore. He thinks everyone is over-reacting. There is something reassuringly anachronistic about Tony. He seems to belong to another time as well as another world. I notice the German's hands shake when he lights each cigarette, but become still as soon as he has taken his first drag.

I keep thinking of last night. The backs of my thighs ache where I sat on the crossbar. Who was he, I wonder? Why was he hanging around the station? Did he get back to wherever he wanted to go? Did I pay him enough? Or far too much? Tony asked me why I hadn't left. I told him, because I'd rather stay, but I'm not sure if that's true. I can leave, of course. I have done what I was asked to do. Soon I will have to leave, unless I can find some means of earning money. I could go home and start applying for jobs. I've been thinking of Canada. Or I could take one of those teaching-English-as-a-foreign-language courses and go anywhere. George suggested that when I told him I was going to China. Or perhaps it was Sally. I could go home and look after mother. George suggested that as well. Dear George. I'm thinking of him now, thinking that I'm quite fond of him, really. Fond of him, I expect, because if he hadn't proved so reliable, filled the space carved out for him so admirably, I probably would never have come to China. But mother doesn't need looking after. How silly, to do something that doesn't need doing, in order to make George happy, in order to fit a suitable space, in order not to do nothing.

It's getting dark now. I left Tony and Kurt drinking duty-free whisky. I am doing nothing, except writing, of course, literally pushing a pen across this sheet of paper, yet I don't feel useless. It's very odd. I am, no doubt deluding myself, but I definitely do not feel useless. Although I am only waiting, without knowing what I am waiting for.

There's a knock on my door and when I open it I find Tony. I can smell the whisky. The knot on his pink tie hangs loosely. He inclines his head – it's almost a bow. There's a Chinese girl looking for you, he says. I follow him to the foyer. There is a woman standing near the door in a patch of dim light. She is wearing a short navy skirt and a white T-shirt. The T-shirt is stained and grubby. She has a red patterned bandana tied around her cropped hair and some gauzy material hanging round her neck. Her eyes are large in her small pointed face. Her hands are also dirty.

As I approach her I raise both my hands. I want to embrace her.

Are you Eleanor? She asks hesitantly.

I nod. She looks like a child, solemn at having been sent on an adult errand, into the adult world. But she is no child. We shake hands – hers is hot and gritty – and she says in slow English, come to Tiananmen, come and help us. Bingshen sent me. I am Suni.

Of course. What can I do?

Help us, Bingshen says. He says, you want to be with us.

Yes, I do, he's right, I say, surprised at myself.

He says, I must tell you, there has been shooting. People are hurt.

I know, I say. But it is instinct that tells me, although I heard the guns and saw the tanks. It is hard to connect those unreal sights and sounds with people hurt and maybe dead.

He says, I must tell you, it is not very safe, but he says it is alright for you, because you are English.

Scottish, I say, and I laugh, though I can see she cannot understand why.

He says, it is for you to decide.

It's alright. I'm coming. I am quite detached, cool. I even wonder if I could be some kind of protection. Wouldn't they hesitate to shoot into a crowd with a white freckled face in the midst of it? Probably not. Probably I'd be lost among the thousands.

He says, you can... bear... witness. Each word is enunciated separately. I wonder if she understands what they mean.

I follow Suni through the door just as I am. Do I imagine it, or do I hear a mild but slightly slurred English voice – Miss Dickinson! – somewhere behind me? I am wearing cotton trousers and a denim shirt, and have a little money in the button-down pocket, enough to buy beers for Tony and Kurt, and a small notebook. Spiral-bound, bought in a stationer's on George Street. George Street. A distant familiarity, reassuring but odd. When I see Suni's bike propped outside, a man's bike with a crossbar, I go back into the foyer and help myself to a cushion from a chair. Yes, Tony is there, a cream blur, and Kurt in a purple sports shirt, with their glasses and their cigarettes. Eleanor! Where are you going? But I am through the door again and balancing the cushion and myself on the crossbar.

Suni takes the back streets, perhaps the same streets I came through last night, but I can't tell. It is dusk. It's quiet at first, but as we get nearer the Forbidden City there are soldiers and armoured cars and more and more people on the streets, on foot, on bikes. They seem aimless. They wander up to the soldiers, bang their fists on the vehicles, wander off again. The soldiers' faces are like stone. People cycle round and round in slow circles. We pass a coat, hanging empty from a lamp post. A bus is parked at an angle, almost blocking the street. We get off the bike. Suni has to lift it to get past.

The huge square is packed. There is a hum of sound. I wonder how Suni can hope to find Bingshen, but she seems to know exactly where to go, both of us off the bike now, weaving in and out of dense knots of people, standing, sitting on the ground, gathered round little makeshift tents and heaps of belongings. Clusters of banners and posters. And the vast ghostly white Goddess of Freedom, two hands raised holding a torch metres above the mass of people. And there's Bingshen, smiling when he sees us, but that looks like blood on his shirt and I notice that his American Levis are torn. He touches Suni's hair briefly, where it springs up from the bandana, and then shakes my hand and claps my shoulder. Eleanor, Eleanor, he says slowly – it is not an easy word for him – and then speaks to Suni in Chinese. Her eyes close as if there is something she cannot bear to look at, and open again.

I have my notebook. But here in the centre of it all I cannot see very much. We hear shots. There are flurries on the edges, spasms of movement, and an acrid, stinging smell of burning. Bingshen disappears and then returns. Suni sits for a while on the ground with her arms clasped round her knees, her eyes closed again, then suddenly gets to her feet and hurries through the crowd. There is no sense of time here, no sense of cause and effect. It is now quite dark. A few small fires have been lit. A few songs are being sung. I am feeling simultaneously hungry and sick, with a taste of beer stale in my mouth. I have eaten nothing since my breakfast bread and jam.

They are kids, these soldiers, Bing says. Some of them have no weapons. I've seen them cry. They are not the enemy.

But people are getting hurt.

Yes. We have to expect that. We are ready for that. We are

ready to die, you know. Some of us have to die.

Don't say that.

Why not? We will all die. Why not now, when it could mean something?

But what use are you dead? What a waste it would be, what an appalling waste.

Bing smiles and shakes his head. I feel like a child, excluded from his world. And then suddenly out of the crowd and the smell of smoke, there is Tang Wei. He is smiling also. He puts his hand on Bingshen's arm. I cannot understand these smiles. What are they doing, these crazy men, smiling? Suni has not smiled.

Well, Eleanor, Tang Wei says, so you are here.

I nod.

I am glad to see you, but I am not sure if it is safe for you. Was this your idea, Bingshen? I am not sure if it is safe for our honoured guest. This is not her battle.

Why not? I say. I'm not likely to find a better one.

I will look after her, says Bingshen.

Where is your wife?

She is with a girl whose arm is broken...

You see? This is real, Eleanor, this is dangerous. Women are getting hurt. I think already people have been killed.

I feel a fraud. I don't think I will get hurt. I feel my difference from these people, as if I am far away from them. The fact that I share the same space seems not to bring me closer. Yet I am grateful to them, for bringing me here, for trying. Whatever their reasons, or mine for agreeing to come.

I am out of time, out of space. But no one looks at me here. Even the quiet knots of people, even those who are not scurrying back and forth, or talking, arguing, singing. Some have decided to leave, to slip away before the square is closed in, before it is too late. I still have the hotel's cushion and give it to Tang Wei to sit on. He looks so thin, so fragile, friable almost, as if he might disintegrate at the slightest breath of wind, let alone the rush of flame from a weapon. He thanks me. And I cannot even offer you a whisky. What a pity. I have drunk all of your gift, Eleanor.

And even if some had remained, I don't think it would have been wise to bring Scotland's water of life to Tiananmen Square.

He sits on the cushion with his long legs crossed. I have come here to die, you know. I think it is time. And I think this is an excellent place to die. Don't you agree? For one of the old guard? An excellent place, an excellent time. I feel very content, Eleanor. Don't look so alarmed. Yes, I would like to be able to offer you a Glenlivet, yet I am very content, myself, without it. It is a long time since I have been content without whisky.

A young man with a scarf partly covering his mouth hands him some crumpled gauze. Tang Wei looks at it quizzically. The young man says something. Ah, tear gas, Tang Wei explains, and shakes his head. I understand. Tang goes on, but there is no need for me to protect myself against tear gas. The young man speaks again and lays the cloth on the ground beside Tang Wei before moving on.

Everyone is talking of dying and I don't know what to say. It is as if death isn't part of my language, although my father dying so suddenly brought me with a shock as close to death as most of us get before it's our turn. I don't know what to think. There is nothing I can do. But I, also, am content to be here. Suni returns, her eyes larger, her mouth tighter. She carries two small bowls of noodles, which we share. I use the same chopsticks as Tang Wei. He eats very little. I am aware of hunger, but I find it difficult to eat. We sit, the four of us, close together, an intimate but strange quartet, Tang Wei on the cushion, legs crossed, his hands on his knees, his face calm. From time to time he closes his eyes, and when they open and see me watching they are full of amusement. Bing has his arm round Suni. On her bare legs are patches of greyish-blue, and I can't tell if it's dirt or bruising. She has black canvas shoes on her feet, which seem tiny beside Bing's American sneakers. I feel the hard ground. When I stand and stretch the dark beyond the crowd is like a wall, and I sense more than see the vehicles, the soldiers, the weapons... Here and there, small fires burn.

The night passes.

What are you thinking about Eleanor? asks Tang Wei. What is it they used to say? A penny for your thoughts? A penny for your thoughts, Eleanor.

I am thinking about... two men, I answer.

Tell us.

A man I loved. And a man I lived with. Now, of all times. Neither of them has a place here.

The comfort of a loved one always has a place.

Suni says, in her slow, careful English, I am thinking of my daughter. Maybe my daughter will pay for her parents' actions. Do you have a child Eleanor? I see Bing's hand tighten on her shoulder.

I shake my head.

Bing says, It is because I have a child that I know it's alright to die.

Suni agrees. I want to protest at this plain assertion, to protect Suni from thoughts of death, but I say nothing, and also realise that any idea of protection is useless. It is I who need protection. I am ashamed of my thought, earlier in this same long day although it feels like an age ago, that I might have offered some protection to my friends.

There is a ripple of sound. A man in a checked shirt approaches and squats in front of Bingshen, talking hurriedly. Suni says something and gets to her feet. Bing puts out a restraining hand and then lets it drop. Suni goes with the young man and they disappear into the patchy darkness.

Bing says, She must go where she is needed. More people have been hurt.

I have picked up my notebook again. Will anyone ever see this? Is anyone watching us? It is all so far away. For a short time I felt quite calm, with the four of us sitting together, almost touching, talking a little but mostly silent. Now I am afraid again. And I can smell fear, too, tension, disturbance. Is something happening on the edge of the crowd? There are sounds, but cloaked somehow, as if a long way away. Bing has jerked to his feet. Tang Wei does not even open his eyes, but rocks ever so slightly, his long fingers spread across his bony knees, clad in flannel trousers. There are lights, movements, shouts, shots.

Bing speaks rapidly to Tang Wei, who almost imperceptibly, and courteously, graciously, shakes his head without opening his eyes. I am on my feet now, too, for I'd felt a tremor in the hard ground, a muffled rumble that seemed to come from inside the earth. But it had come from the earth's surface. Like everyone else, I know it is tanks, although I can see nothing.

Sounds swell from all directions and fill my ears. Bing says something, but I can't hear. I think about Suni, but she isn't there. Tang Wei remains cross-legged on the ground. People are moving, falling back on either side of him. I kneel down beside him.

Please get up. Please don't stay here. There are tanks coming. Guns.

My dear Eleanor. I must stay here, and you must go. Bingshen, you must take our honoured guest to a place of safety. It would not do if anything should happen to her. It would be such a waste if she should die. He smiled, and I was startled. She is not like me – she is not ready for death. And we must not pretend that these are not dangerous times. Dangerous times, Eleanor.

I am sure Bing could not hear him, but I heard him, as I knelt beside his frail body, and I wanted him go on speaking. I wanted to go on hearing his elegant, dry, precise, soothing English.

My dear, you are not ready for this. Go with Bingshen. Go home, Eleanor. These are dangerous times. And we need you to live.

Bing stoops and grabs my arm and pulls me to my feet, but I'm angry at this intrusion and want, and almost try, to throw myself down on the ground again, to cling to Tang Wei's voice.

But he has raised his hand. I turn round and am stunned by a blaze of light and a gut-churning roar of sound. Bing is pulling me away, running. There are shots. Oh this isn't real, it can't be real. I am breathless, and almost laughing. I stumble after Bingshen, trying to run yet not wanting to, instinct and will and terror and laughter all fighting each other.

It goes on and on. Bing's bruising fingers do not let go. He pulls me through people, screams, gunfire, the terrible roar of moving vehicles. We run a few steps, stop, turn, zigzag, run again. I see people flung on the ground. I see blood. I see a girl carried in the arms of a grey-haired man. Lights and sirens rise and fall.

Then Bing stops. My mouth is full of dust and bile. It is darker, and quieter. A few people run past. When I look around I realise we are in a narrow lane. On a windowsill at the level of my eyes is a row of flowerpots and I catch the smell of garlic. Bing pushes me against a wall and says, I am going to look for Suni. Stay here. Do not move. I'll be back, I promise. Don't move.

There is a terrible silence. I can no longer stand, and sink to the ground, where I squat, like an oriental, my back against the rough wall. I don't know how long I am there, without moving, numb. My eyes get used to the darkness. From time to time someone runs past the opening to the lane, but no one turns into it, or even looks, so far as I can tell. My mind starts to move again. At least, I think, I can write something down. That would be a useful thing to do. That's what Tang Wei would like me to do. My notebook and biro are still buttoned into the pocket of my shirt. I remove them, and that simple act allows me to see myself squatting under a windowsill of garlic, my back against the flaking wall of what once was perhaps the fine house of a wealthy Peking merchant, only just able to see the white page, writing painfully, for my fingers are stiff and reluctant to hold the pen. Writing.

The strange thing is that I don't want to write of now. I am thinking of home. The loch at Linlithgow on a winter afternoon with thin ice at the edge and the water birds crowded together. Or in the spring's cold sunshine with ducklings following their mother as if pulled on a string, and the gaunt palace rooted in the grassy bank. Even in the dark it is hot here, and my thighs and back are damp with sweat. I never told anyone about you, my constant companion for so long, always there when I opened my bedroom door, or bicycled to my favourite place on Cockleroy. But if I were to go home now, you would not be waiting, ready to take me back into that imagined refuge.

Arthur's Seat heaving its great hump above the Edinburgh tenements. Daniel's kitchen. He sits at the table with his sleeves rolled up revealing his slender brown arms, his hands folded round a glass of red wine, and I am caught in his magnetic web. Roy smiles in his island of certainty. My mother buttons up her good tweed coat. My father seen from the window turning in at the gate, closing it, checking the latch, walking up the path in his polished shoes.

There is noise again. Where is Bingshen? Where is Suni? I do not ask, where is Tang Wei because I know nothing will move him. Enough to keep you here. Vehicles are passing the end of the lane. I feel them as well as hear them. Voices. Dark shapes. I think they have guns. I know they have guns, for the firing has started.

Some other books published by **Luath Press**

Right to Die
Hazel McHaffie
ISBN 1 906307 21 0 PBK £12.99

Was it only two days ago? Seems like two hundred years. I was still in work mode then. Adam O'Neill, investigative journalist, columnist, would-be novelist. Researching my material. Amassing facts. And today? Yep. Sitting here consciously absorbing it, it's a totally different kettle of fish.

Naomi is haunted by a troubling secret. Struggling to come to terms with her husband's death, her biggest dread is finding out that Adam knew of her betrayal. He left behind an intimate diary – but dare she read it? Will it set her mind at rest – or will it destroy the fragile control she has over her grief?

Caught by the unfolding story, Naomi discovers more than she bargained for. Adam writes of his feelings for her, his challenging career, his burning ambition. How one by one his dreams evaporate when he is diagnosed with a degenerative condition, Motor Neurone Disease. How he resolves to mastermind his own exit at a time of his choice… but time is one luxury he can't afford. Soon he won't be able to do it alone. Can he ask a friend, or even a relative, to commit murder?

Adam's fierce determination to retain control of his own body against insurmountable odds fills his journal with a passion and drive that transcend his situation, and transfix the reader. A startlingly clear-sighted and courageous story, this novel explores the collision between uncompromising laws, complex loyalties and human compassion.

Lively and intensely readable… [Hazel McHaffie] has demonstrated that hard cases make good reading. ALEXANDER MCCALL SMITH

The Bower Bird
Ann Kelley
ISBN 1 906307 45 8 (adult fiction)
PBK £6.99

I had open-heart surgery last year, when I was eleven, and the healing process hasn't finished yet. I now have an amazing scar that cuts me in half almost, as if I have survived a shark attack.

Gussie is twelve years old, loves animals and wants to be a photographer when she grows up. The only problem is that she's unlikely to ever grow up.

Gussie needs a heart and lung transplant, but the donor list is as long as her arm and she can't wait around that long. Gussie has things to do; finding her ancestors, coping with her parents' divorce, and keeping an eye out for the wildlife in her garden.

Category winner at the 2007 Costa Book Awards

It's a lovely book – lyrical, funny, full of wisdom. Gussie is such a dear – such a delight and a wonderful character, bright and sharp and strong, never to be pitied for an instant. HELEN DUNMORE

The English Spy
Donald Smith
ISBN 1 905222 82 3 PBK £8.99

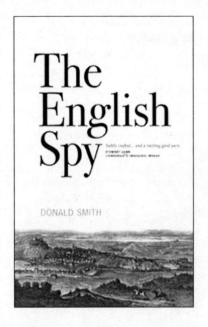

He was a spy among us, but not known as such, otherwise the mob of Edinburgh would pull him to pieces. JOHN CLERK OF PENICUIK

Union between England and Scotland hangs in the balance. Propagandist, spy and novelist-to-be Daniel Defoe is caught up in the murky essence of eighteenth-century Edinburgh – cobblestones, courtesans and kirkyards. Expecting a godly society in the capital of Presbyterianism, Defoe engages with a beautiful Jacobite agent, and uncovers a nest of vipers.

Subtly crafted… and a rattling good yarn. STEWART CONN

Delves into the City of Literature, and comes out dark side up. MARC LAMBERT

Engaging from the opening sentence to the last word, Smith has crafted a novel which captures the essence of Edinburgh during one of its most colourful chapters in history. LIFE AND WORK

Smith's version of Defoe picks his way through it all, arguing, wheedling, scribbling, bribing and cajoling the cast of nicely-drawn characters. Anyone interested in the months that saw the birth of modern Britain should enjoy this book. THE SUNDAY HERALD

Excellent… a brisk narrative and a vivid sense of time and place. THE HERALD

Last of the Line
John MacKay
ISBN 1 905222 90 4 PBK £6.99

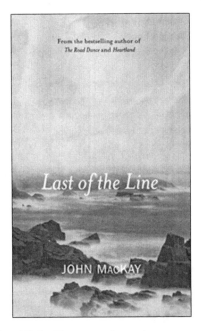

The call came from a place far away where the dark was deep and the only sound was the fading breath of a woman on the edge of eternity.

A summons to the bedside of his dying aunt drags Cal MacCarl away from the blur of city life to the islands where time turns slowly and tradition endures. He is striving for the urban dream of the luxury apartment and the prestige car and has shed his past to get there.

Aunt Mary is his only remaining blood link. She comes from that past. She still knows him as Calum. When she passes he will be the last of the family line. But for Cal, family and history are just bonds to tie him down.

Reluctantly embarking on a journey of duty, Cal finds himself drawn into the role of genealogy detective and discovers some secrets which are buried deep. He begins to understand that Mary is not the woman he thought he knew and the secret she kept buried for so long means he might not be who he thought he was.

The Blue Moon Book
Anne MacLeod
ISBN 1 84282 061 3
PBK £9.99

Heartland
John MacKay
ISBN 1 905222 11 4
PBK £6.99

Love can leave you breathless, lost for words.

Jess Kavanagh knows. Doesn't know. Twenty four hours after meeting and falling for archaeologist and Pictish expert Michael Hurt, she suffers a horrific accident that leaves her with aphasia and amnesia. No words. No memory of love.

Michael travels south, unknowing. It is her estranged partner, sports journalist Dan McKie, who is at her bedside when Jess finally regains consciousness. Dan, forced to review their shared past, is disconcerted by Jess's fear of him, by her loss of memory, loss of words.

Will their relationship survive this test? Should it survive? Will Michael find Jess again? In this absorbing contemporary novel, Anne MacLeod interweaves themes of language, love and loss in patterns as intricate and haunting as the Pictish Stones.

High on drama and pathos, woven through with fine detail.
THE HERALD

A man tries to build for his future by reconnecting with his past, leaving behind the ruins of the life he has lived. Iain Martin hopes that by returning to his Hebridean roots and embarking on a quest to reconstruct the ancient family home, he might find new purpose.

But as Iain begins working on the old blackhouse, he uncovers a secret from the past, which forces him to question everything he ever thoughtto be true.

Who can he turn to without betraying those to whom he is closest? His ailing mother, his childhood friend and his former love are both the building – and stumbling – blocks to his new life.

Where do you seek sanctuary when home has changed and will never be the same again?

A broody, atmospheric little gem set in the Hebrides.
THE HERALD

Cowboys for Christ
Robin Hardy
ISBN 1 905222 41 6
HBK £14.99

The Burying Beetle
Ann Kelley
ISBN 1 84282 099 0
PBK £9.99

A novel of religious sexuality and pagan murder.

If I am a Rabbi, Jehova is my God. If I am a Mullah, Allah the merciful is He. If a Christian, Jesus is my Lord. Millions of people worldwide worship the sun. Here in Tressock I believe the old religion of the Celts fits our needs at this time. Isn't that all you can ask of a religion?

Gospel singer Beth and her cowboy boyfriend Steve, two virgins pro ised to each other through 'the Silver Ring Thing', set off from Texas to enlighten the Scottish heathens in the ways of Christ. When, after initial abuse, they are welcomed with joy and elation to the village of Tressock, they assume their hosts simply want to hear more about Jesus.

How innocent and wrong they are.

Cowboys for Christ inhabits the same disturbing territory as The Wicker Man. Ripping through the themes of religion, paganism, power, sex and sacrifice, it builds to a gruesome, excruciating climax drawn from the terrifying imagination of The Wicker Man's director, Robin Hardy.

Erotic, romantic, comic and horrific enough to loosen the bowels of a bronze statue. CHRISTOPHER LEE

Twelve-year-old Gussie was born with a rare, life-threatening heart disease, but it hasn't hampered her curiosity. When she reads about the Burying Beetle, which has the unusual habit of burying dead birds, mice, and other small animals by digging away the earth beneath them, it becomes her mission to find one. As she searches the Cornish coast for the elusive insect, Gussie learns be like the Burying Beetle, to bury things past and to live.

This is a special book, the one you come across in a hundred, the one you will read and reread, a slow, savouring, enjoyable novel.
ST IVES TIMES AND ECHO

Atmospheric and beguiling.
HELEN DUNMORE

A book I enjoyed so much... both teenagers and adults will find great appeal in this moving story... As one reviewer has said, 'I hope Gussie's story sells a trillion, zillion copies. It deserves to.
PUBLISHING NEWS

Deadly Code
Lin Anderson
ISBN 1 905222 03 3
PBK £9.99

The past meets the future with deadly consequences.

A decomposing foot is caught in a fishing net off the west coast of Scotland and forensic expert Dr Rhona MacLeod is called in on a case that takes her back to her Gaelic roots. But when the Ministry of Defence tries to shut down the story, Rhona refuses to be deflected from her quest for the truth.

As the pieces fall into place, she finds herself up against a deadly international conspiracy of shadowy figures and powerful players bent on manipulating life, death and the future of humanity itself.

The third in the Dr Rhona MacLeod forensic scientist series.

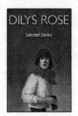

Selected Stories
Dilys Rose
ISBN 1 84282 077 X
PBK £7.99

Selected Stories is a compelling compilation by the award-winning Scottish writer Dilys Rose, selected from her three previous books.

Told from a wide range of perspectives and set in many parts of the world, Rose examines everyday lives on the edge through an unforgettable cast of characters. With subtlety, wit and dark humour, she demonstrates her seemingly effortless command of the short story form at every twist and turn of these deftly poised and finely crafted stories.

Praise for Rose's other work:

Dilys Rose can be compared to Katherine Mansfield in the way she takes hold of life and exposes all its vital elements in a few pages.
TIMES LITERARY SUPPLEMENT

Although Dilys Rose makes writing look effortless, make no mistake, to do so takes talent, skill and effort.
THE HERALD

The true short-story skills of empathy and cool, resonant economy shine through them all. Subtle excellence. THE SCOTSMAN

The Underground City
Jules Verne
ISBN 1 84282 080 X
PBK £7.99

Not Nebuchadnezzar: in search of identities
Jenni Calder
ISBN 1 84282 060 5
PBK £9.99

Ten years after he left the exhausted Aberfoyle mine underneath Loch Katrine, the former manager – James Starr – receives an intriguing letter from the old overman – Simon Ford. It suggests that the mine isn't actually barren after all.

Despite also receiving an anonymous letter the same day contradicting this, James returns to Aberfoyle and discovers that there is indeed more coal to be excavated.

Strange events hint at a presence that does not wish to see the cave mined further. Could someone be out to sabotage their work? Someone with a grudge against them? Or could it be something supernatural, something they cannot see or understand?

This is a new translation of *The Underground City*.

One of the strangest and most beautiful novels of the nineteenth century.
MICHEL TOURNIER

This is a biography, of sorts, and a description of the all-consuming search for that elusive concept known as 'identity'.

Jenni Calder was born Jennifer Rachel Daiches to a Scottish-born mother and English-born Jewish father in Chicago, one of America's great melting-pot cities. This book traces her journey from then to now, a journey that has taken her from America to Scotland via Cambridge, Israel and Kenya, with stops all over the world along the way during her travels as a writer. Throughout her travels, Calder discovers that 'knowing who she is' is only the first step – her true sense of identity develops from finding out who she is not.

This idea of who you are not informing your identification of who you are, and the struggle to find and establish one's identity, will be understood by displaced people and those without the traditional idea of 'roots' from around the world.

explores aspects of her life in a series of lucid, thoughtful essays which examine the concept of identity. THE SCOTSMAN

Scots in Canada
Jenni Calder
ISBN 1 84282 038 9
PBK £7.99

Scots in the USA
Jenni Calder
ISBN 1 905222 06 8
PBK £8.99

In Canada there are nearly as many descendants of Scots as there are people living in Scotland; almost five million Canadians ticked the 'Scottish origin' box in the most recent Canadian Census. Many Scottish families have friends or relatives in Canada.

Thousands of Scots were forced from their homeland, while others chose to leave, seeking a better life. As individuals, families and communities, they braved the wild Atlantic ocean, many crossing in cramped under-rationed ships, unprepared for the fierce Canadian winter. And yet Scots went on to lay railroads, found banks and exploit the fur trade, and helped form the political infrastructure of modern day Canada.

meticulously researched and fluently written... it neatly charts the rise of a country without succumbing to sentimental myths.
SCOTLAND ON SUNDAY

Calder celebrates the ties that still bind Canada and Scotland in cam raderie after nearly 400 years of relations. THE CHRONICLE

The map of the United States is peppered with Scottish placenames and America's telephone directories are filled with surnames illustrating Scottish ancestry. Increasingly, Americans of Scottish extraction are visiting Scotland in search of their family history. All over Scotland and the United States there are clues to the Scottish–American relationship, the legacy of centuries of trade and communication as well as that of departure and heritage.

The experiences of Scottish settlers in the United States varied enormously, as did their attitudes to the lifestyles that they left behind and those that they began anew once they arrived in North America.

Scots in the USA discusses why they left Scotland, where they went once they reached the United States, and what they did when they got there.

a valuable readable and illuminating addition to a burgeoning literature... should be required reading on the flight to New York by all those on the Tartan Week trail.
ALAN TAYLOR, SUNDAY HERALD

Details of these and other Luath Press titles are to be found at www.luath.co.uk

Luath Press Limited

committed to publishing well written books worth reading

LUATH PRESS takes its name from Robert Burns, whose little collie Luath (*Gael.*, swift or nimble) tripped up Jean Armour at a wedding and gave him the chance to speak to the woman who was to be his wife and the abiding love of his life. Burns called one of the 'Twa Dogs' Luath after Cuchullin's hunting dog in Ossian's *Fingal*.

Luath Press was established in 1981 in the heart of Burns country, and is now based a few steps up the road from Burns' first lodgings on Edinburgh's Royal Mile. Luath offers you distinctive writing with a hint of unexpected pleasures.

Most bookshops in the UK, the US, Canada, Australia, New Zealand and parts of Europe, either carry our books in stock or can order them for you. To order direct from us, please send a £sterling cheque, postal order, international money order or your credit card details (number, address of cardholder and expiry date) to us at the address below. Please add post and packing as follows: UK – £1.00 per delivery address; overseas surface mail – £2.50 per delivery address; overseas airmail – £3.50 for the first book to each delivery address, plus £1.00 for each additional book by airmail to the same address. If your order is a gift, we will happily enclose your card or message at no extra charge.

Luath Press Limited
543/2 Castlehill
The Royal Mile
Edinburgh EH1 2ND

Scotland
Telephone: 0131 225 4326 (24 hours)
Fax: 0131 225 4324
email: sales@luath. co.uk
Website: www. luath.co.uk